DRUGGED!

Harry Quinn had come to his feet, and there reeled back and forth like a hopeless drunkard. But the terror that was springing ice-cold in his breast helped to give to his mind an instant of clearness. This was the way the thing had been done before.

The entire testimony that Dave Bates had given to the jury now swept back over the mind of Harry Quinn. Dave had said that he had sat down and had a drink—one drink. And then he had grown sleepy, very sleepy. It was strange that a single drink could overcome the steel nerves and the hard, grim mind of Dave Bates. But, then, perhaps there had been in that first drink—if only Dave had remembered to speak about that—a strange bitterness?

The terror ran wild in Harry Quinn. He knew that a criminal is likely to use the same method in successive crimes. If a man kills with a knife once, he'll use that same tool again. If he kills with a hammer, he'll murder with a hammer the next time. And now the murderer of the Durant Ranch was commencing his work again.

Quinn had to get out of the place. But as he turned toward the door, he realized that he would not be able to take more than a few steps. . . .

MAX BRAND

THE LOST VALLEY

LEISURE BOOKS NEW YORK CITY

A LEISURE BOOK®

May 2002

Published by special arrangement with Golden West Literary Agency

Dorchester Publishing Co., Inc.
276 Fifth Avenue
New York, NY 10001

ISBN 0-8439-5017-X

Visit us on the web at www.dorchesterpub.com.

Table of Contents

D

THE STAGE TO YELLOW CREEK

In 1932 Frank E. Blackwell, editor of Street & Smith's *Western Story Magazine*, informed Carl Brandt, Frederick Faust's New York literary agent, that Street & Smith was being hurt by the Great Depression, as were all magazine publishers, and that as an economy measure Faust's rate (which had been at five cents a word since 1925) would have to be lowered to four cents a word. Faust, who was still living with his family in a Florentine villa in Italy, was displeased with this new policy at Street & Smith and urged his agent to seek other markets. It was while on a long trip to Egypt with his family that Faust wrote three short novels featuring a new character, Perry Woodstock. Carl Brandt sold all three of these Perry Woodstock short novels to Rogers Terrill, editor of Popular Publications' new pulp magazine, *Dime Western*. "The Strange Ride of Perry Woodstock," the first of these short novels, is collected in THE FUGITIVE'S MISSION: A WESTERN TRIO (Five Star Westerns, 1997). The second of them, titled by Faust "The Stage to Yellow Creek" and completed in June, 1932, appeared as "Guardian Guns" by Max Brand in *Dime Western* (8/33). Rogers Terrill, as was his editorial prerogative, in addition to changing the title prior to publication also altered the name of the principal character from Perry Woodstock to Tom Wells and deleted or rewrote certain sections of the text. For its appearance here, both the title and the text of "The Stage to Yellow Creek" have been restored according to Frederick Faust's original typescript.

I

"CACTUS TERRY"

There are so many different kinds of courage in this world that it's a dangerous thing to say right out that this man is brave and that one a coward. Take, for instance, the eleven people who started out that day, many years ago, on the stage trip from Fort Winton to Yellow Creek. I was one of the eleven, and, what is a great deal more important, I was one of the few who lived to tell of that terrible journey. Fear came to all of us before the thing was over. But what I'm trying to get across is that everyone — even the poor devils who died like cowards — showed courage of one sort or another before the end.

Take the three Mexicans whose last names we never knew, Pierre Vernon, the gambler, and the girl, Lydia Vincent. There was never a time when these five. . . . But perhaps I'd better tell the thing as it happened, starting with that fateful moment when Mike Jeffreys, as fine a driver as ever I'd ridden with, eased his six-horse team around a sharp bend in the trail and into the misty darkness of Mule Cañon. Then is when the adventure really began, for we hadn't gone more than a couple of hundred feet between those high rock walls when Mike was forced to yank his horses to a quick stop before an obstruction of branches that had been piled across the trail. At the same time a broad, powerful light, almost like the glare of a train's headlight, shot out at us. It came from the heavy shadows beside the road, and it covered us all with a broad, strong shaft.

When that light struck me, I simply stuck my hands up above my head. There seemed to be no other wise thing to do. Even at that time I wasn't exactly a young man. And, after all, I was only a passenger.

A voice came out of the shadows, strong and high. "Keep 'em covered, boys!" it said. "An' shoot the leaders if they step over that pile of brush. If anybody tries to step off on the far side of the stage, you fellows over there plant him the minute he reaches the road. I'm not over-anxious for bloodshed. But I don't care how many fools we have to kill, if they ask for it. Everybody out, on this side, if you please. That's it!"

All that we could see was a shadowy form behind the light and the gleaming muzzles of a pair of Colts leveled at us. For my part, I had nothing with me that I hated to lose. My name, by the way, is Perry Woodstock. I'd been a cowpuncher all my life up till that time. But the week before, on my fiftieth birthday, my wife, Rosemary, and I'd taken all our savings and sunk 'em in a little spread outside Yellow Creek. So I, for one, had no cash in that hold-up. I felt, anyway, that we were thoroughly trapped and that resistance was useless.

Everybody else seemed to feel the same way. I think it was the cool confidence of the bandit that convinced us we were done for. If he had raved and cursed at us, it might not have chilled our blood so much.

The Mexicans were whispering little, sibilant curses. But old George Vincent, the girl's father, choked back a groan. "God help me!" he said — not as though he were afraid of bodily hurt, but as though there was something else that he could not afford to lose. It didn't take any great stretch of imagination to understand that money must be what he was thinking about, so much money that the loss of it would ruin him.

He got down with the rest of us, and we lined up with our hands stuck in the air, all except Lydia. The robber said to her: "It's all right, lady. You don't need to keep your hands up. I've never robbed women."

He came out from behind his light then, and we saw a black hood over his head, and one gun covering the whole of us. But that gun was enough, to say nothing of whoever might be in the brush on each side of the road, silently giving their chief all the backing necessary.

This robber, I could see, was a fellow with brains, and he used a dodge that was new to me. He went down the line of us, carrying in his left hand a number of black, cotton bags. When he ordered us to put down our arms, one after the other, he dropped these sacks over our heads and shoulders. It was a slick idea. It blanketed us all with darkness. And I stood there in that thin veil of light, suddenly realizing that we had been bamboozled and beaten and fooled by a single man. There were no backers lying in the brush. His talk and the light and our own fear had trapped us. Now, alone and unaided, he was going to go through us.

I heard a yelp from the girl, threw off the black sack without thinking, and there she was, grappling with the robber!

The bandit, of course, could have knocked that foolish girl silly. But he didn't. Instead, he tried to push her away. Lydia, her eyes blazing, was hanging on and fighting like a wildcat when about five of us hit that highway robber in one wave and put him down.

The Mexicans wanted to kill him on the spot, now that he was helpless. And two other hardcase passengers — Chick Dyne and Stuffy Bill Haines, who were little better than saloon bums — would have kicked in his face without any more to-do. But I managed to stop them, although I had to threaten to use the butt of a gun on the face of Stuffy Bill.

Lydia Vincent was standing back against the stage, panting and flushed, with her head up, her lips parted, and the shine of a daredevil tomboy in her eyes. It was a good picture that she made.

11

"I . . . I'm almost ashamed of myself," she said. "He could have killed me, but he wouldn't even use his fist on me, to say nothing of his gun."

There was a lot of sense in what she said. It made me, for one, feel a lot friendlier toward the bandit, to think that there was so much decency in him that he wouldn't use his knuckles on the girl when his failure to knock her away meant capture and maybe death.

Now, as he was lifted from the ground and put on his feet, I saw that he was a tall, loose-jointed fellow with the quietest blue eyes in the world and the calmest expression on his face. He looked surprised and innocent, as though he had been knocked down by a riot with which he had nothing to do.

The Mexicans and the precious pair of bums were for lynching the robber on the spot. But with the backing of Mike, the driver, and the girl and her father, I managed to get him safely into the stage. There was no need to tie his hands, I thought, because he was wedged into the midst of the lot of us, and we were all armed, and his weapons had been taken from him.

I simply said: "Look here, partner, do you want us to tie you hand and foot, or will you promise to be a good boy till we get you safely to the cooler?"

He said: "I like coolers. They're peaceful and quiet. I like 'em a lot."

"And about giving your word?" I said.

"Why, certainly," he said. "I'll sit as quiet as can be, as long as the rest of you sit quiet."

There might be a left-handed meaning in what he said, but I was pretty sure of him, and with his own lantern at his feet to play light on him the stage started on. Our man made himself a cigarette, and, while he was doing it, the sleeves of his coat worked back a little, and we could see that his wrists were criss-crossed with scars. Stuffy Bill wanted to know how he'd gotten them, and if he was covered all over with the same silver marks.

He said: "How'd you get your arms that way, stranger, and what's your moniker, besides?"

"I can answer both questions together," said the prisoner, in a voice the softest and gentlest that you ever heard, and the deepest, too. "When I was a kid, a horse piled me into a cactus patch, and I got cut up pretty badly all over. Ever since then I've been called Cactus Terry. The cactus scars are all over my body, about as close as writing could be crowded."

Stuffy Bill nodded his head as though satisfied with that answer. But across the stage Pierre Vernon, the gambler, laughed. For my part, I thought that a certain round, silver band going around each wrist might have been caused by the friction of a rope or a rawhide thong, working in through the flesh toward the bone. It wasn't a pretty thing to think about.

Just then somebody noticed the rattling of a galloping horse that was coming along behind the stage and said: "What's that? Who's coming up behind?"

"It's only my horse following along, I suppose," said Cactus Terry. He whistled, and pretty soon a black mare ran up beside the stage. Part of the lantern glow reached her head and glimmered over the beauty of it.

"What a beautiful horse!" said Lydia Vincent, her eyes shining at the robber.

"She is," he agreed.

"And how well you've trained her," said the girl.

Old Vincent cut in, asking if Cactus had any information that made him particularly eager to rob this stage. Cactus said that he had. Vincent seemed a good deal cut up by this. "Just what information?" he wanted to know.

"I knew," said Cactus, "that there was a hundred and sixty

13

thousand dollars traveling in greenbacks along with a fellow by the name of George Vincent on this coach. Are you Mister Vincent, by any chance?"

Vincent was knocked in a heap when he heard this, and so was everybody else. I could see Stuffy rolling his eyes up toward the stars, and the flashing teeth of the three Mexicans as they glanced and grinned at one another.

A hundred and sixty thousand dollars! Well, that's a whale of a lot of money in any man's life.

"I thought that I'd borrow some of that money," said Cactus, in his gentle, cheerful way. "There's a saying that money makes money grow, you know. I had some special schemes hatching out to make money grow fast as wildfire, once I had a bit of capital."

I liked his coolness. We all laughed, except George Vincent. He leaned forward and tapped our prisoner on the knee.

"Do you think that anybody else may know, or think they know, that a hundred and sixty thousand is traveling to Yellow Creek on this stage?"

"Oh, sure," said the robber. "A lot of the boys know all about it."

II

"KILLERS AHEAD"

The money was not mine, of course, but, when I heard this, it was as though somebody had tapped me gently under the right ear with a chunk of lead in a nice, soft length of garden hose. As for George Vincent, he sank back in his place and shriveled up like an apple peel that's been too close to the fire.

"Great heavens," he whispered.

"Father," said the girl, "in another moment they'll really begin to think that you *are* traveling with all that money."

It was a good stab on her part, but it was too late. Her father wriggled upright and attempted to laugh and only choked himself.

"Of course, there's nothing in it," he said. "A hundred and sixty thousand dollars! No man would be such a fool as to travel with so much money on him."

I saw that a lot of harm might come out of this if Vincent thought he was pulling the wool over everybody's eyes, so I said: "Nobody would carry that much money on himself unless he knew how often messengers go crooked and how often the mail is robbed."

"Eh? What's that, Woodstock?" said Vincent, blinking at me.

"Well," I explained, "I'd swear that everybody on this stage is pretty sure that you've got the coin with you. Maybe you'd just as well know what we think."

The girl gave me a long, level look, beginning pretty hostile but ending with a sort of friendly, hopeful expression in her worried eyes.

15

Vincent himself glowered at me and said nothing for a moment. Then he turned to Cactus again.

"What makes you think that a number of people know . . . think, I mean . . . that I'm carrying that fortune about the country with me?"

"You've got to look out for freckle-faced men," said Cactus, in his gentle voice. "A freckle-faced boy is all right, but a freckle-faced man is apt to be pretty dangerous, I tell you. There was a clerk back there in the bank you had dealings with, who had freckles across his nose. Remember him?"

"A clerk? I remember, now. There was a man like that in the bank . . . the scoundrel."

"He's a scoundrel, all right," said Cactus. "He's such a scoundrel that he wrote to some old chums that he used to play around with in this neck of the woods. He told them all about your movements, and he suggested that they stop your stage, get your dough, and then split with him."

"Were you one of his former friends?" asked Vincent.

"I don't herd with that kind of vermin," said Cactus softly. "But when a bunch of the boys were talking the thing over in an abandoned shack, I was listening in from the attic, and, before they finished, I knew all about 'em."

"And what did they intend doing?" asked Vincent, wriggling as though he were sitting on top of a hot stove.

"Why," said Cactus, "they intended sticking up the stage, tonight. That was their idea."

"Good God!" said Vincent. "Why didn't you tell us all this before, man? Where are they now?"

"For a man in the hands of the law," said Cactus, "and just about in jail already, there's nothing so dangerous as talking. And I'm afraid that I've talked too much."

"Heavens above us," said Vincent. "Perhaps the ruffians are waiting down the road. Stop the stage, driver! Stop the stage!"

Mike Jeffreys stopped the stage, all right. We were all about as nervous as George Vincent by this time, and the Mexicans were showing the whites of their eyes. If we were stopped a second time, and by a gang, we might not get off so well as we had before. One volley to kill the horses and another to clear out the coach was the way some highwaymen worked.

Stuffy Bill said: "There had oughta be a law ag'in' gents packing around the whole United States treasury in their vest pocket. Look at what it does to a lot of innocent gents that ain't got more'n two bits between them and hell."

At which point Vincent made us a little speech. He said: "Gentlemen, you can see that I'm in a terrible predicament. You also are in danger, so far as I can see. I suggest that we promise our friend, Cactus . . . who, after all, has done us absolutely no harm . . . complete freedom from the dangers of the law if he will reveal to us everything that he knows about the plot that other scoundrels have laid to stop this stage."

Chick Dyne cracked right in with: "I'm dead ag'in' it! When a gent steps out and takes a sock at the jaw of the law, he'd oughta have a broken hand. This here Cactus, he belongs in the jail. That's all there is to it. He belongs in the jail, and that's where I'm going to see that he goes."

The driver pulled at his mustache, and said nothing.

The gambler cleared his throat and then said: "Undoubtedly there is something in what Chick says. I am the last man to wish any other fellow bad fortune, but our friend, Cactus, has broken an important law, and I think that he ought to suffer for it. As for the danger to the money, Mister Vincent ought to tell us where it is hidden, and we will all guarantee him security for it."

I listened to that argument and would have hated him, if I hadn't wanted to laugh. It was a pretty flimsy dodge that he was trying, and even Vincent, excited as he was, paid no attention. The Mexicans picked the idea right up, however. The tall cadaver said that all of our lives were in danger. He suggested that Mr. Vincent should be put on the horse of the highwayman and, together with his money, cut across the rough side of the country toward Yellow Creek. He, Pedro, a man of sense and honor, and a sure guide to all of this countryside, would accompany Mr. Vincent, and make sure that he safely reached his destination.

I looked at the girl. There was a faint smile on her lips, and a lot of thought in her eyes.

Stuffy and Chick both broke in here. They declared that there was something in what the trio had said, except that, of course, the life of a white man and a gentleman could not be trusted to a Mexican, alone in the night. They, however, Stuffy and Chick, were willing to be the guard and guides for Mr. Vincent.

It seemed as though everybody in the coach was suddenly all burned up with the desire to take care of Mr. Vincent — *and* his money.

Mike Jeffreys said, as he still pulled at his mustache: "You pair of tramps would be worse than the Mexicans as a body-guard! Look here, Mister Vincent, have you really got that ocean of hard cash along with you?"

Vincent groaned and looked at the girl.

In that flash, I saw who was the real man of the family. She just nodded, and he admitted: "Yes, I've got it with me . . . fool that I am."

"Now, then," said Mike Jeffreys, "it wouldn't do any good to shell Vincent out of the stage, because if there's a hold-up party farther down the road, they'll stop the stage just the same and load a lot of lead into us, most likely. And if they don't find Vincent, they're likely to start breaking their teeth on our hides. The only thing to do is to keep together. But we've got to find out what Cactus, here, knows."

Stuffy said it was a damned outrage for a freeborn, American citizen to be talked to the way the driver had talked about him and Chick, and that he, for one, would turn Cactus over to the law as soon as we hit Yellow Creek.

I admired the mean, out-and-out way that Stuffy talked. There wasn't anything decent about him, and he hardly made any pretense of decency.

I said: "Of course, Cactus goes free if he'll talk. You agree, Mike . . . and Vincent and his daughter agree. That's four of us. And I think that we're the four that will have to swing this meeting."

"Why," said Pierre Vernon, the gambler, easy as could be, "I agree with you, too, Woodstock."

"That makes five," said Mike. "And that's enough. Look here, Cactus . . . will you out and tell us what you know?"

"Of course, I will," said Cactus, "seeing as how you're not going to turn me over to the sheriff."

He pointed ahead, where two hills rubbed shoulders above the road and blotted out a couple of big half sections of stars.

"They're down in that gorge," said Cactus. "That's about half a mile from here, I suppose. And some of the five of 'em are shotgun boys. One of 'em is Riley Mason, who already has half a dozen killings to boast about."

III

"FLIGHT"

There was not very much doubt as to what would happen now. We could not separate. If we attempted to go down the road, it would be just like writing out our own tickets to boothill. I knew the killer, Riley Mason, and I would rather have put my foot in a nest of rattlers than to ride any farther down the road on that stage. Our best chance, it seemed to me, was to turn the stage off the road and head across country. If luck was with us and we succeeded in finding our way through the hills and arroyos, we might somehow make it across the unbeaten ways of open country to Yellow Creek. It was a pretty long chance, but it looked then like our best bet. I suggested it, and the others agreed almost at once.

Mike Jeffreys nodded his head, then made another suggestion.

"I ought to have somebody scouting ahead to pick the best ways for me," he said. "Somebody who knows this country, and who can tell where a stage can go, and where a stage can't go."

Cactus Terry said: "There's me and my horse. What about that?"

"He'd just fade away, and we'd never see him again," protested the gambler. "I'll take that horse, though, and scout ahead myself."

Every one of the three Mexicans wanted the job. So did Stuffy Bill and Chick. But by this time there was a group of five of us that insisted on voting one way. That party consisted of Mike Jeffreys, the two Vincents, myself, and Cactus Terry. We forced the point through, and Cactus called up his horse and got on her back.

Stuffy Bill was very loud in protesting against this. He pointed out that there was a rifle stuck into the saddle holster and that repeating gun would be used for the stoppage of the coach and the murder of all of us.

However, Cactus not only got the horse, saddle, and rifle, but he also got his own pair of Colts that had been taken from him in the scuffle. I insisted on that. And now that he was fully restored to his horse and his weapons, I can tell you that a shade of difference came in the actions of Cactus and in the appearance of him. I said that he was a sort of long, loose-jointed fellow, on the ground. But when he sat in the saddle, he was a king, right enough. And even the features of his lean, brown face seemed to change.

He looked us up and down, and I was half inclined to believe that Stuffy Bill might be right. He waved his hand in what might be a signal for us to follow, or a gesture of farewell. Then he turned and rode off the trail.

Chick wanted to shoot him from behind. "He's gonna do us dirty!" he said, and the rat went so far as to pull out a long-barreled Colt and level it. It was Lydia Vincent who knocked up his hand with an exclamation of impatient disgust.

He cursed, not at her, to be sure, but at the rest of us and at fate and the world in general. He said: "You don't know what people will do for a hundred and sixty thousand dollars!"

Vincent looked even more worried. But his daughter — she was a good girl, if ever there was one — shook her head.

"We have to take some sort of a chance," she said. "This is the best chance. If we go on down the road, we'll be running into robbery *and* murder. And although Cactus may rob us, he won't murder us. Personally, I think he can be trusted."

She put such a fire into that remark she practically silenced the rest of us.

And now Mike Jeffreys took charge by turning the stage and backing it with a good deal of cursing at the wheelers. Then he drove us, groaning and lurching, up the bank and onto the rough ground above, along the shoulder of the mountain.

Nobody talked. It seemed as though dangers were crowding up close to us, and that guns were pointing through the dark. We got over the shoulder, and there we suddenly saw a big golden moon, with cheeks puffed out, standing up in the east. That was cheering, in a sense, because it would help us to find the way. It was mighty depressing in another sense, because it would show us to anybody who started hunting for our scalps.

Before us, now and then, we heard the voice of Cactus calling back directions, and I thought that he made his voice guarded — letting it be just loud enough to reach our ears. We began to climb over steep slopes and grind with fixed brakes down sharp descents, as we forged ahead through those badlands.

Every now and then Mike Jeffreys swore, and then admired. He said a dozen times: "There's a *man*, that Cactus. There's a man who knows himself and knows a stagecoach, too!"

I felt the same way about it. In the hands of Cactus as a guide and Jeffreys as a driver, I felt that we would get through, if getting through were possible.

The moon, as it got higher, gave us its full light only now and then, for the sky was filled with big sailing clouds, and the moon would plunge into them every now and then and be lost for a minute or two. This changing light made travel a lot more difficult, but the voice of Cactus practically took us by the hand and led us through all difficulties.

Now he would trot or gallop ahead. Now he would call

directions and warnings. Now he would be back beside us, telling Jeffreys just the dangers of a certain slope. And Jeffreys would grunt out — "Gotcha!" — and go ahead.

So we came, at last, to a broad and fairly open tableland, with the moon shining brightly and unstained upon us. We hadn't gone far across that place when little Chick Dyne jumped up and yelled: "Look! There they are!"

There they were, all right. Five riders coming full tilt out of a patch of trees and heading in front of us, to cut off our line of flight. It brought my heart up in my throat. Five of them, counting murdering Riley Mason — and God help us if that crew got us into their hands.

We had men enough and guns enough to make a fight. But in a pinch I could see the Mexicans sneaking off to join the enemy. If Vincent was any good with a gun, I would miss my guess, and that left the gambler, who was likely to take the easiest course. Stuffy Bill and Chick would do the same thing. Jeffreys and myself — practically the last two — were the only ones who counted. While I felt that Jeffreys would make a good accounting of himself, either with a revolver or a rifle, for my part I had never been better than a second-rate marksman, even in my best days.

No, our party looked strong enough to the eye, but I felt that we were a pretty weak ship. Jeffreys gave the mustangs the whip, and we started across that rolling ground like a small boat driven through choppy surf by a hurricane. I never felt such motion. Everybody had to hang on for dear life, and, if ever a Concord was tested out thoroughly in body, wheels, and springs, that coach was tested then. Six mustangs, however well intentioned and however well driven, could not keep pace with five horses that were ridden by desperate and eager men.

Suddenly Chick screamed out: "There goes that crook of a dog's hind leg . . . there goes that Cactus Terry to make up

23

with the five of 'em. We're no better'n dead men. We gotta scatter out of the coach and take our chances!"

In fact, we could see Cactus Terry loping his horse across the plain toward the five racing horses.

But while I was shaking my head, I heard Lydia Vincent exclaiming: "He'll not join them. I know that he'll not join them."

Just then, Cactus got to a bunch of rocks and dropped off the mare, and the mare ducked down out of sight. The next instant rifle fire started, and it did us good to see the five thugs scatter. This side and that, or straight back toward shelter, they rode full tilt, while Lydia Vincent stood straight up, regardless of the danger of being jolted out of the stage. She stood up, and she cheered.

The five had started running as the rifle was turned loose on them. But although it was pretty long-range fire and only by moonlight, suddenly one of those five horses was without a rider. And we saw the dismounted man get up from the ground, try to run, and fall again.

"Winged!" said Jeffreys, as calm as you please. "That Cactus, he's a shooting fool, he is!"

IV

"FIRE AND FLOOD"

That was the kind of a shooting fool to have along, you can
bet. It warmed my heart to see the way Cactus had handled
that job, and suddenly I felt pretty small, back there in the
stage, with one man, and that one a robber by trade, fighting
against five for the lot of us. Presently, as we swung away across
country, we saw Cactus loping the black mare after us, keeping
a good distance behind. And that was the way we went on for
an hour, with Cactus turning back once in another natural little
fort and opening fire once more. What he accomplished that
time we could not tell, for the lay of the land shut him from
view.

And then it came on to rain. And how it rained. I suppose
there are not many parts of the earth where the rainfall averages
less than it does in the Southwest of the United States — that
is, in places that are not out-and-out deserts. But when the
sky makes up its mind to turn black and give a downpour, I
think that the Southwest outrains every record of the tropics.
The drops are bigger, and there are a lot more of 'em to the
square inch.

The moon had disappeared some time before, and lightning
flashes filled the sky. By those flashes of lightning we saw our
way. And presently we saw the rain and heard it coming. There
was a roaring wind behind it, and there was another roaring
of the rain upon the ground that sounded like ten thousand
distant herds stampeding.

It was an awful thing to see, mind you, with the lightning

25

still crackling, and the face of it blurred and smeared across behind the sheets of the driving water. And when that wind and rain hit the stage, I could fairly feel the stagger of the coach and the reeling of the horses that were trying to pull us ahead. They stopped trying for a minute, and we stood still. The weight of the downpour seemed to be breaking the coach and hammering us into the ground. Then we went on again. If we spoke, we had to shout. And when the lightning glared suddenly, peering in on us, we saw frightened, distorted faces.

Presently, with a blaze of lightning over both his shoulders, I saw Cactus ride up to the stage. He was clothed in a slicker that gleamed like golden mail, and the black mare was like polished ebony with the water washing in torrents off her and the lightning glistening along her flanks.

Cactus shouted, and I made out his voice. "You've got to speed up, Mike!" he yelled. "There's a dry arroyo ahead of you, and beyond that there's a fair chance to keep going. But unless you get across the arroyo now, you won't get across at all. It'll be a running river in another minute or two with this storm!"

Mike, for answer, flogged the mustangs. They tried to gallop, but already the mud was deep, and the best they could do was a steady trot. We went lumbering and blundering along, with the wheels making sometimes a crackling and sometimes merely a sloshing sound as they cut their broad tires through the mud.

And so we came to the edge of the arroyo. I'll never forget the moment when we balanced on the rim of the descending slope. Up and down the shallow ravine we saw the wet boulders, illumined by a whole cluster of ripping lightning. There were pools of water everywhere, but no stream was running as yet. As we started down toward the bottom, we heard the thunder pounding in our ears like ten thousand thicknesses of number one canvas sailcloth being torn across by the devil's own fingers. That was a bad minute.

The overlabored coach hit the bottom of the arroyo with a stagger and a groan. Then we went bumping horribly across the flat and got to the far side. But there we found that the bank was steeper than the one that we had come down. It was almost sheer up and down. We turned and went up the arroyo to find a better place for attempting the climb. But we hadn't gone far when the near leader turned with a scream like the death cry of a wounded beast.

I looked ahead, and a white blaze of lightning showed me a six-foot head of water coming straight down that arroyo as fast as a horse could run. The flood was throwing up great muddy, shapeless arms that held big boulders suspended like feathers. Yes, sir, you could see the big rocks, and, while I watched, I saw a tree trunk with all the branches clean off of it thrown up fifteen or twenty feet.

That coach shed us faster than it ever got rid of a cargo of passengers before. I ran out with Mike, and we slashed the traces and set the mustangs loose. We got them free just in time. Those horses, five of them, climbed the bank like wildcats; the sixth one, clean mad with fear and excitement, turned and started racing down the cañon at full speed.

The bank was wet clay where I tried to climb it. I was stuck toward the top, with the water rushing right at me, when a pair of boots appeared under my nose, and I climbed over and up the body of Cactus to the top of the bank. He'd hooked on with his arms at the top and given me a natural ladder. It was quick thinking, and it was a brave thing to do.

I owed my life to the quick brain and the courage of Cactus, because the next minute that roaring water came by and threw a fifty-pound boulder slam on the spot where I had been climbing. All the devils were roaring together now — the thunder, and the wind, and the rushing, trampling rain, and the furious stampeding of the water — so that a person could not speak and hardly be heard if he did, and there was only the lightning to give us glimpses into the storm, and into the wild haggard faces of one another.

At that time I thought that only Cactus Terry remained unchanged. He was on the back of the black mare again, and he suggested that as many of us as could should mount the mustangs and ride along.

Mount them? Yes, we could mount them, all right. But it was a different thing to stick on their backs. They were broken to driving, but that had nothing to do with riding them. They fought like wildcats and spilled us all into the mud, except the three Mexicans and Mike Jeffreys. Mike sat out his bucking devil, and the Mexicans seem to be born with a sense of what's the proper thing to do when on the back of a horse. In the end, there were four of us mounted — five, counting Cactus — which left six of us to trek ahead on foot, leading the fifth of the mustangs that remained to us.

But I want to tell you a strange thing. We pushed ahead through the devilishness of that night. Slickers couldn't keep us dry, for every now and then the wind came around with an unexpected flaw, jerked open our coats, and turned in a deluge on us.

We marched by lightning light. It showed me the three Mexicans, riding last of the party, huddling close together. In front of them came Stuffy Bill and Chick, walking shoulder to shoulder, heads down, cursing so vilely that even my ears got a tingle in them now and then. Next came me and the gambler, Pierre Vernon, walking together, and ahead of us the Vincents, and ahead of the Vincents Mike Jeffreys and Cactus Terry, our two men of action, riding briskly into the storm, cutting this way and that to find a shelter.

Cactus Terry, as one might have expected, was the fellow to find it. He came back with word of having found an old, abandoned ranch. So we followed him through that deepening mud, and after five more minutes the lightning showed up the front of a long, low building. And we all broke out into a feeble, scattering cheer and made a run for cover.

V

"TROUBLE ON HORSEBACK"

It was interesting to see the way the various people acted after we got to shelter. Most of us started in to make a fire, that we built right in the middle of the biggest room on the bare earth, because there was no sign of a stove left, except a few handfuls of rust and a staggering skeleton of iron. Then we left the girl by the fire, and the rest of us herded into the next room and took our clothes off and wrung them out, two men to a garment, to get them dry. We struggled back into the damp garments, then went back to the fire to dry ourselves.

There we found that the girl had gone through the same ceremony. Her clothes looked pretty wrinkled and sagging, but she wore them with just the same air of cool confidence. It takes a rare woman, like it takes a rare hen, to stand being wet and bedraggled. But she stood it and was freshening the fire with old boards and smiled a welcome at us, as though she were the lady of the place and we were house guests. She was all right, that girl. I voted again for her, right on the spot.

I said that the rest of us, after the fire was going, went to wring out our clothes, but I was wrong. Cactus Terry was not with us. The fire had no sooner been lighted than he went right outside again, and he was still gone when we came back from the other room.

Chick and Stuffy sat down together in a corner, muttering to one another. The three Mexicans sat in another corner, not muttering. But now and then the sound of their whispering cut coldly into the ear, like the drawn edge of a knife over the skin. They were an ugly picture, I tell you, like three crows huddled together on one branch and thinking bad thoughts.

The gambler was trying to talk big to the girl now that we were safe for the time in a shelter. He told her what he had done in various cities, and how he had staged all kinds of parties, and how he had laid a bet with the earl of whatnot on a horse race.

She didn't laugh at this blow-hard. She just listened, never smiling.

But there was one center of interest to which all eyes were pulled every now and again. That was George Vincent's pigskin bag. Vincent sat on the ruins of a box, with the bag between his feet, and every once in a while heads would turn and eyes would rest on that pigskin bag.

Of course, that was where the treasure lay. Inside of that leather there was a free and easy life for somebody, and a gay life, too, with plenty of spending money. I found myself, over and over again, figuring out what a hundred and sixty thousand would bring in at five per cent. Eight thousand dollars. Great Scott! In those days that seemed a whole flood of money. Nearly seven hundred a month for sitting still. Seven hundred dollars, and never a lick of work done. More than twenty dollars a day to go and blow in, living at the best hotels off the fat of the land! Not, mind you, that I really ever even dreamed of trying to steal that money. Stealing wasn't exactly my line. But I couldn't help thinking and daydreaming a little, if you know what I mean. It hardly seemed stealing, a job like that. It was so big and important for its possible results, that it seemed more like a big financial adventure. The same difference that there is between war and murder.

Well, if I was figuring things on that scale, I could imagine how the rest of the gang in the corners would be thinking, to say nothing of the smooth-tongued gambler, now rattling away to the girl so swift and easy and sneaking glances at the bag every now and then.

"Where's Cactus Terry?" asked Mike at last.

"Gone to play some dirty trick on us," suggested Stuffy, who was always ready to damn everybody.

Mike looked at him and paid no attention to the remark.

"He's gone to help us out in some way, I suppose," said the girl in her turn.

"D'you think that they'll be able to follow us?" I asked Jeffreys.

"You know as well as I do, Perry," said Mike.

"It's a pretty thick night," I commented. "And if they didn't get across that arroyo before we did, they'll never hit this side before the rain stops."

He shook his head.

"What d'you think, Mike?" asked the girl.

He looked at her and smiled, and his young-old face got very young in fact.

"I don't know," said Jeffreys. "You see how it is. For a gang like that, so much money is enough to give them the scent from halfway around the earth. Besides, they've got a blood grudge by this time. One of their partners has been knocked off his horse, and they'll want to make that even."

"I hope that the man was not killed," said Lydia.

"I don't have the same hope," Mike said. "If he's dead, there's one less thief in the world. But he's not dead . . . not by the way he stood up and tried to walk. He just got it through the leg. I think they've had enough lightning to show 'em the way we came. The arroyo might stop them, but, then again, they might go upstream or down and find shallows that they could ford."

He had hardly finished speaking when Cactus came through the empty doorway and stood within the firelight, gleaming

32

like gold in his yellow slicker.

"What have you been scouting around for?" asked Mike.

"For trouble," said Cactus.

"Find any?"

"Yes."

"What sort of trouble?"

"Trouble on horseback, with four pairs of hands," Cactus informed them.

That did me no good, to hear him say that. It took some of my breath from me.

"You mean they've found us?" said Mike.

"Not yet, but they're going to," said Cactus.

"Then for God's sake, let's put the fire out!" said Vincent.

"Why?" asked Cactus. "They're going to find us, I think, anyway. The lightning is spraying all over the face of the earth. And the tracks we made coming up through the mud are enough to be read from half a mile up in the air. They're going to find us, all right, and we're going to have to fight."

"But not in here . . . with the firelight shining on us!" exclaimed Vincent.

"We won't have to stay in here," said Cactus. "We can go other places." He ran his eyes over the lot of us. "There are enough of us to eat them alive . . . if we've all got healthy appetites. But that's what I'm not sure of. You have to have a lot of hunger to eat boys like Riley and his gang. Mike and Perry Woodstock, we'd better put our heads together . . . with Mister Vincent . . . and see what's to be done. Excuse me, Vernon. I include you, too, of course."

VI

"CONFERENCE OF WAR"

We gathered together and left the three Mexicans in their corner, still whispering and rolling their eyes. Stuffy and Chick went on with their mutterings together, too. I was mighty worried by the look of those fellows. And there was Pierre Vernon, the gambler, who seemed to me just the sort of a crutch that will break when you trust your weight to it.

Cactus took control of things at once. "Riley Mason and his boys are pretty sure to find their way here," he said. "Partly because they know about the money, and partly because they hate me."

"Would they know that it's you?" asked Vernon sharply.

"They would. They wouldn't recognize me in the distance by the moonlight, likely," said Cactus Terry. "But they'd know the look of my horse, Patty. She's pretty well known."

"Why do they hate you?" asked Vernon, scowling. "What have you had to do with Riley Mason?"

Cactus looked at Vernon for a minute as though he were considering making no answer. But then he shrugged his shoulders and said: "You have a right to know because it's the business of all as long as I'm in the party. I've been on Mason's trail for more than a year, and he knows it. I want his scalp, and he knows why."

"What for? Friends that fell out, you and Riley Mason?" asked Vernon.

There was a good deal of sting in the question. Cactus shrugged his shoulders again.

"Riley happened to shoot a friend of mine, and he did it like the bushwhacker he is, through an open window. That's all."

"Who was this friend?" asked Vernon.

It angered me to hear Vernon's questions. But Cactus endured them with a fine self-control.

He merely said: "Jigger Davis. That was the friend."

"I've heard that name," said Vernon quickly, and he looked toward the girl as he spoke. "Jigger Davis was a bank bandit."

"Yes, he cracked safes," said Cactus Terry, as quietly as before.

"And he was a friend of yours?" repeated Vernon, glancing at the girl again.

"I don't see that it matters," said the girl, breaking in. "The point that counts is that Riley Mason has two reasons for catching us. One is money, and the other is hate. And the question is . . . what are we going to do about it?"

"That's the most important question," said Pierre Vernon. "We've simply got to dig in and fight. That's all there is to it."

"If we dig in and start fighting," said Cactus, "we'll have enemies in the camp. The Mexicans and those two loafers yonder will all throw in against us."

"Why, they don't look pretty, but I don't think that they're so bad," said Vernon. "Perhaps they'll stand by and do their share."

"Perhaps," said Cactus, and stopped talking.

Vincent appealed to him at once, recognizing in him the natural leader of us all.

"Go on, Cactus!" he exclaimed. "We need all our hands and all of our brains, too, in a crisis like this. Tell us what you think is the best way out."

"I don't see any good way out," said Cactus simply. "We

can't run far through this mud. And even if we could, our tracks could be seen easy on a night like this."

"True," said Vincent.

"True as the devil!" I agreed. "I wish that this here house was smaller. Then we could defend it better."

"I don't wish that it was smaller," said Cactus. "The way it stands, there's a chance that we may slip from room to room defending the place, if they begin to press us with guns and numbers."

Vincent raised his hand and struck himself on the forehead. "I'm practically helpless with either a rifle or a revolver," he admitted.

"That's no great news to us," said Vernon. Then he glanced toward the girl and bit his lip.

She stared back at Vernon and replied, for herself: "Father is really not much with a rifle or a revolver, but I can handle them both pretty well."

"D'you think that you could shoot at a man?" asked Vernon, smiling a little.

"At some men . . . yes," she said steadily.

The fool ought to have seen that he was being put in his right place, but he was too full of himself to see anything.

He responded with: "What does Woodstock think about all of this?"

I couldn't help it. The words just burst out of me. "I think you're a damn' fool!"

He started, then he recovered himself, and looked at me with a scowl and a sneer.

"You're small enough to say that."

"You big drink of water," I said, "you may be taller than me, but I know how to whittle you down to my own size."

I shouldn't have said either of those things, but you know how you can be irritated until the passion goes right up to your

36

head? That was the way with me, at least. I apologized on the heel of it — not to that scamp of a Vernon, but to the rest of the company.

"I'm sorry, everybody. But this fellow rubs me the wrong way. He's a four-flushing gambler, the way that I make him out. And yet he's trying to talk down to everybody in the room."

It wasn't much of an apology, perhaps, and it was wrong of me to make more trouble when we had more than enough already.

Vernon put on a lot of extra dignity and said that, when our troubles permitted, he would pay attention to me, and not before. He was willing to swallow an insult or two in the meantime. He spoke with a good deal of dignity, I must say. But I looked behind his words and seemed to see a yellow liver. I thought him a coward, out and out.

I saw Cactus turn away from the group and begin to walk up and down, keeping always in earshot of what might be said.

Vernon said, loudly and nobly, that it was simply a matter of fighting to the death when the time came. I said that death was easy to talk about, but damned hard to face. I said that I was badly scared right then, but that I thought I could fight in the pinch. But I would like to have some sort of a plan of defense.

Then Lydia Vincent said: "I think that Cactus has an idea. Will you tell us what it is, Cactus?"

He came back and stood with us, frowning at the face of the girl, and plainly seeing nothing but his own thoughts. Then he said: "Well, I have an idea, but it's not a very cheerful one for Perry Woodstock, here."

He looked at me, and I winced a little. I wondered what sort of trouble he was going to propose for me.

"Will you go on?" asked Vincent, with a sort of nervous eagerness.

"I'll go on, all right," said our friend, Cactus. "My idea is that we're blinded by the walls around us, while we stay in here. I suggest that some of us go out and explore."

"Explore for what?" snapped Vernon.

"For Riley Mason, of course," said Cactus.

"And what's to be done if you can find him?" asked Vernon.

"He's to be killed," responded Cactus gently.

Vernon drew in a quick breath.

"Mason is a dangerous ruffian," he said.

"So am I," replied Cactus.

That gave us all a good sharp turn, I'm sure. One good thing came out of it though: it silenced Mr. Vernon on the spot.

Cactus went on: "I suggest that Woodstock and I go out and scout about, if Perry is willing to take the chance with me."

I swallowed with a good deal of difficulty, before I was able to answer: "Yes, I'll go."

I remember how the eyes of the girl rested on me, understanding my fear and pitying it without despising it. I felt small, but I knew then that I'd be able to go through the motions of filling out a man's part. Anyway, Cactus slapped me on the shoulder and smiled.

"We may be able to wangle somebody important out of this," he said. "At any rate, it's better than waiting here to be surrounded and dropped like a lot of helpless sheep."

I got a rifle. He took another. We waved to the rest of them, and I went out with him into the night, feeling that death was only a step ahead of me.

VII

"PRISONERS"

Things had been letting up a good deal just before we left the house, but, as soon as we poked our noses outside, the wind squatted and jumped straight in our faces with a howl, and the rain came and clawed us. And then on a flood of lightning the mountains seemed to rush at us out of the darkness. The thunder seemed to be spilling off those mountain heads straight above us.

My courage was knocked in the head, right then and there. I got my companion by the arm, and I said to him: "Look here, old-timer, is it right for us to go away alone and leave the girl and her father back there with those hounds?"

He listened to my shouting, then he put his lips close to my ear. "I know that it's dangerous to leave 'em," he said. "But there's no way out for us, I'm afraid. We must catch the Riley Mason outfit off guard and smash them. If we just wait here for whatever may happen, we'll be caught between the Mason gang on the one side and our own crooks on the other, and we'll be done in."

Of course, I could see that there was a lot in what he said, but, nevertheless, that didn't make the howling devil of a night any more satisfactory to me. I kept going forward, steadily enough, wherever he led, but my heart was not in the work, and my eyes were trying to look in four directions all at once.

We edged around to the rear of the house, then climbed a little hill into a thicket of trees and big brush. Up there on the hill, with every spurt of lightning like the scratching of immense matches on the ceiling of the sky, we would have a chance to look across the lowlands all around us. But I wondered what would happen if, while we walked up the slope, the Riley Mason outfit were lying in wait for us, within the brush, ready to mow us down when we got within a good, easy distance. Fighting men have to take chances like that, and they're welcome to them. I only fight when I have to.

We had got right up to the line of the bushes when the sky broke in two and let through four or five cascading streams of lightning along with peal after peal of thunder that came bumping and banging down like ten thousand barrels rolling downstairs from the moon. And in that second or two of bright light I saw two men standing in the bushes just ahead of us.

My partner saw them, too, and his gun cracked quicker than I could have snapped my fingers. Then the noose of a rope jerked tight around my chest, and I was yanked forward on my face into the mud. By the time I got my wits about me, I was tied in a bundle. I looked aside, and the light of the storm showed me that the very same thing had happened to Cactus. I can't tell you how incredible it was to me, when I saw that he had gone down almost as easily as I had. Because, up to this moment, he had seemed pretty nearly invincible to me. I took off my hat to Riley Mason, though, scared as I was. Shooting at a target by lightning flashes, of course, was not likely to accomplish half as much as reaching for it with a forty-foot rope and a big noose on the end of it.

They carried us back into the middle of the grove and put us down in a place where the beat of the rain was kept from our bodies. Then they worked up a fire, not big enough for much heat, but big enough for light. Riley Mason stood over the fire, holding out his hands to warm them, and the shadows of his hands kept brushing back and forth across his handsome, vicious face.

We were in the center of a group of five or six big trees whose branches interfaced and made a green roof over us. The firelight showed us very little more than Riley, because the others kept in the background. But when the sky opened and spilled half a million quarts of electricity at a splash, then we could look around into the depths of the wood about us and see the three other men in the gang.

I knew them all, and knew no good of them. Big Josh Carey had been a bad actor all his life, and Slugger Watts, with his dark, broken face, was known to be a bank bandit and all kinds of a scoundrel. Then there was Stew Bailey, who was one of those happy, round, little, fat men who are capable of smiling their way through all sorts of villainy.

Mason seemed to be content just to stand there and look us over for a long time.

Slugger Watts was the first one to speak. "Look here, Riley," he said, "you got the two of 'em at once. Why not clear 'em away. Then we'll go on and gather in the cash. No use wasting time."

Riley did not turn his eyes from Cactus.

"There's plenty of time," he said quietly. And then he laughed.

You could see that he felt the way a cat does, when it has the mouse between its paws. No use hurrying with the meal.

"I'm for hurrying," said Watts. "No use lingering over a gent like Cactus. He's got too much slickness up his sleeve."

"That's why I wanta linger," said Riley Mason. "I wanta see if he can work himself or talk himself loose from those ropes before he gets a slug through his brain." And he smiled again. "You didn't think that it would come out this way, Cactus, did you?"

I waited for the voice of Cactus, hoping that it would be steady. It was, all right. It was as steady and calm as could be.

He said: "Why, Riley, I really thought that it might wind

up like this. I thought so from the first."

"You did?" exclaimed Riley Mason. "Come now, Cactus. That don't sound likely, does it?"

"Why not?" said Cactus. "I'd been chasing you so long, and you'd been running away so fast, that I knew you'd never stand and make a fair fight of it against me."

Riley's hands, stretched above the fire, turned suddenly into fists.

"I been on the run before you, have I?" he asked fiercely.

"Well, what would you call it?" went on Cactus. "What would *you* call it, Josh?"

Josh called it nothing at all. The three in the background smiled a little, however, I noticed. Riley did not look to see what their facial expressions might be. Perhaps he guessed.

"I never ran away from anybody in the world!" he said harshly.

"All right," said Cactus. "There's no use arguing. I simply knew right from the first that you'd never stand up to me. You'd have to back up and get a chance at me through a trick that would hand you an advantage."

"You knew that right from the first, did you?" Riley Mason said, with a whining note in his voice.

It was rage, that whine. Some dogs make the same sound when they start a fight. In Riley Mason, it simply meant that he was ready for murder, and I got even sicker than I had been before.

"I knew it right from the first," said Cactus Terry. "If you were afraid to meet up with Jigger, then you'd be afraid to meet up with me. That was plain enough."

"Me? Afraid to meet up with Jigger?" shouted Riley Mason, maddened with shame and with anger. "Why, I met up with him and bumped him off, didn't I? That's how much afraid I was of him."

Cactus shrugged his shoulders. "Why do you keep on whining such lies as that, Riley?" he asked. "Everybody knows that you're no fighting man . . . you're just a murderer that takes advantages and shoots in the dark."

"You lying fool!" yelled Riley Mason.

"It's pretty easy to call names, when you got the other fellow tied up," said Cactus. "But the facts are what everybody knows. You found poor Jigger sitting down with a light in the room and an open window, and you just rested your gun on the windowsill and shot him."

"You lie!" yelled Riley again.

He was so enraged that he began to shake and shudder all over.

"There was a mark on the windowsill, you sneaking throat-cutter," answered Cactus. "There was a mark made by your gun when you fired. So that's proof enough."

"It's a lie. Everything that you say is a damned lie," cried Mason. "Look what I tell you . . . this time you lie biggest and loudest of all. I didn't rest the gun on the sill of the window."

"You must have. You couldn't shoot that straight without a rest," declared Cactus.

"Couldn't I? Couldn't I?" exclaimed Riley. "Now, I'm gonna tell you something, you bright guy . . . you fat-headed fool. I was standing a good three paces outside of that window, when I shot Jigger. And I used up only one bullet on him!"

I saw, of course, how Riley Mason had been trapped into the confession. Now Cactus allowed himself a slow smile of contempt.

"So it's out at last," he said. "Everybody knew it before, though."

"What?" said Riley Mason.

"That you stood outside the window and killed him. That

you didn't dare to come into the room and fight it out with poor old Jigger."

"I didn't . . . ," began Riley Mason. And then he paused, and made a choking sound.

He saw that he had let himself in for it with his own foolishness in talking so much. But I didn't see how this victory in words helped the position of us two captives at all. We were dead men — any way you looked at it.

VIII

"TREACHERY"

It's a bad thing to have to jump from one place to another, but, unless I do that, I don't know how I can bring all the threads together. For while things were happening out there in the muddy dark of the night to me and Cactus Terry, other things were happening inside of the house that promised to turn out just about as bad.

It was Pierre Vernon that started the trouble going. I had had him most in mind when I told Cactus that, if I were he, I would think twice before going off alone and trying to tackle the Mason gang. And the minute that Pierre saw us disappear in the black night, he started his work going. He got very blustering and familiar, at first, and assured George Vincent and the girl that he would be able to take care of them, and that, although he was not a man to display weapons and skill, he always went armed in this rough part of the world. Then he slicked out a brace of pistols and put a slug as neat as you please right through an old tin can that stood rusting in a corner of the room.

The sudden explosion wasn't any too good for the bad nerves of Vincent, and he snapped out a wish that Pierre Vernon would stop showing off. There would be time enough for shooting, he said, when the bandits showed up and attacked them.

Vernon seemed glad to get a chance to talk about the danger that threatened and what they ought to do about it. He said that, for his part, he never had really approved of the halt in the ranch house. He, for his part, thought that they should leave the house at once and continue the march toward Yellow Creek.

George Vincent said that he would not dream of stirring from the ranch house except with Perry Woodstock and Cactus Terry along.

Vernon took another line then and began to show his hand. He turned to Stuffy Bill and Chick.

"Well, boys," he said, "you hear what Mister Vincent says. But it seems to me that we all have a vote in this matter. It's his money that's bringing danger and not on his own head only, but on the rest of us as well. We ought to be able to cast our votes about what's right, and what's wrong. What do you boys think?"

Of course, Stuffy and Chick were only waiting for a chance to horn in, and I can imagine the grin that must have come on the black, greasy face of Stuffy when he was appealed to in this way.

He said: "Why, there ain't anything to it, from my way of thinking. We just ought to get out of the house at once and march."

"And what," put in the girl, "will become of Cactus and Perry Woodstock when they come back and find out that we've moved on?"

"Maybe they won't come back," said Stuffy, with relish in his voice. "Maybe they won't come back at all. And if they don't, it's better for us to be on the way than just to be sitting here waiting for Riley Mason's gang to eat us all alive."

The three Mexicans rose then like one man. They said they were for marching at once. Vernon, of course, was delighted.

He turned back to Vincent. "You see how it is," he smiled. "We get six votes against the two of yours. That settles it. This is a democratic country, Mister Vincent."

It wasn't hard to guess how those democrats would work together. Before they had been long on the way, a tap on the head would finish poor Vincent. And that precious pigskin case would then be in the hands of the six thugs, led by Vernon. And the girl would either stay behind or follow them.

That was clear enough to Vincent, and he, saying nothing at all, but cornered and desperate, got ready to fight. His face was white and his hands trembled, but he pulled out a revolver.

Stuffy simply laughed out loud. "You gotta come where the majority votes," said Stuffy, the democrat.

Lydia Vincent picked up a rifle that had been leaning against the wall and threw it expertly into the ready position. She stood close to her father, saying: "There's nothing but a fight that will accomplish anything, Father. Keep back from me, Stuffy, or I'll. . . ."

She jerked the butt of the gun to her shoulder, and Stuffy walked straight in upon her, an odd, sneering smile on his face. He came with one hand stretched out toward the gun.

"If you come another step . . . !" she cried out.

"Get back, you scoundrel!" cried George Vincent.

But Stuffy answered: "I know you kind of birds. You ain't got the nerve to shoot. Gimme that rifle!"

He closed in on Lydia Vincent, and grasping the muzzle of the rifle, while she, with face white and contorted, seemed striving to pull the trigger, tore the weapon from her hands. It exploded in the midst of this flourish, and the bullet clipped through Stuffy's coat, close to his ribs. A yell of fear and rage came from him and from Chick who, being just behind his friend, was almost struck by the same bullet. As Stuffy staggered back from the danger that had threatened him so closely, Chick, with a wild yell, threw himself in and flung his revolver into the face of George Vincent.

The older man went down on one knee, his hands pressed

47

against his face. The blood from a cut across his forehead made by the impact of the heavy gun streamed down and blinded him. Half stunned, totally helpless, he crouched back there against the wall.

Stuffy leaned over and picked up the fallen pigskin case, then made for the door.

I suppose that Lydia hardly knew what had happened to the valise that held the money. She was more than stunned by the attack that had taken the gun from her. And then she saw the gleam of the gun as it whirled through the air and beat against her father's head. She was on her knees at once, beside him, paying no regard to the rest of the world, when the Mexicans, Stuffy and Bill, and big Pierre Vernon got through the door of the house and out into the open.

The rain was beating on them as they ran, but they felt as though they had gone out into the spring sunshine — a hundred and sixty thousand dollars, and only six ways to divide it.

Inside the house, poor Vincent recovered his wits a little, and his girl tied a handkerchief as a bandage around his bleeding head.

It was he himself, as his eyes cleared, who cried out: "And the money, Lydia? The money?"

She looked about her with a gasp. "They have it! They've gone with it," she groaned.

George Vincent, throwing his hands above his head, suddenly ran out from the house.

At the door Lydia overtook him, crying out that it was useless for one man to pursue six scoundrels, all armed.

But he only struck her hands away from him and ran on furiously through the mud and the whipping rain, with the lightning to show him the path.

And she? Well, what could she do but follow him?

The last man to leave that place was Mike, the driver. He

48

had been standing against the wall, in a trance, all the while. I think I know what was going on inside of him. He was a good enough fellow, but he was terribly tempted to cut in with the thugs and get away with a share of the spoils. Between that and the decent heart of him wanting to help the Vincents, he had been paralyzed. One call from the girl to him, by name, might have got him out of the trance and into proper action. But he didn't get that call. Only after all the others were gone did he come to with a groan. And he went lurching out into the darkness after them.

IX

"BLUFF"

And now I must go back to the situation out there among the dripping trees, in the dull, trembling light of Riley Mason's little fire.

I couldn't see what Cactus was driving at with all his talk about the murder of his friend, Jigger, except that perhaps he wished to enrage Riley Mason to such a point that he might kill us instantly and so spare us the agony of whatever tortures they might cook up for us.

"Come along, Riley," Big Josh Carey bawled out impatiently. "Bash in his head and finish his tongue wagging."

Riley turned savagely on the speaker. "Shut your face, will you?" he snarled.

"There you are," said Cactus. "Bluff again. Always bluff. There's nothing to this fellow's reputation for standing up to gunmen. He's killed his men, but he's always done it when they were helpless."

"I never stood up to any man, eh?" growled Riley Mason.

"Come, come, Riley," said Cactus. "Why keep up the bluff among men who know you?"

"I'll tell you this," said Riley Mason, ". . . and you know damn' well it's true. I was the only man that ever dared stand up to Jim Welch, when he was shooting them up pretty near every week in old Fargo."

"Jim Welch?" asked Cactus, smiling. "Why, Jim's the fellow you shot down in the Perkins Saloon in Fargo, wasn't he?"

"He was. It wasn't night, neither," said Riley, boasting. "It was broad daylight, and there was twenty men that seen the draw and the shooting."

"I know all about that," said Cactus sadly. "It's too bad for you, Riley, that you have to pick out cases I know so well."

"It wasn't daylight, eh?" said Riley Mason. "And there wasn't eighteen or twenty men in there that saw the shooting?"

"Yeah, and I've talked to some of those men," said Cactus.

"You have? And what did they say?"

"You oughtn't to ask me to tell what I know of the shooting of Jim Welch in the Perkins Saloon," said Cactus. "It'll be bad for the hold that you have on these fellows."

"Will it?" said Riley Mason, his lip curling.

I got the strong idea, right then, that Riley Mason hadn't lied about the killing of Jim Welch, and that he knew that he was in the right. Otherwise, he wouldn't have stood his ground and let Cactus go on talking and plaguing him.

"Yes, it will," said Cactus. "They'll find you out one of these days, and one of 'em will turn you over his knee and spank you."

"One of 'em will, eh?" said Riley Mason.

He was a pale, mean green, now. He turned his head slowly and looked from one face to another among those fellows who were sitting back on the outside rim of the firelight.

I noticed, pretty carefully, that they were looking straight back at the leader. Not as though they were defying him, mind you, but as though they were mighty interested in anything that he might have to say to 'em. And as though they wanted to hear some more about the past history of this fellow, and about what had happened in that fight between him and Jim Welch.

Something in the looks of those three men at the edge of the firelight must have turned Riley Mason's head for a minute. After all, he was a gunman and a killer, and like all such men

51

he was proud of his reputation. What he should have done, of course, was kill Cactus Terry and me at once. And once we were out of the way, it would have been no trick at all to laugh off a dead man's charges.

But Riley Mason saw the growing doubt in the eyes of his men, and that must have got under his skin and turned his head for a minute. He had killed Jim Welch in fair fight — and his pride made him want, more than anything else in the world, to prove Cactus Terry a liar. He licked his dry lips and grinned crookedly.

"I'll tell you all what happened," he said. "And I'll make Cactus swallow his lying tongue before he dies!" He took a deep breath, and the grin left his face. "I had a friend by the name of Chile Smith," he said. "Chile, who was only a kid, barged into Fargo one day and got into an argument with the redhead, Jim Welch. Welch throws a chair at him, knocks him down, and then kicks him in the head while he's lying there. And the kid dies of that kick. It cracked his skull for him. When I heard about it, I buckled on my guns, got on a hoss, and rode right into town."

"Regular hero, eh, going out to revenge a friend's death?" Cactus commented. "Listen, boys, to the way he tells it. He could always tell things pretty well."

"And when I'm through telling this," continued Riley Mason, "I'm gonna cut the ears off your head so you won't hear much more before you die, and, after that, I'm gonna cut the tongue out of your lying black mouth and make you eat it."

He meant what he said.

"Well, then," said Cactus. "Why not go ahead with your story and get it over with?"

"This is what happened," said Riley Mason, controlling his anger with a mighty effort. "When I got into town, I inquired around, then sent out word that I was after Jim Welch. When the sheriff heard that, he rode out of town, because he said that a fight between us two would be a good thing, no matter who was killed."

"Anyway, I finally got wind that Welch was in the Perkins Saloon, and that he'd wait for me there. I looked my guns over, walked down the street, and went in. And just as I stepped through the swinging doors, I see Jim Welch taking a drink that he don't finish. He spots me, throws the glass of whiskey at my head, and pulls his six-gun with the same move.

"That's about all," went on Riley Mason. "The whiskey didn't get in my eyes and blind me, as Welch had hoped it would, and I beat him fair and square to the draw. I put a bullet through his right shoulder.

"That spoiled his gun hand, but he was game, all right. He picked his gun out of his useless right hand with his left, and took another shot at me. But the bullet only plowed up the floor, while I put my second slug straight through his stomach."

"Well," said Cactus, "I've heard liars before, but I never heard a better lie than this one, because most of it is the truth. Everything happened the way he said, except that there was *more* happened!"

"What?" said Riley.

"You really want me to tell?"

"Why, damn you, you've got nothing to tell," snarled Riley.

"You knew a fellow called Steve Pepper, down there in Fargo?" asked Cactus, calm and judicial in his way of speaking. And then, before Riley could answer him, he went on in a quick rush of words. "Yeah, you bet you did," he snapped. "And it's him that told me the truth that you left out!"

X

"GUN TALK"

It's hard to give an idea of the suspense that was eating at my heart while I listened to the way Cactus was badgering that man-eater, Riley Mason. The killer's three gunhands, you could see, were by now just as much interested in what my partner had to say as were Riley and myself.

"You met with Steve Pepper the day before you killed Jim Welch, and you talked to him like this," said Cactus. " 'Steve,' you said, 'I'm going to meet Jim Welch, and it's better for me to find him drunk than sober. You've got all night and tomorrow morning to do the job.'

" 'How am I going to get that Welch drunk?' said Steve, 'when I have no money. I couldn't get him drunk except on free liquor, and nothing's free in Fargo but the air.'

" 'That's all right,' you said to Steve. 'Here's a hundred bucks. Take it and get Jim plastered. But mind your own hooch and how you handle it. Understand?'

"So Steve, he said that he understood, all right, and he went and did a good job. The party started one afternoon and went on to the next, and during that time it cost Steve the hundred bucks. They were so plastered that it took two weeks before Steve Pepper's hands stopped shaking. Two weeks before he could drink coffee without spilling it onto his vest. That's how much hooch was in the pair of them . . . and that's the condition that big Jim Welch was in when you stepped through the swinging door into the Perkins Saloon. You knew damn' well that Welch was paralyzed, or you'd never have dared to come in sight of him. Even then you were scared white, just to stand up and face a helpless hulk like him."

Riley Mason, too angry for words by now, had begun a sort of choked-up growling, deep in his throat. His right hand was on his gun.

"Don't talk to me like that," said Cactus, seeming sort of disgusted. "You can cut my throat now, and I suppose that you'll do just that. But I've told the truth about you, and I know damn' well that you never stood up to any man in your life, except some green kid of a tenderfoot that didn't know one end of a gun from another. You've shot gents from behind, and when they were drunk, and all that. But the reputation that you've built up as a gunman is all wrong. You're no gunman at all. You're just a plain, dirty, cheap murderer!"

That last was what did it. The words hit me with a slam and a bang — and I saw Riley Mason beginning to lean a little toward Cactus — just leaning gradually and slowly, without moving his feet. I knew then that when he leaped, he would jump like a wildcat. Sick? Yes, I was sick all right. I was so dog-gone sick that I could hardly see. After Cactus was clawed to death, my turn would come. All I could think to pray for was a quicker finish than would come to poor Cactus. I prayed for that, and hoped that no matter what happened, I would be able to keep my jaws locked and not howl or beg like a dog.

But just as the knees of Riley Mason sagged a little — just as he was about to spring for Cactus — I heard Stew Bailey say: "Aw, leave him be, Riley."

Suddenly I understood everything, and it staggered me — the brilliance of it, and the cool thinking of it. You see the idea. Cactus had set out to talk down Riley Mason so much that his three pet man-killers would all despise their chief. They would despise him so much that they'd find the nerve to make a stand against him. And when they made the stand — why, then, of course, friend Cactus and I would have some sort of a chance.

Chance? I saw then that we'd have better than that. For as Stew Bailey spoke, I noticed Cactus's right hand. It was free and stealing down into a pocket of his coat. And his hands had been bound with rope at least as tight as the ones that now bit into my arms and worked toward the bone with a bulldog grip.

Riley Mason, in the meantime, had been stopped in the very act of leaping at Cactus. And now he whirled, in a blind, devilish temper.

"Did you tell me to leave him be?" howled Riley.

"I told you that, and I meant it," said Stew Bailey.

"You fool! You crack-brained fool!" cried Riley Mason. "Do you believe the lies he's been telling?"

"You were just now gonna prove him right by murderin' another helpless gent," said Stew Bailey. "That's why I say . . . leave him be."

"I got a good mind to leave him be and get at *you*," said Riley Mason. "Except that I see what he's after now. He wants to get me scrapping with the three of you. Then he'll be happy. He wants to see the four of us murdering one another."

Slugger Watts, his hideous face more ugly than ever, said: "Look at that! Riley sees that *your* hands ain't tied, Stew, and he's gonna make sure that he don't mix with you . . . not where both of you have got an even chance."

"You, too?" shouted Riley Mason.

He stammered, and his teeth beat together. I never saw a man in such a wild fury, and yet I've seen plenty in the craziest rages. I think that the others may actually have thought that it was fear that was working in Riley Mason.

Josh Carey said suddenly: "Aw, shut up, Riley. You've

four-flushed long enough. There ain't anything to you but bluff."

"My God, all three," gasped Riley Mason.

Yes, he might have seemed afraid, but he was *not* afraid. I could tell, looking at him, that the story Cactus had told about Steve Pepper, if ever there was such a man, must have been one long lie. At any rate, I know that Riley had no fear as he stood there before his men. No, I think that he was almost glad — glad that, being in such a rage, he had three new and fresh victims to tackle.

"You started this, and I'll take you first," he snarled at Stew Bailey.

Then I saw that Cactus, armed with a knife, was slashing at the ropes that bound his legs. A minute later he slid his hand across and cut the cords that bound my hands together. I'll never forget how I felt then — as hope rushed in on me, like a bright river, a river of glory worth drowning in. I could have laughed or cried, like a baby.

Stew Bailey was talking now. "I started it first, and I'll finish it first, too. I always had a hunch that we were fools to work for you. Cactus is right. He's bound to be right. He's got brains, and he sees what we all ought to have seen long ago."

"He's got brains, has he? Oh, damn him! He's got brains, has he?" Riley Mason yelled. "I'll have those brains out where they can be weighed and looked at, pretty soon. I'll have them opened up so that the buzzards can enjoy 'em. But he comes after you, Bailey. Fill your hand!"

Even then the three of them didn't understand that Riley Mason was all they'd ever dreamed him to be — and a lot more. He might have murdered in the dark, but he was able to fight in the open, too. And he was about to show that trio of devils the truth about himself.

Free of the ropes that had bound me, I gathered myself to

jump for cover when the explosion came. Right then I was appreciating Cactus as no man was ever appreciated before.

This fellow, Bailey, stood with his hands on his hips, sneering at his boss. "Don't go and invite me to fill my hand first," he snarled. "Fill your own, you damned fake. I'll match you at the draw."

"You will, will you?" screamed Riley Mason, the pitch of his voice jumping up the scale a notch or two with every word. "Take it, then, and be damned!"

It wasn't a draw he made. He just wished, and the gun was in his hand.

Fat Stew Bailey was quick enough, quick as a tiger, in fact. But he seemed to be slow as molasses compared with the gun speed of Riley Mason. The poor fellow didn't even have his shooting iron clear of leather when Riley Mason finished his draw and fired.

I was jumping for cover at the same moment, but I couldn't take my eyes from what was happening.

Bailey was hit, and hit hard. His body jerked halfway around. He threw out his hands and started falling sidewise, just as the second bullet hit him.

I was behind a tree, then, and turning to run. Back in the clearing I heard Mason screaming like a man gone mad: "Who's next? Who's next, damn your eyes!"

Stew Bailey, on hands and knees, was dragging himself away from the devil that raged there in the firelight. And the other pair, Josh and Slugger, had seen enough to make them realize that they'd been sadly deceived. They were diving blindly for the deepest shadows.

I heard more gun shots behind me, rapidly fired. Then I started making tracks so fast that the wind of my own running blurred everything else for me — even the rumble of the thunder, that began just then to roar and beat more heavily than ever. I ran faster then than I ever ran in my life, before or since. But there beside me was Cactus, taking time to look back and running easily.

"No use getting winded," he said at my ear. And he touched my arm, and made me slow down.

I saw, in the flare of lightning, the smile on his face. And it seemed to me, just then, and it has always seemed to me since, that it was the proper sort of light to show one the smile on the face of Cactus Terry.

XI

"CACTUS GOES TO PIECES"

"We've had the luck, and we've done our job," said Cactus to me. "If Riley Mason comes on tonight, he'll be coming alone. And maybe he won't come at all. Maybe one of those boys will tag Riley with a lucky shot, while he hunts for them through the trees."

I could hardly think about anything else, I was that taken up with wonder concerning this fellow who stepped along so cheerfully beside me.

But I said: "They won't hurt Riley Mason. They're numb, they're so scared. I'll never forget the way he drove the three of 'em before him. He's a great fighting man, Cactus."

"You bet he is," said Cactus. "He's one of the best in the world. He can be a sneaking devil, too. But he's also a grand, fighting man."

I swallowed hard. "That stuff about Steve Pepper," I said. "That was all made up, wasn't it?"

"Of course," said Cactus. "There never was a fellow by that name, so far as I know. I wouldn't have named a real man, unless I was sure that Riley would be dead before he got a chance at him." Suddenly he was laughing. "Pride is the worst of all faults, Perry," he told me. "Pride is the thing that knocks us over. Look at Riley there, with three good men behind him, and you and me in his hands safely. Then, when his pride was touched up, he turned blind as a bat and went all to pieces. He's lost us . . . he's lost his mob. And for the first time, we've got a fighting chance."

"Cactus," I said, and I talked from my heart, "a few minutes back I knew that I was a dead man. I knew it so well, that I don't feel that I *can* be here, walking back to the ranch house. And I owe it to you that I'm alive. You're the smartest devil in the world. I never met anybody like you."

"If you had, you might have lost your wallet. Don't make me proud, Woodstock. You keep on talking like that, and I'll be as blind as our friend, Riley Mason."

We came at last to the house. As we paused before it, Cactus said to me: "We haven't much time. Riley will probably run the three of 'em to death, or lose all track of 'em in the woods. And then he'll come like a greyhound after us. And you've seen what he can do when he cuts loose.

"Now our job," said Cactus, "is to move fast and make decisions. We've got to split up the party. The Mexicans, Stuffy and Chick, and Pierre Vernon are spoiled meat, I guess. We'll cut them out and leave them alone. The rest of us . . . that is, Mike and you and I and the Vincents . . . are going to march along together. No matter what the weather is, we've got to go. And as for the bad eggs, we'll hold them off, if we have to, with a little shooting. We've come to the crisis, old son."

We had come to the crisis, all right. For he'd hardly finished saying this when we got through the door of the old deserted shack of a house, and, inside, we found what I've already prepared you for — nothing but the flicker of the shadows that the dying fire threw along the walls. It was a shock for me, but what I went through seemed nothing compared with what happened to Cactus. There was the man of steel nerves, iron mind, and adamant will now with a hand against the wall and shaking all over.

He saw something glimmer on the floor, ran suddenly, and picked it up — a revolver, not far from the fire. He looked down at it, then up at me.

I knew what it meant. People don't rush out of a place and leave their guns behind them unless there's a good deal of excitement in the air. I went over and lifted a rifle that lay in the dust. A bullet had been fired from it. I told him so.

He seemed totally dazed, and he began to walk up and down with an irregular step, simply saying: "I'm too late. I'm too late. And she's gone. My God, Perry, I'm too late!"

A terrible panic began to rise in me. It wasn't, I'm afraid, so much concerning what might have happened to the others, as it was the sight of what was happening to Cactus. He came up to me suddenly and grabbed my arm, looking at me with a wild, unknowing eye, like a crazy man.

"Perry," he said, "what if something should happen to her? What if something should happen to her?"

He stood there with his mouth open, looking as though I could tell him about the end of the world.

I got colder and colder. I said: "Pull yourself together, old son. Now's the time when we have to do something."

"Yes, but what?" he asked me.

I grew more panicky still. Think of a man like Cactus, with the brain he had in his head — think of him asking directions of me.

"Why, man, we ought to try to find out where they went . . . they've certainly left a trail in the mud."

He gripped my arm hard. "That's it," he said. "God give me light enough to follow her. God give me luck enough to find her." And he made a rush out of that house.

I felt that I was tagging along with a man partially mad. And through my fear and disturbance, I did a little thinking. It was plain as your face that Cactus had lost his head and his heart over the girl. And what would that lead to? It was a dizzy thing to think about. A girl like Lydia Vincent, and a stage robber — well, just the saying of the problem was enough to finish it. But just the saying of it would not finish it for a fellow like Cactus. If he could talk himself out of ropes and the hands of Riley Mason and Mason's gang — what would he do when it came to talking himself into the good graces of Lydia Vincent? Well, the future, I decided, could take care of itself. We had a job ahead of us that was like looking for bats in the dark.

One thing, there was plenty of light for seeing now. The storm was breaking up, and its breaking was even wilder and grander than its coming, for the whole western half of the sky tumbled into separate clouds, and the solid wall of leaden gray and black retreated toward the east rapidly, letting the moon show through again. So by moonlight we started out to find the trail left by the Vincents and the others.

Right at the start Cactus went down on his knees, cursing because one pair of high-heeled Mexican boots made tracks almost as small as those of the girl. However, he disentangled the two quickly enough, and then began one of the hardest trips I ever made. It was a job, let me tell you, just keeping up with that fellow while he raced along like a foxhound on a hot scent. I paid no attention to the trail, because I was too busy following my companion.

He ran stooped over a good deal, staring at the ground. And once he came to a full stop on a gravelly patch where the sign practically disappeared. I was glad of the pause, because my lungs were burning up. And I heard him say: "There're not together. Most of the gang have gone on ahead. The girl's behind with one man . . . that must be her father. They're trailing the rest of 'em. You see what that means?"

"What?" I panted.

"Why," he said, "it simply means that the crooks have the loot, and the Vincents are following along after 'em. Might as well set a pair of puppies to following the trail of a pack of wolves."

Then he was off again, at the same hot pace, with me staggering along behind. Finally, after what seemed hours, I heard a wild yell of joy from Cactus and saw him pointing. And well off ahead of us I made out the figures of two people who were going quite slowly up the slope of a rain-drenched hill. The Vincents?

We put on steam, both of us. But that fellow, Cactus, he left me behind the way a greyhound might leave a cocker spaniel. As I came up to them, panting, I saw that it was, indeed, the Vincents, father and daughter, that we had run down.

XII

"TWO AGAINST MANY"

There was plenty of light from the moon to show us that George Vincent himself was close to a collapse. I'll never forget the look on his face, the grim and set jaw of him, and the way his head was canted to the side with sheer exhaustion. He had to keep his fists clenched in order to force himself on. But you could see that he would rather have died than give in — and dying was what it looked like he might do.

We learned from Lydia Vincent what had happened in the old ranch house. She told us the whole thing in about ten words. I never saw anybody as cool and calm as that girl was on that crazy night. There are a lot of girls who need to be housed and warmed, delicately fed and watched over, and loved and tended every moment. Those girls may be all right. But give me a girl like Lydia Vincent. She could be a helpmate for a prince or a pauper. As the wife of a pauper she would share his poverty, put her shoulder to the wheel, and make her weight felt in working uphill till they got to better times.

There was this girl out in the middle of hell with her father, and not looking a bit out of place — because her place was the exact moment of his greatest need. Where he was in trouble, that was where she would be. I also thought that if a girl like this hooked up even with a man like Cactus Terry, it would be all right. He had plenty of strength, and strength was what she knew how to handle. If he was a wild hawk, why, she might tame him into a hunting falcon that would bring all sorts of wonderful things out of the sky and right down to her hand.

Vincent began to break out into a tirade to Cactus Terry. But the girl got me to one side and said in my ear: "You've been a kind friend to us, Perry. Be a still kinder one, and make my father stop this rush through the mud and the night. He's exhausted, and exhaustion and exposure can kill a man of his type . . . as quickly as water can kill a hen. He's got to be stopped."

I could see that she was right. And I noticed that even as she made this appeal on behalf of the father who meant so much to her, there was no tremor in her voice, and her eyes met mine without any frantic entreaty.

I went up to Vincent and said: "Look here. We've got to try to get on the trail of those rats, but there's only one good way to do that. We've got to have a center for our operations, and then we've got to throw out feelers."

"What do you mean by that, Woodstock?" he said to me.

"Why . . . ," I said, talking with a little irritation, as though what I had said ought to be perfectly clear to any sensible man, "why, Vincent, what's the use of all of us swarming into the mountains in one party? That's a crazy idea. The best way is to locate them. Then the lot of us can go ahead and close in on 'em and smash 'em up."

Cactus looked at me and said nothing.

Vincent began to shake his head and argue. He said: "I've got to keep on. There's nothing to compel you fellows to keep on with me. The affair is mine. It's caused you trouble enough already. I know that. But I must go on. I'm not tired."

"Of course, you're not," Cactus said suddenly. "But Woodstock is right. We've got to have a central point. Right here . . . right yonder in that patch of poplars. That's the place. You stay there, and, if the thugs try to double back from one of those ravines, you can block 'em and turn 'em back toward us."

I thought of poor George Vincent trying to block and turn back that herd of well-armed scoundrels, and wondered how I kept from laughing.

Cactus went on: "You'll hold the center, that way. You'll be the point from which old Perry Woodstock here and I can go out and rummage through some of those ravines. Then, when we find them, we'll come on and get you, and the whole lot of us will go ahead together, just as Woodstock says. He's got a head on his shoulders."

"I don't like it," said Vincent. "I don't like it a bit. There would never be time to come back and get us. We're lucky enough if we can overtake 'em, by going straight on with the march." He swayed as he talked. He was ready to drop with fatigue.

"We have plenty of time," said Cactus. "They're sure to camp. They'll never dream that we'll follow 'em . . . a handful like us against their army. They'll want to camp when they get off to a good place, because they're all keen to divide the spoils."

That was a good argument, and it was a settler to Vincent. His weariness must have been fighting on our side all the time. When Lydia horned in and said the plan was the only thing to try, George Vincent gave in at last.

We got him to the poplar grove and started a fire for him that would keep him warm and gradually dry him off. Then we went off together, Cactus and I, and the last thing I heard from them was the crackling of the fire and the cheerful voice of Lydia Vincent talking to her father.

Cactus strode along with his head thrust forward. I said: "Damn it, if there's plenty of time, why d'you want to run the legs off of me?"

He slowed up a little, but only to say: "I made a fool of myself. Why did I go storming along at her like that? I came

67

rushing up to her . . . I played the fool. She was as cool as could be. I made a howling fool of myself. Damn it!"

I thought it was as well to pretend not to hear him, for I could see that he was writhing with shame.

"Now," I said, "what do we do? Here's the trail, pointing as plain as day straight toward that cañon yonder. But what's the good of going up there, just the two of us? Even if we could overtake the gang, what's the good of that, anyway? They could eat us as soon as they saw us."

"Maybe they won't see us," he said. "Anyway, we'd better go on and get in touch with 'em. You don't have to, though, Woodstock."

I said that I would go along, just the same. So we trekked on together, and came into the cañon's mouth. It was one of those dry cuts that saw into the side of a mountain, without a drop of water in the bottom in ordinary weather and a whole river running after a heavy rain. We had had the rain, and now there was a booming stream that came galloping through the gorge and made the ground tremble under our feet. We had gone a good distance up the gorge, when we came to a branch gully that ran off to the left and turned a corner and went out of sight. Down that branch went the trail we were following.

Cactus Terry paused and pulled up his belt. I knew he felt that we were about to run straight into a lot of trouble.

He said to me: "You've got a gun there that you know how to use, Woodstock, haven't you?"

I said that I was a fair hand with a rifle, but that a long-range gun might not be of much account in a hand-to-hand scrap. He nodded. He was thinking his own thoughts and not about me.

"If the pinch comes," he said, "you try to account for one of 'em. That's all. I may have luck with a couple more. And when you salt away two or three out of a dozen at the first fire, the rest may break up and run for it. Come on."

I was wondering how often he had dropped "two or three out of a dozen, at the first fire," when, walking up, we rounded the corner of the branching ravine and saw the fine, strong flare of a fire before us, with the dark shapes of men all around it.

XIII

"DEATH ON THE WAY"

I'll never see a campfire in my life without thinking about that scene up there among the rocks of that little cañon. It seemed to me that the light fell right on me and showed me to every eye around the fire. But that fellow, Cactus Terry, walked straight on. I got to my hands and knees long before he suddenly took the same posture. Even then he worked carefully forward, straight on toward the fire.

Finally he waited for me to come up to him. Already the voices of those around the fire were pretty loud and clear in our ears. Cactus said, in a whisper: "They've picked up a new man. I wonder which one?"

I gasped as a sudden thought sent new fear through me.

"There are the two bums," said Cactus, "and the three Mexicans. And there's Mike Jeffreys and Pierre Vernon. That makes seven. But there are eight fellows around that fire."

"And there's only two of us here," I reminded him.

He shrugged his shoulders as though what I had said could not be considered important in the least. He began to edge again, until we got to a perfect spying station, between two boulders, with a screen of brush before us that would hide our faces, but let us look through the irregular veil of branches and see what was happening around the fire.

Then we could see who the eighth man was. And it didn't cheer me up a bit to find myself staring at the handsome, weak, vicious face of Riley Mason. He was standing making a cigarette, rolling it in one hand. I could see at once that he was in the middle of an argument — an argument that looked as though it might have to be finished with gun play. He was talking to Pierre Vernon, and the gambler, not knowing his danger, was sneering openly at him.

"If you could talk money out of our pockets, you could have a split of the cash," said Vernon, and I saw that the pigskin case was resting at *his* feet.

The three Mexicans and the two tramps seemed perfectly happy to let Vernon play kingpin. They would let the talking be done by the slickster, Pierre Vernon, while they themselves just waited for the dividing of the coin. I wondered how even a tiger like the great Riley Mason would be able to cut in on such a deal as this. There was only one uncertain card in the pack, and that was Mike Jeffreys. That big fellow sat on a stone with his chin resting on a fist, and his face puckered with thought and doubt. I couldn't help feeling that Jeffreys wanted to be on the right side more than he wanted a cut in that money.

Riley began to answer the last remark of the gambler. "You boys think, then, that I don't deserve a cut in the money, eh?" he asked quietly.

"You don't," said Vernon tersely. "And neither does Mike Jeffreys. The only good thing he did was not helping the Vincents when the pinch came."

Jeffreys looked up with a scowl. His forehead was like the forehead of an angry bull.

"Well," said Riley Mason, "I don't guess that me and Jeffreys yonder could force you boys to divvy up, could we?"

"You could try," said Vernon, sneering.

Riley Mason only nodded in answer to this invitation. At last he said: "I can't force you. But I can persuade you, because you fellows are a good enough bunch. You'll see reason."

"Go on and make us see what your cut should be," sneered Vernon.

"I'll make you see, all right. What give you your big chance . . . the chance that let you get the coin from the Vincents without any real trouble, eh? It was because the two fighting men of the gang . . . the only two that didn't want to rob the Vincents, according to the lot of you . . . had gone out to look for me. They found me, too, and a sweet hell of a time I had with 'em. But the reason that you're here with the coin is because I was working on that pair."

"That sounds kind of reasonable," admitted Chick, the tramp, breaking in.

"Does it?" snarled Pierre Vernon. "You going to make a fool of yourself, maybe?"

"Oh, maybe I am, and maybe not," said Chick. "He done a good job for us. I wish that he'd cut their hearts out . . . that would have been a better job still."

"Look!" exclaimed Vernon. "You tell what you've spent to get us here, will you? We took chances, and we grabbed the loot, and here we have it. What did you spend that you should get in on the split?"

"I'll ask you right back," said Riley Mason, "what was the chief job you had in getting the coin for yourself?"

"Why, our job was to get Cactus Terry out of the way," said Vernon. "What of it?"

"Well, you got him out of the way at last. And how? Because I spent all four of my men on the job. There ain't a one of 'em that ain't got a bullet sunk through him, somewheres."

"You mean to say that Cactus shot 'em all?" demanded Vernon.

"He didn't shoot 'em all," said Mason, his face contorting with fury at the memory. "He talked. That's what he did. His tongue does more for him than his guns. Anyway, there's one of the three likely to die, and two more pretty badly winged."

That, then, had been the final outcome of the dive that

72

Mason took after the others into the dark of the brush. The devil had wounded them all before his senses came back to him. He seemed to me as dangerous a man as ever I had seen in the world as he stood there by the fire and admitted that his entire gang was down.

"You lost some men, and it just happened to be useful to us," said Vernon. "You weren't thinking about us, my friend, while you were spending your men so free and easy. You were thinking about the hard cash."

Riley Mason did a strange thing then. He lifted his right hand to the sky and shook his fist at the moon.

"I swear to God," he said, "that I'd rather have a slice of the heart of Cactus Terry, and eat it raw, than have all the money in the valise yonder!"

He meant it. He was shaking with the earnestness of his passion. And I looked aside at the face of my friend, and saw that Cactus was smiling gently, almost tenderly.

"The job's done. It's too late to get your hand in," Vernon said tersely.

"The job's not done," answered the great Riley Mason.

"What d'you mean?"

"Why, you fool," said Riley Mason, "ain't Cactus still loose, along with the other gent? I don't give a damn about the other one, but so long as that fellow, Cactus, is loose, he's on your trail. And so long as he's loose on your trail, you've just got your hands on the cash, but it's not yours. He'll run the lot of you down, and he'll bring you to time."

Stuffy Bill stood up and struck his hands together. "By God," he said. "There's a lot in what Mason says."

"You lie," said Pierre Vernon. "And Mason lies, too."

I gathered my muscles tight, waiting for the noise of the shots that were bound to follow.

XIV

"MEN DIE"

Of course, there had to be a gun play. There was nothing else for it, when things had got to that point. I don't know why it is that in the West a man will let you call him by any name in the world so long as you call the names in the right way. But the moment that you call him even the mildest bit out of the way and do it in the *wrong* manner, then there has to be a fight. And a fight, among people like these, could only be with knives or guns.

It's easy enough to sit still in a comfortable room and talk about a gun fight, but it's a mighty different thing to stand close by and see the guns actually come into action. I remember that I crouched there, shuddering, and kept saying to myself: *One of 'em is going to die . . . maybe both of 'em are going to die.*

Now all of this thinking and this talking to myself occupied only a second or so. During that time, Pierre Vernon and the great Riley Mason stood and glared at one another. The gambler was the fellow who amazed me. I had taken him to be simply an ordinary crook who stole from working men with the cleverness of his fingers and the aptness of his wits. But now I had to guess at something else. He knew who Riley Mason was, and, therefore, he knew what Mason could do with a gun. And yet he was not afraid to face him. It was a pretty awful thing to see the pair confront one another, each of them so sure and calm that he was in no haste to put the battle into actual progress. Each delayed and was foretasting the death of the opponent.

In the meantime, the bystanders were quietly occupied in their own ways. It seemed as though every one of them expected that trouble might rain on his own head in very short order, and, therefore, they all set about shifting themselves into positions of defense. The tall Mexican cadaver pulled out a gun almost as long as his arm. One of his friends got out a knife just as generously built as the gun, and the other let the light glint on a little stiletto that he held like a weltering white flame in the palm of his hand, ready to throw. The two tramps, Stuffy and Chick, backed off together, each with a revolver in his hand. Only Jeffreys did not stir. He remained as before, with his chin resting on his fist, and his eyes looking far away beyond all of these petty troubles at something else.

Just then, the fire laid hold on the tips of a big pine branch, or some such thing, that had not been fed into the flames. With a great crackling, it blazed up in a huge, yellow sheet of illumination.

"Now!" yelled Riley Mason, his voice high and shrill. "Now, you damned . . . !"

I watched them with eyes frozen to hard glass and saw everything. A great man was Riley Mason and wonderfully quick on the draw. But on my word of honor, he was not a shade faster than that unknown gambler, Pierre Vernon. They got out their guns at the same moment. But then Riley's practice stood him in good stead. He got the bullet away from the muzzle of his gun a thousandth part of a second faster than the gambler fired his, and the body of Pierre Vernon felt the shock of the heavy slug pounding home against his flesh and jerking him off balance, just as he pulled his own trigger. He missed, but he did not miss by far. His bullet took the hat off the head of Riley as slick as you please.

The weight of the .45-caliber slug had knocked Pierre off balance. He managed to fire, as I said, but then he toppled backward, and the agony of his wound made him yell from the pain of it.

Riley Mason went over and kicked the gun out of the hand of Pierre Vernon. He leaned over and smiled like a devil into his eyes.

"You ain't seen or heard the last of me, neither, Mister Vernon," he growled. "I've just started to open up hell for you."

Vernon didn't howl any longer. Neither did he speak. He simply made a face like a cat about to spit, and he grabbed his wound, that was in his thigh, with both hands, to stop the flow of the blood.

"You made all the trouble, you sneak thief," snarled Riley Mason. "You wanted to get your hands on the coin and keep it all for yourself." He laughed, still leaning over Pierre Vernon. "I'm gonna make an example out of you," said the gunman. "And then. . . ."

Now I had no liking for Pierre Vernon. But for the first time since I started to look on at this scene, I really felt a desire to cut in and take a hand. However, there were other things beginning to happen just then. I saw the two tramps had come a little closer with their guns. And the three Mexicans made an oblique movement that put them shoulder to shoulder with the tramps. I could understand that. It was plain that Riley Mason was of a higher order, and being the lion among them, the rats and the jackals would unite against him. I could understand the five weaker crooks, well enough. But I'm confounded if I could understand the actions of Mike Jeffreys, for he had not changed his attitude, even during the actual moment when the guns exploded. Instead, he remained there like a statue of thought.

Then I saw, suddenly, that the five who had gotten shoulder to shoulder meant to act. I half rose, but Cactus was on his feet before me.

"Behind you, Riley!" he shouted, in a voice that would have cracked the very gate of hell.

Riley Mason, acting on the instant, wheeled and fell on his face, as the guns of the crooks spat fire and lead. And he was shooting as he dropped. That was a thing to see and remember. His first bullet smacked right into the middle of the tall Mexican and folded him upon the ground. His second knocked the hat from another Mexican, and his third took Stuffy the tramp clean between the eyes. It was fast and beautiful work. But the three remaining were not stopped. They came in, and they came fast. And what chance had one man, no matter how good he might be, against three?

I didn't think of what I was about to do. I only know that instinct made me do it. I didn't like Riley Mason, but I liked the three against him still less. At any rate, with one step I was beyond the rocks and had caught up the thick end of the blazing pine bough. I swung that flaming branch straight across the faces of the three, as they came on in a line with nothing but the great Riley Mason in their minds.

The effect was terrific. All three of them had their fur singed, I suppose. And they acted like madmen, falling down and springing up again, and then turning tail and running off into the darkness, still yelling and groaning and jumping as they ran, until the darkness swallowed them up. As they disappeared, I was taken with a crazy fit of laughter. And the great Riley Mason, I discovered, was standing beside me, with an arm on my shoulder, laughing, too — as though he would die of mirth.

What I saw from the corner of my eye removed my laughter with one gesture. It was big Mike Jeffreys, who had come to life at last. And now he sat on the same rock that had been his chair before, and the pigskin valise was between his feet, and in his hand he held a long-barreled .45 Colt revolver. And

77

as we eased up in our noise-making, Jeffreys spoke quietly.

"Boys," he said, "it was a good fight, but all that's over now. The coin is going back to Vincent, where it belongs."

I understood, then, what it was that had been working so hard in the mind of Jeffreys all this time. He had been fighting against temptation from the start. He had wanted his split of the loot as much as anybody else. But when the pinch came, the honest soul of him stood up and rebelled against crookedness. I think it's that way in the West. Honesty is closer to the heart than crookedness. Anyway, here we were brought to a full standstill.

Then Riley Mason looked around and saw the man he hated most in the world, Cactus Terry.

XV

"THE GOLD COMES BACK"

Everything else went out of the bandit's brain, plainly enough, when he saw Cactus. Here before him was his major enemy, and I don't know whether I saw fear or joy in the face of Riley Mason, or both combined.

There was no question about Cactus, though. He was simply the happiest man in the world. He had his man after a long, long trail. Now he was ready to eat him.

"It's been a long time, Riley," he said. "But now I have you where I want you. Get out your gun . . . fill your hand, you dirty scoundrel!"

I waited to hear Riley Mason protest that he would not take the draw from any man. I was wrong. He had no intention of refusing any advantage that he could get from the savage generosity of Cactus Terry. Half crouching, he stared at Cactus, and I hardly blamed him for having no more honesty and integrity than a wildcat in that moment.

For when I looked across at Cactus Terry, I could see that the man would not be beaten, even by tricks.

He said again: "Fill your hand whenever you're ready, Riley."

Riley Mason nodded. There was no doubt about what was in his face now. It was sheer despair and savage rage and terror combined. He knew that his time had come. He was willing to face it and fight until he dropped.

I heard Pierre Vernon snarling with deep content at the side, where he swayed his body back and forth and gripped with both hands upon his bleeding wound.

Then, for the second time, Mike Jeffreys stepped in.

"The minute you pull a gun, you're a dead man, Mason," he said sternly.

I was amazed. It hadn't seemed to me possible that any human being could interfere between two such men as faced each other there in the firelight. But here was big Jeffreys standing up now, his head lowered and thrust forward, his face an ugly thing to see. He was coming into his own. All his doubts and indecision were left behind him. He seemed more important, more dominant, than the great Cactus Terry himself.

Riley Mason did not answer, did not move his glance from the face of Cactus. But Cactus himself turned squarely to the side, giving Riley a terrible opening for a snap shot, and faced Jeffreys.

"Mike," he said, "are you crazy? Are you asking for trouble from the pair of us?"

"I don't ask for trouble from nobody," said Jeffreys. "But I'll tell you this . . . there's been shooting enough. The coin's been swiped, and now it's come back again. The job's done when this satchel gets back to George Vincent, and I get my horses together. I've lost a lot. I ain't gonna have the reputation of a snake in the grass. When folks find out that I've lost a lead hoss and my stage, it'll be bad enough. But, anyway, there ain't anybody more gonna lose a penny tonight, or an ounce of blood, except them as rate the losing of it."

There was a good deal in this speech. There was authority behind it and confidence — and the strength that comes with being right.

Suddenly I saw Riley Mason turn his back on the scene and walk off, saying over his shoulder: "I'll find you some day when you ain't got three cronies hanging around you, Cactus.

I'll shoot it out with you then."

"Mason, I'll let the world know that you're a sneaking, murdering coward!" shouted Cactus Terry.

But already the form of Riley Mason was dim in the moonshine. We heard his laughter come back to us, like the distant snarling of a beast.

"By God," said Cactus, "I'm going after him."

He had leaned forward to break into a run when Jeffreys spoke again. "You want to go back and see her, when you've got blood on your hands, Cactus?" he asked.

It stopped the great Cactus, I can tell you. He halted in his tracks, then turned about and clapped a hand on Jeffreys's shoulder.

"You've got a brain in your head," he said. "You've got the kind of a brain that I envy any man having. And I'm going to start in and try to pile up some common horse sense."

It was like the break-up of the storm in the sky, sudden and swift, and unexpected. While we'd been rubbing elbows with all sorts of death and danger the moment before, now we were suddenly free from all trouble. There was only the long hike left before us, all the way to Yellow Creek.

When I get this far, it always seems to me that the story is finished. But other folks never think so. My friends have heard the yarn a thousand times, I guess, because it's one of the most exciting things that I was ever neighbor to. But still they linger over the ending. As a matter of fact, I think they like the ending better than any of the action, because they roll the tender morsels over their tongues, and particularly they like to hear about how we came back with the money and found poor George Vincent sound asleep with his daughter watching over him, a rifle in her hands. And they like to hear how she hushed us, and wouldn't let us disturb her father from his sleep, and how we gave her the valise.

And in the morning — but what's the use of telling of the doubt and the joy of George Vincent when he saw that his life's work had been brought back to him? Or how he wrung his hands and couldn't speak a word? No, that is not what folks most want to hear about. Like my wife, Rosemary, they prefer, generally, that I should tell how Cactus Terry gave up the wild life and became a thorough-braced, honest rancher in the hills. They beg me to take them to see him and his wife and his kids, the way Rosemary and I've done. But, somehow, I'm sorry to think that the robber who held up the stage to Yellow Creek is no more, riding, masked, along the dim trails.

THE WHISPERER

A Reata Story

Frederick Faust's original title for this story was "The Whisperer." Street & Smith's *Western Story Magazine*, where it was first published in the November 25, 1933, issue under the byline George Owen Baxter, changed the title to "Reata's Danger Trail." This was the second short novel to feature Reata, who proved to be one of Faust's most popular characters among readers of this magazine, harking back to the enthusiasm that had met a previous, very different Faust character, Bull Hunter, in the same magazine a decade earlier. Like Bull Hunter, who was accompanied on his adventures by the stallion, Diablo, and the wolf dog, The Ghost, Reata also gains a mare and a mongrel, but they are very different from those found in the Bull Hunter stories. There would be seven short novels in all about Reata. The first, "Reata," appears in THE FUGITIVE'S MISSION (Five Star Westerns, 1997). This is the second and continues Reata's adventures after he successfully accomplishes the first of his three labors for Pop Dickerman.

I

"QUINN'S RETURN"

The scattered length of Rusty Gulch drew the whole heart of
Harry Quinn. By the roofs of the houses he knew them. His
brow puckered at the flat top of the jail, and his mouth watered
when he identified the saloon. He could hear, merely through
the power of the mind, the clicking of dice as they rattled and
rolled, the whisper of shuffled cards, and the clinking of ice in
the glass. As he looked across the town, he was biting his teeth
into the fat of a good cigar and lifting one finger to tell the
bartender to set them up all down the line.

There were not many elements in the heaven desired by
Harry Quinn; he could find them all in Rusty Gulch. But
instead of riding straight into the arms of that paradise, he
knew that it would be wisest for him to turn aside, at the
outskirts of the town, to what looked like a barn from a distance
and only appeared as a dwelling when one came up close to
it and saw the high, wooden wall pierced by a few shuttered
windows.

The gate to the yard was open, so Harry Quinn jogged his
mustang inside and looked over the familiar heaps of junk that
were arranged in ordered piles. It always seemed to him that
Pop Dickerman's junk yard was a cemetery for the entire range.
The rags and tags of everything used by a cowpuncher, lum-
berman, or farmer could be found in these outdoor heaps, or
in those that filled the huge mow of the converted barn where
Dickerman lived.

Pop himself was now unloading a wagon in front of which

stood two little down-headed skeletons of mules. He must have been out early to collect this load, the relics of some small shack among the hills, the sign that one more family had moved away. Pop Dickerman, buzzard that he was, had come to the emptying house and picked up for a song an entire load, in which Harry Quinn could notice the joints of a stovepipe and the dingy gray-black of the stove, a little single plow with toil-worn handles, a heap of old furniture, the clustered handles of brooms and spades and axes, a mound of saddles, and even a pair of chicken coops had been added.

On top of this load or rubbing against the legs of Dickerman on the ground were a score of cats. A Maltese giant sat on the driver's seat and luxuriously licked a forepaw and washed his face with it. Harry Quinn thought of rats so strongly that he could almost sniff the odor out of the air. He thought of rats, too, when he saw the long, grizzled face of Pop Dickerman, furred over with curling hair like the muzzle of an animal. Harry Quinn came up close and dismounted, calling out: "Hello, Pop. How's things?"

He began to untie the lead rope of the wiry roan mare he had brought in with him.

Pop Dickerman went straight past Harry Quinn as though his arrival were a matter not worthy of comment, as though he had not schemed day and night for the delivery of him from most imminent death. But Dickerman went by him and first greeted the mare, stroking her ewe neck with his grimy hand.

"How are you, Sue, old gal?" he asked. "How they been treatin' you, honey?"

She pricked one ear and looked at him with lazy eyes.

"And where's him that was ridin' Sue?" asked Dickerman.

"He's gone," said Harry Quinn.

"Dead?" asked Dickerman.

86

"He ain't dead. But he's gone. He brought me all the way along the trail until we come in sight of Rusty Gulch, and, when he seen the roof of your house, he looked like he was smellin' rats under the roof of it. He hopped off Sue and throwed me the reins. He ain't dead, but he's gone for good."

"If he ain't dead, he'll come back," said Dickerman. "He's swore to me, and he's got a conscience. Maybe he thinks now that he won't come back, but a conscience is a funny thing. You dunno nothin' about it, Harry, because you never had one, but when the night starts and the world gets dark, a gent's conscience will come out with the stars. Yeah, we'll have Reata back here with us not long after dark. Here . . . gimme a hand unloadin' this stuff, will you?"

"I ain't hired out to handle junk," protested Harry Quinn. "I'm goin' to put up the hosses and go have a snack of sleep. I stopped sleepin' when the hangin' day got closer."

Pop Dickerman did not argue. He merely stood there with a rusty bale of plowshares in his hands and watched Quinn lead the horse away.

Afterward, Quinn entered the barn. He so hated the sight of the piles of junk on the floor of the old mow and the great bundles that hung down on ropes from the rafters of the place that he half squinted his eyes and hurried on to the little rooms at the end of the building. There he entered the kitchen, found the five-gallon jug behind the door, helped himself to a large slug of good whiskey, and then went up to a room where bunks were built in two tiers against the wall. Those bunks were heaped with disordered, second-hand blankets of all colors, but the taste of Harry Quinn was not at all fine.

"In jail again," was all he said, and, pulling off his tight boots, he lay down and rolled himself in one blanket. He stared for a moment at the window, dusted over with cobwebs, and then went to sleep.

When he wakened, it was near the end of the day. He went down and discovered Pop Dickerman cooking supper. On the oilcloth covering of the kitchen table, three places were laid out.

"Who's goin' to chow with us?" asked Harry Quinn.

"Reata. He'll be back," said Dickerman.

"Yeah? And the devil he will," answered Quinn. "That *hombre* was so fed up when he just seen the roof of your barn, Pop, that he looked sick at the stomach. He couldn't come no nearer."

He went to the stove and lifted the lids from the pots. He found boiling potatoes, stewing chicken that gave out a rich mist of savor, and a great pot of coffee. Inevitable bacon simmered in another pan. He opened the oven door. A hot breath of smoky air boiled out at him, but he saw a deep pot of baking beans, brown-black and bubbling at the top, and two wide pans of baking-powder biscuits that were just coming to the right golden brown.

"You feed a man," admitted Harry Quinn, slamming the door shut. "I gotta say that the chuck is all right here. Dog-gone my heart, though, but it must nigh kill you to part yourself from so much good grub."

"A good man has gotta have good grub," said Dickerman. And he lifted an eyebrow at Harry Quinn.

"Meaning that I ain't so good, eh?" said Quinn. "That's all right by me. But hop to it, Pop. It's sundown, and I get a regular appetite at the regular hour."

In fact, food was presently on the table, and Harry Quinn sat down to it with a capacious grin on his bulldog face. He held a fork in his left hand, but it was poised in an attitude of attention and only made vague dipping motions toward the plate from time to time. Sitting well slued around in his chair, far enough back to have leaped to his feet at any moment,

Harry Quinn leaned forward and with sweeping gestures of a broad-bladed knife conveyed quantities to his mouth.

Opposite him, at the other end of the little table, Pop Dickerman ate some stale pone he had found in the bread box and drank small sips of some milk that had just gone sour. He seemed half revolted, and one could not tell whether it was the taste of his own portion or the vast appetite of Quinn that disgusted him. Certainly, Quinn's manners made no difference to him. He kept his shoulders hunched up a little in rigid disfavor as he lowered his hairy face toward his sour milk. Now and then he put out a hand and stroked one of the cats that rubbed against his feet. One or another of them was continually jumping onto his lap, the half-starved creatures reaching their paws out in vain, tentative gestures toward that richly loaded table.

"This kid . . . this here Reata," said Quinn, when his mouth was only occasionally filled, "what I'd like to know is how you ever tied him up to you, you old blatherskite?"

"Brain work . . . brain work is the thing," answered Pop Dickerman thoughtfully. "I seen him workin' in a crowd at the rodeo the other day with his reata."

"Yeah, the damnedest thing I ever seen," declared Harry Quinn, "the way he handles that rope of his. It ain't no bigger'n a pencil, but it'll hold a hoss. It looks like rawhide, but there's gotta be something stronger than leather inside it. Is it wire?"

"I dunno," answered Dickerman. "I seen him playin' his tricks with it and pickin' the pockets of the gents that stood around him while he was workin', as slick as you ever seen."

"Him? Pickin' pockets? Hey, I wouldn't think him that kind of low-down," declared Quinn, amazed.

"There's a lot of things that you wouldn't think," answered Dickerman, "and one of 'em is that young gents is often young fools, not meanin' no real harm. I watched him, and his style was mighty fine. His hand was faster than any eye but mine, all right, and I seen that he didn't lift nothing off anybody but the gents that looked like cattle kings and what not. You take a young fool like Reata and he wouldn't steal enough to harm a man. What happened was that when he gets his loot, he looks it over and finds Tom Wayland's watch that has a picture of Tom's gal in it, and she's so pretty that Reata is ashamed of stealin' that watch and goes and puts it back in Wayland's pocket.

"And while he's puttin' it in the pocket, puttin' it back in . . . the poor fool! . . . Tom happens to catch him at it and raises a holler and downs him. But you can't keep a cat like Reata down, and he eases through that whole crowd and swipes a hoss from the rack and gets away. And he ropes a new hoss pretty soon out of a field, and goes on. He leaves the whole gang away off behind him till he comes to the river, and there he sees a fool of a little mongrel dog on a bit of a chicken coop on a rock that's been washed down the river. And he can't leave that dog, but has to ride in and get it, and by that action he lets the sheriff and all come up to him.

"Well, they take and put him in jail, but on the way I give him a handshake, and I leave a good saw and a key to the back door of the jail in his hand. So, when he gets out that night, he comes to me and asks what can he do to pay me back. And I say that he can do for me what I've done for him, with three hundred percent interest, because I've got three men in a jam, and want to get them home. So he says he will and shakes hands on it."

"That's what he done, is it?" said Harry Quinn. "Well, conscience or no conscience, he's done enough to pay you back already. When he got me loose, he did what nobody else in the world could 'a' done, bar none. Not even Gene Salvio could 'a' done it. Those Gypsies were goin' to hang me up the next day, and they kept two men watchin' me night and day. But Reata stepped in and fixed things."

"Without a gun!" exclaimed Dickerman.

"Aye, with only hands and brain."

"And how did he do it?"

"Well, I hardly know. But he sold himself to Queen Maggie, the head of the tribe, and she let him into the gang. Then he manhandled a couple of the Gypsies that was jealous of him, and they try to cut his throat, and he dodges that. And he picks out the prettiest gal you ever seen, which is Miriam, their bareback rider that hauls in the dough for them when they give their show at a town, and he gets her pretty dizzy, and he gets her to tell him where I am. Then he goes and just ties up the two mugs that are guardin' me . . . and here I am. But here he ain't, Pop, and here he's goin' to never be. There's something kind of clean about him, and he wouldn't stand the dirt around here."

With irritating assurance, Pop said: "Conscience, it comes out with the stars. I'll get some of this food back into the stove."

He set about it as Quinn said: "Leave me another slab of them biscuits, and I'll mop up some syrup with 'em. Gimme some more coffee, too. You think Reata is goin' to come back here, do you, and keep on with you till he's got Dave Bates and Salvio both loose?"

"He'll try," said Pop Dickerman.

A shrill sound of barking came stabbing through the night, small and thin.

"There," said Dickerman, his little eyes glistening. "There he is now, with his dog, Rags, tellin' him not to come back inside here, and Reata comin' along just the same. You'd think that a smart feller like him would have sense enough to listen to a dog, wouldn't you?"

A moment later the back door opened, and Reata stood on the threshold. The little dog, Rags, crouched, whimpering at his heels.

II

"REATA'S PRIDE"

The welcome for Reata was very effusive. Quinn called out: "Hey, Reata . . . dog-gone me, if I ain't glad to see you! Dog-gone me, old boy, but it's good to see your mug ag'in."

Dickerman kept grinning and pointing to the third place at the table. "I knew that you'd be along," he declared. "Set down there and feed."

Reata pulled up his belt a notch. "I'm not hungry," he declared.

Two or three of the cats began to stalk little Rags. He backed against the feet of his master and looked up. Reata held down his hand and caught the slender body as it jumped. Rags, with great dexterity, ran up the crooked arm of his master and perched himself on the broad shoulder.

"Not hungry?" gasped Harry Quinn. "Hey, you *gotta* be hungry when you take a look at chuck like this here. This is food, old son."

Reata pulled back the waiting third chair and sat down. It's a bad job when most of us sit down, bending our bodies, slumping our weight suddenly off the legs. But Reata sat down as a dog might sit — when it is waiting for the start of the race. When he leaned back, no one would be deceived into thinking that this was a lasting inertia. The sleeping wolf is only a second away from the naked fangs and bristling mane of full consciousness. Reata, reclining in the chair, making a cigarette with an idle twist of his fingers, made one think of the same static power. One touch of need could discharge all the danger that was in him.

"Looka here, Reata," urged Dickerman, "I'm goin' to take it pretty hard if you don't join us. These baked beans, they're prime. Ain't they, Harry?"

"Yeah, they'll grow hair on the palm of your hand," stated Quinn, grinning with much kindness at his rescuer. "How's every old thing, kid? Dog-gone me, but it's good to see you again. Pop here, he said that you'd come along, all right. Pull up the old chair and have a shot at this here chicken stew. It's the goods."

Reata took from his pocket the snaky handful of his rope, and his unthinking fingers made swift designs with it in the air. The thing seemed alive, as always, under his touch.

"I'm not hungry," he insisted. "But I want to know something, Dickerman. I don't think I would have come back, but all at once I remembered that I'd finished one third of the job, and it seemed a shame not to finish the trip. Tell me the next item on the list, and I'll start again. There were three men. Well, here's Harry Quinn back with you. What's the next one?"

"Dave Bates . . . he hangs next month for murder," said Dickerman.

"Yeah," murmured Quinn, "and the funny thing is that he didn't do that job. Am I wrong, Pop?"

"He sure didn't do the job," answered Dickerman. "It's like this, Reata." He looked into the gray eyes and the brown face of Reata for a moment, gathering his thoughts. "It's like this. My big man . . . Gene Salvio . . . he's in a terrible jam. I send out Dave Bates to get him. Dave starts, all right. The next thing I know, Dave is bein' tried for murder. Charge is that he got drunk and killed a rancher by name of Durant. They find Durant dead, Dave asleep and drunk in his chair, and on the floor is Dave's gun with two bullets fired out of it. Looks like a good case, and they sock Dave. He hangs next month, and he's in the pen, waiting for the noose."

"The funny thing," said Harry Quinn, "is that Dave never gets drunk."

"I'm to break open the penitentiary and bring Dave Bates out with me, is that all?" asked Reata ironically.

"No, no. I'm not such a fool," said Dickerman. "All you do is get up there and find out who really *did* kill that rancher. You see? Hang it on the right man so clear and heavy that the law is goin' to turn poor Dave loose. That was what Quinn was riding north for when he snagged himself on those Gypsies."

The eyes of Dickerman burned as he stared at Quinn.

Reata stood up and threw the butt of his cigarette out the window.

"I'll start now," he said.

"Wait for the morning. Harry'll go along with you and show you the way, tell you everything we know," suggested Dickerman.

"I'll go now," insisted Reata. Suddenly his lip curled a little. "I'd rather sleep in the open," he added.

"Yeah, and I told you," remarked Harry Quinn, "that he had the smell of the rats up his nose."

"Take Sue, then, and get started," said Dickerman.

"All right," said Reata. "One more thing. What price do you put on Sue?"

Dickerman frowned.

"He'll never sell Sue," said Quinn.

"You'll sell her at a price," said Reata. Suddenly scorn welled up into his voice. "You'll sell your own hide . . . for a price. What do you want for Sue, Dickerman?"

The contempt of Reata made very slight impact upon Dickerman. He kept squinting his little eyes for a moment and stroking his hairy face. Then he said: "When all three of 'em are back here . . . Harry and Dave and Gene Salvio . . . then I'm goin' to throw in Sue and let you have her free."

A little glint of yellow light came into the gray eyes of Reata as he nodded.

"If you're coming with me, build your pack," Reata told Quinn. "I'm starting now."

He walked out into the open night, leaving Quinn and Dickerman to stare at one another for a long moment.

"Don't seem so dog-gone good-natured as he was on the road," said Quinn regretfully

"Any sharp knife is goin' to give you a nick now and then," said Pop Dickerman. "But he wouldn't eat none at my table. You notice that?"

"Hey, and how could I help but notice it? And him pinched in the gills, too. He pulls up his belt when he tells you that he ain't hungry. There's a kind of a pride about Reata, all right."

"Pride's the grindstone that rubs the knife sharp," said Dickerman.

"Maybe he's steel," admitted Quinn, "but how's he goin' to cut into that big cheese up there at Boyden Lake? How's he goin' to have a chance to cut in and find out who really done the murder? There ain't a chance in a million, Pop. You oughta know that there ain't a chance in a million."

"Sure I know it," said the junkman. "It ain't an easy job, and I ain't offering low pay. Sue . . . if he gets out all three of you . . . Sue is what he gets from me. Go on now and get your pack."

Harry Quinn rose with a sigh. He went to the stove, picked the iron spoon out of the pot, and loaded a large heap of dripping beans into his mouth thoughtfully. He was still munching these as he left the room.

When he came downstairs again, carrying a roll over his shoulder, he said to Dickerman: "I'm takin' the big gray."

"You wanta advertise that you're a real man, do you?" Dickerson sneered. "You take the same hoss that you rode down here originally. It's plenty good enough for you. And it won't draw no attention."

Harry Quinn looked sullenly at his chief for a moment.

"Aw, all right, then," he said.

That was the only farewell.

III

"THE DURANT RANCH"

By the time, two days later, that Reata and Harry Quinn had come close to the Durant ranch, Reata knew very little more about the killing of Cleve Durant than Pop Dickerman had told him. All that Quinn knew, in addition, was the testimony of Dave Bates at the trial. Bates had said that he had asked hospitality at the ranch while he was traveling through the country, and that during the evening he had taken a drink of the whiskey that was offered to him after dinner. When he had drunk the stuff, he began to get very sleepy. He was about to go to bed when sleep overwhelmed him in his chair. He awakened to find the deputy sheriff shaking him by the shoulder. On the opposite side of the room lay Cleveland Durant, dead. On the floor beside his chair was Bates's gun, with two chambers of the revolver empty.

Quinn's comment on the story was characteristic. "Think of the poor sucker tellin' a yarn like that," he said. "Long as he was goin' to tell a lie, why didn't he cook up a good one? Dog-gone me, but I was surprised when I read that yarn in the paper. Dave Bates ain't a fool. He's a pretty bright *hombre*. But for a lot of gents, when the law gets hold of 'em, it sort of freezes up their brains, and they can't think none."

"Maybe it was the truth?" suggested Reata.

Quinn stared as he answered: "You mean that Dave was doped? They couldn't dope Dave. He's a bright *hombre* . . . he's real bright, is the facts of the case."

It was a broad, flat-bottomed valley in which the Durant

ranch lay. The naked hills surrounded the district with walls of cliffs. Little trails like chalk marks and a few narrow, white streaks that were roads wound through the country and focused on the town of Boyden Lake, that got its name from the little blue patch of water beside it. So the scene appeared to Reata from the top of the southern hills. It was a bare land without a tree. Patches of shrubbery could get rooting in that stubborn soil, but nothing larger. And the grass grew in mere spots, not solidly. The cattle that grazed were hardly ever clustered in spots of color, but were scattered as dots here and there. Two or three creeks trailed lines of light across the landscape — the ranches of that district at least had water.

"It's a tough spot," said Harry Quinn, as he surveyed the broad map. "Yonder . . . that oughta be the ranch house. We'll go down there and take a look. The word is that old Sam Durant will pay high for the right kind of a cowhand, but the right kind for him is hard to find."

They got a cross trail that swung onto a road that ran between fences of barbed wire. Harry Quinn was indignant when he saw the fences.

"Look at a free country," he said, "that's said to be free and all the gents in it equal, and along comes a lot of bums and checks off the free range with fences. Is it right? No, it ain't right! Is it free? Look for yourself. Suppose you was in a hurry. Suppose you had to make a quick break across country, with maybe a deputy sheriff or something behind you . . . why, what chance would you have? You'd be jammed ag'in' a wire fence in no time, and they'd have you. And what kind of a life is that?"

Reata gave no answer. He had a way of keeping up his end of a conversation merely by smiling and nodding, assuming at the same time a look of such interest that the other fellow was sure to be drawn out. He had had plenty of chance to estimate

Harry Quinn on the trip north, and he did not think very highly of his traveling companion. Harry was a good hand with a gun, and probably his nerve was excellent. Otherwise, he was a brawler, a noise maker, and gifted with a very loose mouth. For what important affairs could Pop Dickerman use a man of this sort except actual fighting? And why should Pop Dickerman need fighting men around him?

He asked Harry Quinn bluntly: "What did you and Bates and Gene Salvio do for Dickerman when you were all together?"

Quinn simply answered: "Hey? What didn't we do?" He laughed, but did not offer any more details. It had been crooked work of some sort, that was fairly apparent. Certainly Pop Dickerman was far more than a mere collector of rags and junk.

A sudden lane opened from the battered road, and at the mouth of the lane there was a board tacked across a post, and on the board, roughed in with red paint, were these words:

$100 a month for the right man.
Try the Durant Ranch.

This sign moved Harry Quinn very much.

"A hundred bucks!" he said. "Why, dog-gone me, that had oughta raise every cowpuncher on the whole countryside. How can a sign like that keep stayin' up?"

In fact, they had hardly gone down the long line a quarter of a mile before they saw, coming toward them, a big man on a tough, little mustang. He was gripping the pommel of the saddle with both hands. His body was slouched low. When he came nearer, it was seen that his clothes were badly torn and dust covered, and that his face was decorated with a greatly swollen eye already discoloring from red to black.

Harry Quinn ventured to halt him.

"Are you from the Durant Ranch?" he asked.

The big man did not stop his mustang. He allowed it to jog along as he slued himself around in the saddle and shouted: "It ain't a ranch. It's an Injun massacre. I'm goin' to come back with friends and wipe that place up. I'm goin' to take it apart! I'm goin' to . . . !" Here his rage overcame his vocabulary, and he could merely curse. He began to talk and wave from a distance, but his words could not be made out.

"I'd say that gent was kind of peeved," suggested Harry Quinn. "Looks like he's been in some kind of a ruction. But if that's what they want on the Durant Ranch, you and me oughta get on pretty good there. Gun or knife or hands, I don't mind a fight . . . and when they bump into you, Reata, they're certainly goin' to find themselves tied."

He laughed very cheerfully at this idea, but Reata shook his head a little. Rags, who was riding over the withers of Sue, the roan mare, was now put down on the stirrup leather by Reata, and the dog jumped to the ground and ran happily on ahead.

"Rags might smell out the trouble," said Reata. "And here's Sue, cocking her ears. We'll see what we see."

"That Rags, now," said Harry Quinn, "you mind tellin' me what that dog-gone mongrel pup is good for?"

"He's not a worker," answered Reata, chuckling. "He's a thinker. He's like me."

They came out of the lane to the ranch house itself. There was nothing much to it. It was long and low, with an open shed between the kitchen and the rest of the house. This being close to midday, two men were idling in the shade of the house, waiting for the cook's call. One of them — tall, lean, middle-aged, grizzled — was whittling a stick. The other sat on the ground with his back against the wall of the house. He was a red-headed fellow with a fat, round, good-natured face.

"Howdy, boys," said the older man as Quinn and Reata swung down to the ground.

"Howdy," they answered. And Quinn added: "We're lookin' for the boss. We seen that sign on the board down the road."

"I'm Sam Durant," said the tall man, "and when I put the sign out there, I wanted to get me a real man for the place. How about you?" He looked at Quinn.

"Aw, I can daub a rope on a cow now and then," said Quinn, "and in this kind of a country I guess that I could stretch a wire, too, if I have to."

The rancher smiled a little as though in sympathy. And the red-headed fellow sat up and nodded violently.

"We got a lot of snakes and coyotes and what not around here," said Sam Durant. "How would you be with a gun?"

"Fair. Pretty fair," said Quinn, brightening.

"There's a chicken over there that we might use for supper," said Sam Durant. "Suppose you take a whack at that?"

There were a dozen or so chickens scratching holes here and there, and Durant had indicated a speckled Plymouth Rock twenty yards away.

"We'll sure eat him, then," said Harry Quinn, and in a flash he had pulled a gun and fired from the hip. The first bullet knocked a spray of dust into that bird. As it rose into the air with a flop and a squawk, beating its wings as it jumped, the second big bullet smashed into it and through it. It was hurled along the ground, scattering feathers and blood, and lay still without kicking. All the other chickens fled, squawking loudly.

"Hi! That was a good shot!" called the red-headed lad. "That was sure a beauty. You can do it, stranger." He began to laugh, rather too loudly, and walked over and picked up the dead rooster.

"Give it to the cook," directed Sam Durant. "Tell him to stew it for supper, Porky. And thanks," he added to Harry

Quinn. "That was a good shot, all right. A fellow that can shoot as straight as that wouldn't ever go hungry, eh? No, sir, you'd never have to look around very far before you ate. No use in tyin' you down to life on a ranch and drudgin' all day long for the sake of three squares. No use at all. And there's a whole lot of country all around here, partner, and a whole lot of game on it . . . from sparrows to buzzards. You go out and make yourself welcome to anything you can shoot. I'll have to keep the place here open for a gent that ain't so sure with his Colt."

Harry Quinn, who saw that he had overshot his real mark, took in a quick breath in order to make a hot answer, but the hard, cold eye of Reata caught him and stopped him.

Sam Durant said to Reata: "Now, maybe you're the man that I'm goin' to use, but I'll have to try you first. It's a kind of a mean job, too. You see that bay gelding out there in the corral?" He pointed out a well-made mustang in the corner of the corral with dropped head and a pointed rear hoof, taking a noonday nap in the sun.

"That gelding looked so damned good to me," said Sam Durant, "that I bought it from Bill Chester for a hundred and fifty dollars. But after I got it over here, I decided that I didn't like it, and I been meaning to return that mustang to the Chester place and get my money back. Somehow I ain't got around to it. Suppose you just saddle up that hoss and take it over to the Chesters for me. Tell 'em I'm damned sorry to send the hoss back, and that I'd like to have my money."

"All right," agreed Reata. "But why shouldn't I lead him over, instead of riding him?"

"Well, son," said the rancher, "it's just an idea that I had . . . that Chester would be a lot more pleased, sort of, if you rode that hoss over there today. I think he'd be a pile more likely to take the mustang back and gimme the money that I spent."

Reata nodded. Something, of course, was in the air. But he obediently pulled the saddle and bridle off Sue, leaving her with only a lead rope that he tied up around her neck. She would follow, unguided, even as she followed her master now to the gate of the corral and remained there, stretching her ugly neck and scrawny head between the bars to see what was going on.

Porky had come out of the house and stood by with a brightly cheerful smile to watch the proceedings, while Reata, leaving his saddle near the gate, took the rope that he carried from his pocket and crossed the corral. There were a dozen other horses in the big enclosure. They herded up around the big bay colt that watched impassively until Reata was near. Then, as the other horses spilled to one side, the bay flashed to the right.

He ran fast, head down, as though he knew what might be the target, but the thin, heavy line of Reata's rope shot like a bullet from his hand. A small noose opened in the head of the rope and snagged the mustang fairly and squarely. He came up gently on the rope, far too trained to risk a burn.

Moreover, he stood with perfect calm while Reata saddled him. Even when the leg of Reata swung over the saddle, the gelding stood with pricking ears, as though delighted. But at the last instant he shifted with a cat-like spring to the side and let Reata drop in the dust of the corral.

IV

"HANDLING THE OUTLAW"

A loud, howling cry of glee came from Porky, who now sat on top of the corral fence. Reata, on one knee as he had fallen, watched the bay colt fly into a fine frenzy, racing around that corral and pitching in every style Reata could remember. A fine, free-hand improviser was the bay, and his object was to buck that saddle off his back. In fact, the saddle presently was loosened and began to twist to the side. At this point Reata intervened with another perfect cast of his rope. The forty feet of that lithe and sinewy lariat went out like a shadowy extension of Reata's will, and at the touch of it around his neck the bay was instantly still again.

He stood with head up and the red blaze of deviltry in his eye — the perfect picture of the untamable outlaw. The cloud of dust that he had raised slowly blew away and left his beauty and his deviltry both unveiled. From the fence boomed the loud, looney laughter of Porky, the red-headed cowpuncher. Harry Quinn was grinning by the fence also, but the rancher remained seated on the chopping block near the kitchen door, whittling his stick, and apparently unimpressed and indifferent to what was happening in the corral.

The mouth of Reata jerked a little to one side as he came up to the bay. This time, when he loosened the rope from the neck of the horse, the mustang stood as still as before, and now Reata tied the slender thong under the fetlock joint of the off foreleg and passed it with a single half hitch over the horn of the saddle. He tightened the cinches once more and mounted. It was not the leisurely effort he had made before. This time it was the spring of a cat that clapped him on the back of the bay, and his two feet instantly slammed into the stirrups.

The mustang, at the same instant, shot up into the air. As he rose, Reata pulled up by a few inches the length of the rope that was fastened to the leg of the horse and secured the slack with a jerk on the half hitch. The result was that the bay landed on three feet instead of four, staggered, and almost fell. He tried to buck, but he could only hobble with the right forefoot lifted. And, presently, he stopped and crouched a little, shuddering, unable to realize what had happened to paralyze his strength.

Reata, at this, let out the rope once more, until the gelding had four feet on the ground. The bucking started again; and again it was stopped after the first flourish. Here, deliberately, slowly, the bay put down his head and sniffed at the rope that imprisoned his foot. After that, lifting his head, he calmly submitted to the bridle and was content to jog quietly to the corral gate.

Porky, standing up on the fence, whooped with amazement, holding up both hands in a rather feminine gesture of astonishment.

"That's a good one, kid," said Harry Quinn, opening the gate for his companion. He added in a low voice: "But where do I get in on this show?"

"You don't get in," answered Reata. "Ride down the road with me. We can talk there."

He guided the bay across to the rancher, whose head was still bowed over his work.

The gelding went on calmly and smoothly, except that there was a slight limp in his right foreleg, where the reata flapped and snapped tight with every stride, just measuring the length of that limb.

"You tell me where the Chester place is," said Reata, "and I'll take this broncho over there. But why do you want to send him back? He looks like a right good one to me."

"You don't see anything wrong with him?" asked Sam Durant gravely.

"No. Got four good legs under him, and he's sound in mind and body. He can jump like a wildcat, and he looks as tough as rawhide."

"He's got a good eye, too," said Durant. "Now that I notice it, he's got a nice red eye. I never seen a redder. But what I don't like is the color of the rest of him. I dunno why. It just doesn't fit into my eye. You take him down the road east and turn off on the first north trail. It'll take you bang into the Chester place. Just leave the colt there, and, when you come back here with the hundred and fifty bucks, you'll find some hot lunch waitin' for you."

"Thanks," said Reata. "I can see you're the sort of a boss that does everything for your cowhands. See you later, Durant."

He jogged the bay gelding down the lane with Sue following and Rags running out in front. And every minute or two a start ran through the bay, and his whole steel spring of a body flexed and trembled a little. He was not tamed; he would never be tamed. The instant the vise-like grip of the reata on his leg was relaxed, he would be at his deviltry once more. That was the comment of Harry Quinn as he rode at the side of Reata.

"He's all one grain, and it's bad all the way through," said Quinn. "But how you goin' to get a hundred and fifty bucks out of this here Chester *hombre?*"

"I'll know when I see him," answered Reata. "Maybe I can talk him out of it."

"And what about me in the rest of this game at the ranch?" asked Quinn.

"You lie low, off the place," said Reata. "You can come in

at night, and I'll tell you what's happening. There's going to be plenty for you to do from the outside, I think. It's a queer layout, Quinn. What do you think about it?"

"The gent called Porky is a kind of a loud-mouthed half-wit," said Harry Quinn. "And this here Sam Durant is as sour as they make 'em. I wouldn't blame anybody for socking a dose of lead into him. He needs it for softening."

"There's a lot more in the air than I can make out," said Reata. "I'll have to see this place by day and night. There's a lot you can see by night that never shows in the daylight."

"Like what?" Harry Quinn frowned.

"Ghosts and things." Reata smiled. "Here's the north trail, and I'll follow it. You cut off wherever you please, and come in after dark. I might have something more to tell you by that time."

"You know what I think, Reata?" declared Quinn. "I think there's goin' to be hell popping around that place before the finish."

"I think that there's hell popping now," answered Reata. "So long, Harry."

He kept the gelding at a jog. He loosened the rope so that the horse could gallop freely. And it was at a gallop that he came up to the Chester house. Here, too, the hands were in for lunch, and, as Reata drew near, he saw the cook come to the kitchen door and howl through cupped hands — although the men were not five steps away.

"Come and get it! Hi! Come and get it!"

The men did not troop instantly in for their food, however. They began to stare and point at the bay gelding and at the mare that cantered softly in the rear, stretching out in a long and perfect stride that made her standing ugliness disappear. Little Rags, running at his best, fell well behind those long legs.

Reata, as he came up, decided to trust the bay for the last few strides. Therefore, he shook loose the noose that bound the gelding under the fetlock and jerked the lariat up into his hand. The mustang ran on, unheeding. Perhaps for a moment he could not tell that the pressure was gone. At any rate, he allowed Reata to bring him up in fine style to a sliding halt in front of the hitch rack. There Reata dismounted, tied the gelding to the rack, and shifted saddle and bridle onto the roan mare. The whole group of six men crowded about him.

"Hey, brother," said one, "you ain't found this bay a spooky devil, have you?"

"Me? Not a bit," said Reata. "He just takes a little handling."

"Aye," said the man, rubbing his right shoulder absently. "He takes a little handling, all right. A fifth chain is all that he needs to be handled with."

"Bill Chester here?" asked Reata.

"Yeah, he's inside the house somewhere. He'll be coming out to lunch in a minute. Here he is now."

Bill Chester came out of the house with a mighty stride, slamming the door heavily behind him. He was not a tall man, and his legs were too long. They seemed to hitch onto the bulge of his chest and leave no space for a stomach. On this singular underpinning there was mounted such a pair of shoulders as one seldom sees in this world and vast, dangling arms. He was an ugly but a perfect machine, and he had the brute look of one who has used nothing but strength all the way through life.

He came up to the bay gelding and called out: "Is that there a saddle mark that I see on the broncho?"

"This *hombre* rode him over as easy as you please," said one of the men. "They've gone and busted him, all right. He runs right along like a dog on a lead."

"They never busted him. Nothin' ever busted him," said Bill Chester. "Who's been lyin' to you about it, eh?" He strode up to Reata. "You been sayin' that you broke that gelding?" he demanded.

"I rode him over," said Reata modestly.

"You don't look to me like you could break nothing," declared Bill Chester.

"No," said Reata, smiling at him, "but sometimes I can bend things a little."

"What could you bend?" asked Chester.

"Something worthwhile," answered Reata.

"You could, could you? Well, unbend the rope that's holding that gelding to that hitch rack and take him off this place, will you?" He added: "What does that mossy, old fool of a Durant mean by sendin' back the gelding?"

"What would you guess, partner?" asked Reata.

"Guess? I don't want to guess. It ain't any business of mine to guess," said the rancher. "Get this hoss off my place, and get him off quick. You hear me talk?"

"The fact is," said Reata, lowering his eyes so that the little yellow light might not be seen, usurping the place of the gray, "that Mister Durant wants to make a deal with you, and he thinks it would be to the advantage of both of you. Can I talk to you inside the house?"

"Deal with me?" said Bill Chester. "I'll deal with anybody. And I ain't seen the man yet that's ever got the best of me in a hoss trade. Come in here with me."

V

"REATA'S BARGAINING"

He led the way into a bunk room, long, low ceilinged, with two rows of bunks built into the walls on two sides and windows and a door at either end. A dozen men could sleep in these quarters. The stale smell of tobacco and old clothes oozed constantly into the air. A thousand odds and ends of apparel and horse gear lay in corners or hung down from pegs in the walls.

"Now," said the rancher, turning sharply around and planting his huge fists on his hips, "now, what you want, kid? What's Durant's idea? Make it quick, because I got a hot lunch waitin' for me."

"Mister Durant," said Reata, "had in mind making another exchange with you."

"What kind of an exchange?"

"He thought he'd give you the bay gelding back and take a hundred and fifty dollars in exchange."

"Hey? He what? He thought what?" demanded Bill Chester. "He thought he'd make another exchange, did he? The moldy, old fool . . . I took and trimmed him good and proper, and he thinks he can talk me out of the bargain now. He can rot first!"

"Oh," said Reata, "seeing that he's had a lot of trouble gentling the mustang, he thinks that you might be glad to throw in an extra ten dollars or so for the work he's done on the horse and call it a bargain price at a hundred and sixty dollars."

"A hundred and . . . ! Say, kid, are you tryin' to make me

111

laugh or cry? Or are you just wastin' my time? Get out of here before I throw you out!"

"The more you argue, Chester," said Reata, "the higher the price goes. You'll have to pay twenty dollars to boot to take that horse back now."

"Who'll make me?" asked Chester.

"I'll make you," said Reata.

"You? You make me?" shouted Chester.

He opened his mouth, his eyes, his hands, and then he charged, speechless with rage, words too large for his great mouth making it work big and small as he rushed, hitting out with his mighty right hand.

Reata staggered, or seemed to stagger. The huge fist missed him. Chester, checking himself with both hands against the wall, thrust around and charged again at the reeling, unbalanced form that seemed to have been unsteadied by the very wind of Chester's passing. A savage glow of joy worked into Chester's eyes. He was a man who loved fighting, and, more than fighting, he loved punishing. The biggest Spanish curb was not too big for his use. The longest Spanish rowels were just right for his spurs. And when he had a chance to manhandle a human victim, it was the supreme moment of his life. He could not be called a brutal man. He was simply a brute with some small smack of humanity in his features.

So he raced at full speed at that staggering, retreating, helpless Reata. With the full length of his arm, all his weight behind it, all the thrust of his massive charge, he struck at the head of the smaller man. But Reata had swayed — bowed with fear, as it were — under the drive of the blow. He had dropped almost to one knee. It seemed the sheerest accident that, when the weight of Chester hurled against him, the lean, rubbery arms of Reata locked around the legs of the big man just above the knees. But the truth was that, as Reata straightened, lifting with all his might, Bill Chester hurtled on through the empty air, making vain passes at nothingness, and crashed head and shoulders against the wall of the building. He fell in a heap.

Reata took a pair of revolvers from him and hung the guns on two pegs against the wall. Then he sat down on the central table, all littered with the carved initials of cowpunchers, and made a cigarette. He was smoking it at leisure when Bill Chester got to his feet with one hand clasped against his bruised head.

Vaguely he saw the slim figure of Reata, seated on the edge of the table with feet crossed. Only by degrees the truth dawned on Chester. He made a vague, moaning sound deep in his throat, like the first noise a bull utters before it begins to bellow. Then he started forward to resume the fight.

Something checked him. It was the negligent attitude of Reata in part, and in part it was the little yellow point of fire that had turned the eyes of Reata from pale gray to hazel. So Bill Chester paused — and reached for his guns. His hands came away empty. His face, at the same time, emptied of all meaning also. Gradually, very gradually, fear began to occupy the big void.

."Now that we've had a chance to talk things over," said Reata, "you can realize that the bargain's made. But the price is a little higher. Mister Durant is a little queer about that. The longer people bargain with him, the more the price goes up. He'll have to have two hundred dollars for that first-rate gelding, Chester."

Such anger raged in Bill Chester that he balled his fists and started to bellow an answer. The bellow turned into a groan. He stood swaying from head to foot, wanting to lay his grasp on this will-o'-the-wisp, but was checked by a mystery. He had confronted at last, he dimly knew, a being of an order superior to his, and more dangerous by far.

"I'll go . . . and I'll get some cash," he said. "It's . . . I'll go and get some money."

"You don't need to go," said Reata. "You've forgotten about it. I know how a fellow is when his mind is full of cows and horses and business, the way yours is, Chester. But now, if you'll feel in your upper left-hand vest pocket, you'll find a little roll of bills that ought to have all the money I want in it."

Chester stared. His glance gradually fell to the little dog, Rags, who sat in front of the feet of his master, looking up with bright eyes and canting his head to one side.

Even to kill the dog — even to wring the head off that small neck — would have been a delightful consummation to Bill Chester. But, instead, his huge brown hand pulled out the money. He could not believe the thing that he found himself doing as he counted out the money and threw it on the table. Two hundred honest dollars — or more or less honest — he had abandoned to this slender wildcat of a man.

"There's law . . . there's a law for robbery," said Bill Chester.

"And there's a laugh for bullies and fools," answered Reata. "So long, Chester. Treat that gelding well. He's worth a lot of treatment. And when you want the sheriff to arrest me, he can find me at the Durant place. I'll tell him exactly how I got this money."

He left Chester swaying from foot to foot, stunned, and went out to the mare. Little Rags bounded up to the stirrup and, under the steadying hand of his master, gained the pommel of the saddle. So, in a moment, the roan mare was stretching in her long canter down the trail that led back to the main road. Seven pairs of eyes followed him agape. For strange sounds had been heard issuing from the bunkhouse — and if there were any bruises, it seemed plain that the stranger was not wearing them.

Reata went straight back to Durant's and found that tall,

lean rider in the act of mounting a mustang for the afternoon's riding of the range. Durant pulled his foot out of the stirrup, hooked the reins over his arm, and turned with his hands on his hips.

"You left that colt . . . and then you got out, eh?" he demanded.

"That's what I did," said Reata, nodding.

"It won't do, son," said Durant, shaking his head. "You got a brain in your head, and I know it. But I gotta have more than brains working on this ranch just now. I gotta have *men*. I told you to bring back a hundred and fifty dollars in trade for the colt."

"Bill Chester wouldn't have it that way," said Reata.

"Sure he wouldn't," said Durant. "I kind of had an idea when you started over, that he wouldn't have it that way."

"He wouldn't have it that way," repeated Reata. "He thought that, considering all the time you'd put in taming that bay, he ought to add something to the price. A hundred and fifty wasn't enough. He gave me two hundred, and here it is." He held out the money.

Durant counted it, one bill at a time. When he reached a hundred and fifty dollars, he handed the rest back to Reata.

"What's this for, anyway?" asked Reata.

"Why," said Durant, looking earnestly at Reata, "when I hire a good man, I like to give him a bonus to start with. It's something that makes him want to keep living up to his reputation."

"Am I hired?" asked Reata.

"You knew that before, son," said Durant. "Go pile your pack on a bunk and come out here again."

VI

"DURANT TALKS"

In the kitchen Reata found Porky seated at one end of the long table, still consuming food with the waning of an enormous appetite. The cook was also at the table. He was an old man, so old that the wrinkles on the back of his neck were criss-crossed by deep, vertical incisions that looked as though they must give pain. But his face was ennobled and lengthened by a pointed, white beard. It was a severe face, full of dignity and repose, with a magnificent forehead. One could not help wondering how such a man came to be cramped in by the labors of a ranch cook.

Porky, when he saw Reata standing in the doorway, gaped at him widely enough to show the mouthful of beans he was eating. Then he ran his hand over his head and made his red hair stand up in confusion.

"Look, Doc. He's got back. He must 'a' collected the coin from Bill Chester."

"Nobody collects nothing from Bill Chester," said the cook. He turned aside toward Reata.

"Durant sent me here to eat," said Reata.

He had washed his face and hands at the pump outside the house. Now he took the place that Doc indicated.

"Set down here," said the cook. "I'm going to feed you fine if you got anything out of Bill Chester except kicks."

Porky stopped eating, and, picking up his coffee cup, he moved over opposite Reata and sat down.

"I ain't met you proper," he said. "I'm Sam Durant's

nephew. Porky's my name."

He held out his hand. It was damp and soft to the grip of Reata's lean fingers.

"I'm Reata," he said.

"Damned glad to know you, Reata," said Porky. "This here is Doc. He's a bang-up cook, too."

Reata stood up and shook hands with the cook. No head boss or straw boss is so dreaded a tyrant as the cook at a ranch. Doc accepted the hand of Reata with dignity and composure. He began to heap a large portion on a plate.

"You tell us what you done to Bill Chester to collect that hundred and fifty," said Porky. "I wish I'd been there. That's what I wish. Hey, Doc, suppose we'd been there?"

Porky leaned back in his chair and laughed till his eyes wrinkled almost shut. He was not an altogether displeasing sight; there seemed to be so much brute simplicity in him. Now he was choking his laughter for fear of losing a word of the narrative to come. The cook also, having put the liberal plateful in front of Reata, came to the end of the table and rested his knuckles on the board, all attention.

"Well, there was an argument," said Reata. "You see, Bill Chester seems to be the sort of a fellow who likes to argue a little."

"Yeah. With his fists he likes to argue . . . or with a gun," said Porky. "Go on."

"And he took a run at me," went on Reata, "when I said that Durant wanted the money back. He scared me so that I dodged, and he sort of tripped over me and slammed his head against the wall. After he came to, he seemed to be thinking about everything in a different way. He seemed to think that he owed not only a hundred and fifty bucks, but a bonus, too. So he gave me fifty more for a bonus, and Durant, who seems to be a pretty big handed sort of a boss, handed that fifty dollars on to me. It's a lucky day for me, I should say."

Even if he had had more to say, which he did not, he would have been drowned out by Porky, who was howling with delight.

"Listen to him!" shouted Porky. "Ain't he a wonder, Doc? Bill Chester tripped over him, eh? I bet he picked Chester up and slammed him. I bet he knows *how* to slam. Look at him, Doc. He ain't so big all over, but he's got it in the shoulders, ain't he? He sort of fines down around the hips, but he's got it in the shoulders, ain't he? By jiminy, Reata, I'm glad you're on the place. We're goin' to have some larks now."

The cook continued, all during this speech, to rest his knuckles on the board and look steadily at Reata. Now, as though he had made up his mind about something, he turned away to his duties of cleaning up the dishes.

Porky remained at the table, drinking coffee, spreading his elbows wide, admiring Reata, and talking busily. He wanted to know all about everything. Every man who has been long in the West knows that personal questions are rarely advisable. But Porky, with the license of one who never can know better, poured a shower on Reata.

"Where you from, Reata?" he asked. "And where you been that we ain't heard about you a whole long time before this? You been around wearin' another name? Because I bet you been in the newspapers a lot before this."

"Maybe I have been," said Reata, "but I never recognized my name. They must have spelled it differently."

The cook began to chuckle. "Shut up, Porky," he said. "He's just kidding you, and you don't know enough to see through it all."

Porky stopped his happy chuckling and looked sad. "Aw, are you makin' fun of me?" he asked, with his eyes big.

"No, no," answered Reata. "You just don't want to judge

118

a man by his lucky day. That's all."

When he had finished the meal, he asked for food for Rags and fed that small warrior a bite or two before he carried the dog to Sue, mounted the saddle, and joined Sam Durant, who appeared suddenly, riding around from behind a feed shed.

"I'll show you the layout," said Durant, and led the way straight up a big swale of ground that was almost a hill to the charred and brush-grown ruins of a building that must have been very large when it was standing.

"This is the old house," said Durant. "The folks used to live up here when I was a kid. You see the stumps of them trees? They were the only stumps anywheres around Boyden Lake. You could see 'em on the hill here for miles and miles, and the roof of the house stickin' up over them all."

"What happened? Accident?" asked Reata.

"I suppose so. One day it caught fire and burned down. There's the grave of my father. You see back there in that berry tangle? My mother's there beside him and my brother, Cleve, too. That's where I'll be planted."

"Your brother, Cleve? I've heard something about a Cleve Durant," said Reata.

"Yeah, he got into the papers by being murdered," stated Sam Durant. "That's the only way that he could 'a got up to headlines. He was a simple sort of an *hombre*, was Cleve, and never done much good. What for would they take and kill old Cleve for? Unless they were just tryin' to keep their hands in."

"I heard it was a stranger that came along to the ranch," said Reata.

"Maybe it was him. A fellow with half a face, twisted a little. Dave Bates, he's called, and they're going to hang him for that job. But I dunno, Reata. It wasn't Dave Bates that killed Big Ben. He's planted back there in the berry patch, too."

"Who was Big Ben?" asked Reata.

He could not help feeling that there was a distinct, though obscure, point about the manner in which Sam Durant was opening up and talking with such frankness.

"Big Ben was my dog," said Durant. "Kind of a cross between a greyhound and a mastiff and a bull moose, if you know what I mean. He wasn't handsome, but he had a brain and a big lot of teeth in his head. And one day, not long after Cleve was killed, we were all out on the range, even the cook, and we'd made up some coffee, and I'd just finished pouring a lot of canned milk into my cup. And a mountain grouse busted out of some brush near us, and we all took a shot and missed.

"Well, when I turned around, I saw that Big Ben had lapped up my coffee for the sake of the milk that was loaded into it. I swore at him and washed out the cup, and we were all settling down again when Big Ben began to act sort of queer. He pretty quick was acting queerer and queerer, until it looked to us like the best thing we could do was to try to find out what was wrong. But there was nothing we could do. He died right there, *pronto.*"

"Poison?" asked Reata, feeling his flesh crawl at the thought.

"We gave some of that tinned milk to a chicken afterward," said Sam Durant, "and the chicken died *pronto*, too."

"But how could they get the poison into a can of milk?"

"Stick a needle into it and work a drop of solder into the hole afterward."

"You think that they did that?"

"I don't think. I know. We had to do some looking, but we found the place, all right."

"Poison?" said Reata breathlessly.

"Poison enough in that can of milk to kill a team of horses. They would 'a' wiped us all out . . . the cook and poor Porky and me."

"But who's after you?" urged Reata.

"How would I know, old son? I'm just telling you things so maybe you'll see why I want a real man on the place."

"A man good enough to drink poison?"

"Yeah, and it might come down to pretty nigh that, for all that I know."

Afterward, he led the way all around the ranch. The soil was not very good, the stand of grass small, but the dimensions of that place were surprising, and the number of cattle. Two creeks crossed its boundaries. They came by the shelving banks that were the favorite ways of the cattle down to the streams, and they saw how the myriad of hoof prints drew out from the central blur into uncountable little trails that led away toward the dry pastures in the distance. The ranch was so big that, as Sam Durant pointed out, some of the cows had to trot for the greater part of a day to get from their outermost posts to the nearest of the creeks. This was wealth spread out very thin, but, gathered into one heap, it would make a very big pile, indeed.

"Now you know the lay of the land," said Sam Durant, "tell me just how good you are with a gun."

"Give me plenty of time and a rifle, and I can knock over a deer now and then," said Reata.

"Give you a Colt and no time at all and you can knock over a man?" asked Durant.

"I never shot at one," answered Reata.

Durant jerked up his head. His jaw set. There was a grim glittering in his eyes.

"You didn't pull a gun on Bill Chester?"

"No," said Reata.

"You used your hands on him, eh?" asked Sam Durant.

"Yes," said Reata.

At this reiteration, Durant stared more keenly than ever at his new man.

"What else do you use?" he asked. "Just brains?"

Reata shrugged his shoulders.

"All right, all right," muttered Durant. "If you don't want to tell me about yourself, you don't have to. I've got to be thankful for a small blessing, it seems. I thought I might be getting a man that I could lean on. But . . . well, have *you* any questions to ask?"

"You're convinced that Dave Bates didn't kill your brother?"

"I'm not convinced. I'm only convinced that there was something behind Bates. That was what put poison into the milk later on."

"There's nobody on the ranch you could suspect?"

"My honest nephew," said Sam Durant, "he ain't much better than a half-wit. Nobody would try to buy that kind of a fool for any sort of a real job. And the cook's too old. He's too old to be taking chances. These things have been done by people from the outside. It's not an inside job."

They started riding home. Durant said: "You take your blankets out of the bunkhouse. Bring them up and bed down in the room next to mine. Even if you can't use a gun, you're going to be better than nothing, I suppose."

"If you wanted a good man with a gun, why didn't you take that fellow who showed up along with me?" asked Reata.

"Because he's a crook. He's got the face of a crook," said the rancher. "And if he shoots straight, he'll be bought up by the others behind the scenes to use his gun on me. Nobody can help me except an honest man. That's all I know about it."

"That's all you know, but how much do you guess?" asked Reata.

"I guess," said the rancher, "that I'll be dead inside of forty-eight hours."

VII

"THE STRANGER"

The limited section of the house that was given up to the family was two stories high, and the bedrooms were not a great improvement over the comforts of the bunkhouse. They gave a bit of privacy, to be sure, but not a great deal, because the partitions everywhere were paper-thin, and a footfall in any part of the place was sufficient to send a squeaky tremor to the farthermost limits of the building. Reata rather regretted that he had been put into the room next to that of his employer. Yet it gave him a chance to sit down and think things over undisturbed.

He was by no means certain that he could accomplish anything in this case. He put Rags on the table that stood in the center of his bedroom and sat down to consider the problem, because the bright little eyes of Rags encouraged optimism and seemed to suggest that light was about to fall upon the most obscure details of the mystery. He stroked the fuzzy head and the strange, sleek body of the little dog and added up what he knew. The mere knowledge was not much. But there is a feeling about things that should give to the strong mind the extra sense that leads to far-cast hints and guesses at a buried truth.

Sam Durant, by leading him up to the ruins of the old house, had seemed to suggest a number of things. One was that he, Durant, was the last of his family except the half-witted Porky. Another was that the same source of malice that had caused the death of Cleve Durant might be that which had

123

destroyed the dog, Big Ben, and burned the old house in the first place. The idea seemed to be simply that the Durants would be wiped off the face of the earth, and then the total possession of the property would pass — to whom? That was a point to be discovered.

Inside the house, the agents that could have been employed to murder Cleve Durant and poison the dog were the cook, who seemed less trustworthy to Reata than Sam Durant considered him, and Porky, whose extreme simplicity ought to remove him from all shadow of a doubt, and finally Sam Durant himself.

Brothers have murdered brothers in this world. Yes, and they have afterward gone many years undetected, suspicion diverted by the very enormity of the crime and the ghastly unnaturalness of it. Sam Durant might be the man for such a job. His sour dryness might cover the most honest of hearts. It might also be the face of a fiend. As for the poison story — perhaps that poison was directed at poor Porky, who, rubbed off the slate, would limit the inheritance to the hands of Sam Durant alone. The dog's part in the affair would have been equally inopportune in any case.

As for suspicions, therefore, Reata was inclined to place them against Sam Durant, unless there proved to be some other relative in the world. He determined to ask that question as soon as possible.

So, when he saw Sam Durant that evening, after they had all come in from the range, he took the first chance of saying to him: "Got any relatives anywhere?"

"No," said Durant. "So far's I know, there ain't a soul outside of my sister's boy, Porky. There ain't even so much as the first cousin of an uncle's sister's aunt. I don't know of anybody in the world that would ever have a claim to this here place except me and Porky, if that's what you're driving at."

And his keen eyes held fixedly upon the face of Reata, obviously reading his mind with ease.

"All right," said Reata cheerfully. "We'll have to tackle a different angle, then."

But in spite of the keen, steady glance Sam Durant had given him, Reata determined on the spot that Sam himself must be the guilty man.

He carried that conviction with him through supper. He held it while he was smoking his after-supper cigarette in the gloom of the evening. Then, putting out the cigarette, he looked up at the house and saw that Durant already had gone to bed and put out his light. Porky still manipulated a mouth organ, wheezing out foolish tunes with a great lustiness, until the cook thrust out a head from the bunkhouse and shouted for silence. Porky's music was instantly still. That was the amiable quality in the poor fellow. He might be simple, but he was willing to be checked and rated into his proper place by anyone.

Now that the house was black and silent, Reata went out for a walk. He did not go very far from the house, and his course led him from one patch of brush to another. At each one he paused and whistled softly. He could not help thinking how very strange, to say the least, this proceeding would have seemed to anyone who crawled after him through the darkness. He had come to the fourth of those small clusters before a stocky form rose up to meet him.

"Back up, Harry," he said. "You're up here on the top of a hill, where you'd show as clear as a light against the stars if anybody looked at you from the house."

"Yeah, and I didn't think about that," said Harry Quinn, hurrying back into the shallow hollow behind the swale. Rags followed him, sniffing suspiciously at his heels, and Reata joined him.

They sat on the ground. Quinn would have smoked, but

125

Reata would not permit it. The scent of the smoke might reach to any passerby, he said.

"Who'd be passing?" asked Quinn. "Ain't everybody else in the house asleep?"

"They may all be asleep, and they may all be awake," answered Reata. "You never can tell in a house where there's been a murder."

"Hey," muttered Harry Quinn, "are you trying to give me a chill up the spine?"

"I'm not trying to give you a chill up the spine," answered Reata. "I couldn't give you that unless you caught it from me, and I've had gooseflesh right in the middle of the afternoon."

"What's the matter?" asked Quinn.

"An old cook they all trust, with an eye that might do murder as soon as look at a sheep. And a half-wit that could be a tool, but never a good one, and Sam Durant himself, who could be anything you want."

"Him," said Harry Quinn. "I been thinkin' all day, while I was roasted back there in the brush. I been thinkin' all the day that it might be Sam Durant himself. I ain't seen him much, but I hate the heart of him already."

"Because he gave you a run," answered Reata. "But there's something else for you to pay attention to. I want you to do the rounds about the house tonight, Harry."

"Keep a long watch, you mean?"

"Yes, till the sky gets a little gray. If there's outside work taking a hand in this, it may show up this same night, the first night a new man comes on the job. If there's a murderer inside of the house, and a tool outside of it, or vice versa, it may be that they'll get together tonight and talk things over. They may want me out of the way and choose tonight to talk it over. They can't find a time any sooner than this."

"So I'm to walk the rounds?" groaned Harry Quinn. He

broke off, lamenting: "Why do I stick with Pop Dickerman? I never get a real easy job from him, and even if I get good pay now and then, I sweat blood for it in the long run. Why do I stick with him?"

"Because you're afraid to leave," suggested Reata.

"You know that much, do you?" said Quinn. "Then you know a whole lot."

"You start the rounds," said Reata. "My job is to be there in the house, asleep in my bed, not suspecting anything. They may want to try their hands on me this same night."

"Great thunder, man," said Quinn, "are you goin' to go in there and lie like the bait in a trap and sleep?"

"I'll lie there. I may not sleep," said Reata. "Keep out at a distance. Stop and squat and look along the ground now and then. That's the way to spot things at night."

"I know it, and I'll do it. When do I see you again?"

"I don't know. Maybe not till tomorrow night. If I want you, I'll make a cross at my window with a lighted lamp. You see? Like this."

"Which is your window?"

"The second one from this end. Up there in the second story. I'm moved in to be bodyguard."

"And him you guard is the one that may stick a knife in you, eh?"

"That's the idea exactly."

"Well," said Quinn, "so long. It's a rotten job. I never had a worse one. Good luck to you, Reata. I hope you're goin' to be alive to throw me the flash tomorrow night, but . . . I got a chill out of the air, now. You've passed it to me. Maybe you'll be so cold you'll be stiff by tomorrow night."

Harry Quinn got up and moved away through the night, disappearing at the next cluster of shrubs and remaining permanently out of sight.

Reata remained for a moment, looking away from the blackness of the earth to the white and scattered fields of the stars overhead. Little Rags gave him the alarm at last. The dog jumped from the knee of his master, ran to the top of the little swale that sheltered Reata from spying eyes, and then whisked quickly back to the man.

It was too plain a signal to be overlooked. Reata, crouching to keep his body from outlining against the stars of the horizon, went cautiously up the little slope and instantly saw a shadowy figure coming toward him from the direction of the house.

The cook, half-witted Porky, or Sam Durant himself? All three of them had pretended to be silent in sleep a long time ago. If he could catch one of them, the result might be the solution of the entire mystery — or, at least, it would be a long-pointing arm down the road of correct suspicion.

Crouched almost flat on the ground, he stared at the advancing figure. It was not Porky. There were too many inches to him for that. It was not the cook, unless Doc had been able to put strange suppleness into his knees and step out like a youth and an athlete. Was it Sam Durant? Even he could hardly have a step like that, swift and rising lightly on the toes. No, the whole outline of the head and shoulders was different from that of Durant. It was, in fact, a man who had not been seen at the house during the day. Had he been hidden there, then? Had he come in from the outer night long before this and was just now departing? The latter alternative did not seem very plausible. It had not been long after twilight when Reata himself began his vigil. If the man were leaving in this direction, he probably had approached the house in the same line. Instinct would make him do that. At any rate, it was certainly an unnamed stranger. If he had been at the house in this manner, perhaps it was he who was responsible for the murder of poor Cleve Durant?

128

The stranger went by, stepping lightly, easily still, his feet almost soundless on the ground, for the very good reason that he was carrying his boots in his hand. Reata could see them, now that the man had gone by. He half rose, shook out the noose of his reata, and cast it with that sudden, subtle movement that he had learned south of the Rio Grande. The thin coil opened in the air with the softest of whispers. It fell true, and with one jerk Reata had pinioned the arms of the stranger to his hips. The pull on the line made the fellow stagger backward, but he uttered not a sound. And that, strange to say, completely convinced Reata of the guilt of his prisoner. He advanced, throwing over the other two rapid coils of the lariat that secured him as well as ever the sticky silk of a spider secured an insect in its web.

"Who are you?" asked Reata.

He got no answer. So he scratched a match on his trousers and moved the dim blue light of it across the face of the other. What he saw was the handsome features of Anton, the Gypsy.

VIII

"THE GYPSY'S STORY"

Reata dropped the match to the ground. It made only a dim streak of light and a glowing spot, on which he stepped. He was seeing many things out of the immediate past — the round of the Gypsy wagons, and the masculine bulk of Maggie, the queen, and Anton himself, riding his horse and swinging his bright saber, and Miriam, whom Anton loved, dancing on the bare back of her gelding. It seemed to him that Miriam was the happiness of that past moment, and Anton was the poison point of the evil.

"Do you know me, Anton?" he asked softly.

Anton hissed like an angry cat. But he spoke the Gypsy dialect, and his words were unintelligible to Reata.

"Say it in English, Anton," he suggested.

"Sure, I'll say it in English," went on Anton, getting easily into range vernacular. "I'm sent here to find you, Reata. And when I get to you, you throw a rope around me. Well?"

"Ah, you're sent here to find me? By whom?"

"By Queen Maggie."

"What does she want with me?"

"She says that she wants to see the fellow who made a fool of her and walked off with Harry Quinn. But that's not the main reason."

"Tell me the whole thing, Anton."

"Miriam wants you to come back because Miriam is no good since you left. She sits and moons. We went to a town two days ago, and Miriam couldn't do her tricks on the horse.

130

She slipped and fell, and wouldn't try again. Maggie came sashayin' into her tent. Maggie had a quirt in her hand, and she swore that she'd give Miriam a beating, and, Miriam, she pulled out a knife and waited for the fun to start. Hi," breathed the Gypsy softly. "That was a thing worth seeing, Reata! But Maggie wants you back, and Miriam wants you back."

"And so do you, I suppose?" said Reata. "The whole tribe of you want me back, eh?"

"Why should I want you?" asked Anton. "You made a howlin' fool of me. You tied me up and pulled me off my hoss and dragged me in front of the tribe. You took my girl away from me. Why should I want you back? But I come on the errand when Maggie sends me."

"Why should she have picked you out unless she wanted to have a knife dug into my back?" asked Reata.

"Because if I came to you, you'd know that the whole tribe really wants you. I hated you more'n the rest of 'em. If I came to ask you back, it'd show that we all wanted you to come."

"You think that I should come, Anton?"

"Why not?" asked Anton. "There ain't a better job in the world than doin' nothin' and eatin' fat, is there? You can lay in the shade all day if you want to. Miriam'll be there to keep you happy. She gets plenty of dollars throwed at her when she rides bareback at the shows. And you can do your rope tricks, if you want."

"How did you know you'd find me here?" asked Reata.

"That I can't tell. Maggie knows pretty nigh everything. She's always got her ear to the ground."

"What room do I have in the house?"

"The one next to Durant's."

Reata was amazed.

"Did you go in?"

"Yes."

"Through the window?"

"I picked the lock of the door. A Gypsy in Maggie's outfit . . . well, we gotta know how to do all kinds of things."

"Anton," said Reata, "you've told good lies, standing here. A lot of 'em, and good ones, too. Maggie didn't send you at all. Miriam didn't send you. If you came for me, you'd only come with a knife in your hand."

"All right, all right," said Anton. "You tell me why I came, then, eh?"

"For the sort of work a Gypsy would be hired for. Murder, Anton, or stealing."

"Murder! Hi!" cried the Gypsy softly.

"We'll go back to the house and have some light on you," said Reata.

"All right," said Anton.

Reata was amazed again by the calm of the Gypsy. He could see his shoulders shrug up.

"Nobody knows me there," said Anton. "And you won't believe me. I go back to Maggie and tell her. Well, she'll see that it's better to keep to the pure Gypsy blood, eh? Or if she takes another man in, swear him in blood first. Come on, Reata. We'll go back to the house."

Reata was of half a mind not to fulfill his threat, but he knew that Gypsy tongues can lie faster than a clock ticks, so he marched Anton back to the front of the house and then, under the windows, called out: "Hey, Durant!"

There was an answer so instant that it proved Sam Durant had not been asleep so far during the night.

"Who's there?" he called a moment later, leaning shadowy from the window.

"Reata and a friend of his on a rope. Come downstairs and light a lamp, and we'll come in for a chat."

Suppose, thought Reata, *that Sam Durant had actually worked*

*with this handsome scoundrel in planning the death of his brother,
and then shifted the blame for that act upon the innocent shoulders
of Dave Bates? Well, if that were the case, it would be strange if
he failed to surprise some flash of a glance as it passed between the
two allies.*

As he waited, he could hear the rancher's steps as the latter
moved about his room, dressing, no doubt. A light had
bloomed behind the window of Sam Durant's room. Now his
footfalls came down the stairs, and their squeaking was accompanied by the deep, bass snore of Porky. A bit of pity entered
the soul of Reata as he thought of that poor fellow of the
deficient mind, closed up here to rub elbows with murder that
was in the air. The light entered the lower part of the house.
It shone through the windows of the kitchen.

"All right," said Durant, opening the kitchen door.

"Walk in," Reata invited Anton, and, again to his surprise,
Anton walked jauntily forward, as though there were not a care
in the world on his mind.

As he passed through the doorway, Sam Durant drew back,
his eyes working keenly, deeply on the handsome face of the
young Gypsy. Reality like this could hardly be counterfeited.
Reata was instantly sure that the eyes of Durant had never
rested on the Gypsy before this moment.

133

IX

"THE SILENT DEATH"

When they were in the kitchen, the young Gypsy showed perfect unconcern. His eyes were bright; his color was clear; he even seemed to be enjoying his position at the center of the stage.

"Where'd you get this?" asked Sam Durant, sleeking his long face with one hand.

"He was coming out of the house. He's somewhere in the game that we want to find out about," answered Reata. "Name is Anton. He belongs to a gang of Gypsies that drifts around under a woman called Queen Maggie."

"I've seen 'em do their show," said Durant.

"This is the fellow who rides the horse and swings the sword," explained Reata.

"Have you frisked him?"

"I'll go through him now," said Reata.

He got from Anton one compact little .32-caliber revolver and a slim bit of a knife, a stiletto with a weighted handle, evidently meant more for throwing than for stabbing. Reata took it across the palm of his hand and smiled down at it.

"You see this?" he said to Durant. "He can hit a patch as big as your hand at ten steps with this knife. It's better than a gun, in some ways. There's no sound except a whisper in the air, and then you're dead with a needle jabbed right through your heart, so to speak."

"He's got a good, sleek look about him," said Durant. "I sort of remember him from that show. A fine bit of riding was what he done. Anton, what brought you here?"

"I come along for Reata," said Anton. "He was in our band, and Queen Maggie wants him back. I came here. I looked in his room. He was gone. So I left to go away, and he stood up out of the ground and roped me like this."

"Queen Maggie wants me? She wants me dead," said Reata. "The point is . . . how did he know which room was mine? He says that he got up there and picked the lock and looked in. But I was away. If I'd been asleep there, he would have slid that knife through my back, I suppose."

"Who told you which was Reata's room?" asked Durant.

"Maggie told me."

"Where did she find out?"

"I don't know. Maggie finds out anything she wants to know."

"You were goin' to bring back Reata to your gang, were you?" said the rancher. "How were you goin' to bring him?"

"By telling him that a girl in the tribe . . . she is waiting for him. You have seen the show, Mister Durant. Maybe you remember the bareback rider? She told me to talk to him."

"That's a loud lie," answered Reata. "She's a wild little devil, Durant. But she's a proud little devil, too. She wouldn't send for any man and ask him to come back."

"I kind of remember her, all right," said Durant. "She danced on a gallopin' hoss like she was on a big floor. I can remember the sleek and slim of her, all right. If she called a man, he'd foller."

"She sent for Reata," insisted Anton.

"She'd never do it in the world. She'd rather choke first," declared Reata.

"Reach into the inside pocket of my coat," said Anton. "There's something to see, Reata."

Reata dipped his swift fingers inside the coat and drew out a small brown envelope. From the envelope he took a picture of Miriam, the bareback rider. There was only the face and the slender round of the throat smiling at him. Under the picture, written in a small, swift hand, like that of a man who uses his pen a great deal, had been scribbled:

Reata, it's a long, long time.

He stared at the snapshot for a while, and then passed the picture into his pocket.

"You see him?" said Anton to Durant. "You see how she put her hand on him from a long ways off? Now . . . is it true that I came from Queen Maggie to call in Reata?"

"I dunno," remarked Durant. "What good would a fellow like Reata be to your group?"

"If they can pull me away from this house, they'll have a freer hand to tackle you, Durant," suggested Reata.

"Aye, that's straight," agreed Durant. "But would that tribe really get anything out of Reata, Anton?"

"More cash than for anything, except Miriam's riding. He can do more tricks. He can snatch the hat off your head and the gun out of your hand. Well, people like to see such things. Besides, he's a very good pickpocket. He could take your watch and your wallet while you watch his rope jump like a snake in the air. Gypsies need people with quick fingers."

He laughed, not without malice, as he said this. Reata merely shrugged his shoulders.

"Well," said Durant, "it looks as though he might be telling part of the truth. Not that I care a crack what you do with your fingers, Reata. Hadn't we better turn this *hombre* loose?"

"No," said Reata. "We'll keep him here. He hasn't told the whole truth. Before morning, maybe I'll be able to make him talk. Maybe he'll say something that'll interest us a whole lot. Maybe it'll even interest the sheriff, eh?"

"You think that he's in it?"

"I know that he's in it. Maybe he was hidden away in the house all day, and that's why he knows about my room. But wait a minute. What did you find on the table in my room?"

"Matches, a sack of tobacco, and an old magazine," said Anton.

"That's right," agreed Reata, shaking his head.

"Let him go," urged Durant. "I believe what he's said, mostly. He came to take you back to the Gypsies."

"I'll try working on him tonight," said Reata. "I may not get anything out of him, but I'll try. The Gypsies are the best liars in the world, because they have the most practice at the game. Anton, you're going up to my room with me."

Anton chuckled. "You want to know more about Miriam, is that it?"

"It's no good," insisted Durant. "You ain't goin' to get a thing out of him. He don't know a thing about what's happened here."

"Because you haven't seen him, that doesn't mean that he hasn't been around. You'll see, Durant. Up this way, Anton."

He made the Gypsy climb the stairs in front of him to the room on the second floor. There Reata, in fact, found that the door was unlocked. He pushed it open, entered, and kept taut the rope that held Anton while he lighted the lamp on the little center table. After that, he set Anton free, shut the hall door, and locked it.

The Gypsy sat down by the table and picked up the makings of a cigarette, that he manufactured with quick, skillful fingers. He had an air of suppressed smiling about him, and it was plain that in some way he considered that he held powerful cards up his sleeve.

Reata walked the floor with an irregular step, trying to think his way to a conclusion. His hand in his coat pocket presently found the picture of the girl, and that suggested something to him. However, he would try other measures first. He paused and leaned against the wall, partly facing Anton. The Gypsy was a bigger man and a dangerous fighter, but he had tried combat once before with Reata, and he would not attempt to fight him again. Of that Reata was certain, and for this reason he had taken the rope from the arms of his prisoner.

"Anton," he said, "the fact is that I've got you, and you know it."

"So?" said Anton, smiling and blowing a cloud of cigarette smoke toward the open window that he faced.

"But it's going to be better to talk to me than to talk to a sheriff. Durant is slow in the head. He doesn't fully understand what you're up against."

"You tell me," Anton grinned with the utmost insolence.

"There's a burglary charge," said Reata. "You've broken into a house and picked a lock. That's burglary, Anton, and they send 'em up for a long time for that. Eight or ten years for you."

Anton shook his head. "I took nothing. There ain't a way to railroad a man for taking nothing. It's too far west for that, Reata." Then, still grinning, he added: "Try another way to scare me."

"I've got a mind to beat it out of you," said Reata. "I've got a good mind to beat it right out of you."

Anton said nothing. But he shook his head in silence, as though to indicate that he knew perfectly well that there was not enough brute in his captor to permit Reata to use cruel measures.

Reata took a deep breath and controlled himself.

"There's another way to look at it," he said. "There's money, Anton. You could make a good bit of hard cash out of talking to us."

"So?" said Anton again. "What do you want me to say?"

"Who killed Cleve Durant?"

"That other Durant? How could I know that?"

"You could know it if you thought for a minute."

"Well, I can't think."

Reata wanted to smash a fist into that smiling face. But he held himself in check. "You could make enough, Anton, to buy yourself the finest horse ever seen in the tribe."

"I have the finest horse already," said Anton.

"You could have a gold watch, jewels in your ears, diamonds on the hilt of your knife. You could have a thousand dollars, Anton, for telling what I want to know."

Anton shook his head. "Let Bates hang," he said.

At this sneering remark, that proved how completely Anton understood the reason for the presence of Reata on the place, the latter felt like giving up the task on the spot. However, he persisted grimly. There was one last chance for him.

"Anton," he said, putting the picture of Miriam on the table, "suppose that you knew I'd never come back to the tribe?"

Anton sat straight, suddenly interested. His bright eyes narrowed.

"To stay away," he said huskily, rapidly, "all the time? *Never* to come back?"

"Never," said Reata.

"Aye, but she'd come to you," said Anton. "She says that she belongs to you."

"She'll forget me quick enough," said Reata. "She's not meant for me. I never could marry her. My trail hasn't stopped winding uphill. And . . . suppose I say that I'll never come back even so much as to see her? You understand that, Anton? Would there be any other man in the tribe for her except you?"

"No," said Anton, leaning forward from his chair. "But if

you promise never to see her again . . . then how could I trust your promise?"

"Because you know I'd stick to it," said Reata.

Anton, staring at him with feverish eyes, at length nodded. "Yes," he said, "I could believe you."

"Then talk," said Reata. "You'll have to say enough to make it worth my while. I want to know who killed Cleve Durant, and I want to be able to hang it on him. Can you tell me enough for that?"

"Yes," said Anton.

Reata sighed. "All right," he said. "It wasn't Dave Bates, to start with?"

"No, no. It was the last man you would think of." Anton began to chuckle a little. Then he leaned forward from his chair. "I whisper it, Reata," he said. "His name was. . . ."

Something flashed in the air. There was a soft, thudding sound as a weapon penetrated the throat of Anton. He leaped up, trying to scream, but was only able to bubble blood and, tearing the knife from his throat, he dropped on the floor the weighted hilt and the slender blade of the same knife that Reata had taken from him only a few minutes before.

X

"THE MURDERER'S NAME"

Reata got to the window in a single leap, the lariat in his hand, but only in time to hear the thud of feet on the ground beneath. As he leaned out, he saw a dark form scud around the corner of the building. He slithered over the sill of the window, hung a second by the tips of his fingers, and dropped cat-like. In his turn he sprinted around the corner of the house, scanning all the while the ground beyond. But he completed the entire circle of the house without seeing the fugitive. He dropped to one knee, controlled his breathing, listening either for the beating hoofs of a horse or for the pounding feet of a running man. But it seemed that the fugitive had dissolved into nothingness.

There was no use in hurrying back to Anton in that bedroom. He was dead before this, stifled by his own blood. So Reata stepped out into the night and whistled until he heard a faint response. And Harry Quinn came quickly up to him.

"You saw somebody come out of the house. Why didn't you stop him?" demanded Reata.

"Because I didn't see nobody," said Quinn.

"Harry, you were asleep. Tell me the truth. It's important."

"Nobody left that house, and I certainly wasn't asleep," vowed Quinn. "That's the straight of it."

Reata was stunned. For the only other explanation was that the murderer had simply circled the corner of the house and run back into the dwelling.

He merely said: "There's a lot of queer stuff in the air, Harry. Stay out here. I'm going to see if I can call you in

141

tonight and tell Durant that you're on the job. But I have to go easy with him, because he's a hard man."

"Aye, and maybe he'll be softened before a long time," said Harry Quinn.

Reata returned to the house straightway. He moved slowly. In that house, he felt sure, was the murderer of Anton. In that house, as far as he knew, there were only three people — Sam Durant, Doc, and Porky Durant. Perhaps the cook was not too old to have clambered up the side of the house and dropped again to the ground. Porky had probably been asleep through the whole affair. In fact, now that Reata listened, he could hear the deep, soft snoring of Porky, making a mournful sound through the house. And as for Sam Durant — well, of course, if it were he, then the murderer of Cleve had been found.

It was Sam Durant also who had been present to see the knife and the other things taken from the clothes of the Gypsy. It was Sam who had heard the remark about the excellence of that knife as a missile weapon. And still it would be very strange if the big, horny, labor-hardened hands of Sam Durant were able to use a knife in this fashion, for knife throwing is an art that can only be mastered by indefatigable practice.

In the door of the house, Reata paused. The obvious answer was that the crime had not been committed by any of the three inhabitants of the place. It had been done by another man who might still be lurking inside the premises. If that were true, then he could search the place in the morning, when daylight shrank the dimensions and dismissed the mysteries of the house.

He went to Porky's room and, standing outside the door, listened for a moment to the snoring. He felt equal parts of disgust and reassurance as he heard that deep, regular sound. Then he went to his own room and set his teeth hard before he entered.

He hated blood, and there was plenty of it. It was streaked and smeared on the floor in a great circle where Anton had writhed around and around. Now he lay face down, his head doubled under his shoulder. One hand was still fixed in his hair. The other arm was thrown out to the side.

And, leaning against the wall with folded arms, calmly looking down at this spectacle, was Durant.

The rancher lifted his eyes grimly from that picture on the floor and stared at Reata. He said nothing. He simply kept watching and waiting for some sort of an explanation. Driven inches deep into the floor was the small stiletto that Anton, in his last agony, had drawn from his throat and plunged into the wood as he stifled in his own blood.

"I was talking to him," explained Reata curtly. "Someone threw that knife from the window and caught him in the throat. I dropped out the window and chased the fellow. I saw him dodge around the corner of the house, but I didn't come up with him. Whoever threw that knife is now in the house. He must have run back into the house. The reason the knife was thrown was that Anton was about to give me the name of the man who killed Cleve Durant."

He brought out these facts slowly, dryly, watching Sam Durant with a merciless eye, ready, in fact, to see the rancher pull a gun. But Durant was motionless.

"He didn't get out no part of the name?" asked Durant.

"No part of it," said Reata.

"It was somebody from the outside," said Sam Durant. "He managed to sneak away across the open ground. You missed him, was all."

"I wasn't very far behind his heels. Besides, I've got another man out there watching the open," confessed Reata. And again he narrowed his eyes at the rancher. This time he saw the big man start.

"You've got a sidekicker out there?" said Sam Durant.

"Yes," said Reata.

"The gent that rode up to the house with you?" asked the rancher.

"That's the one."

"What's your game, you two?"

"Dave Bates is going to hang for a job he didn't do," said Reata. "I'm here to discover the real crook."

He rather wondered to find himself speaking so frankly to the rancher. But as he looked at the big fellow, it seemed certain to him that Sam Durant could not have killed this man, dropped from the window, circled the house, and then, stealing back, come to the very room of the murder to look silently down at his handiwork. Besides, trying to remember how the shadowy fugitive had seemed as he ran around the corner of the house, it appeared to the memory of Reata that the figure had been rather shorter and stockier. However, that would be hard to make sure of, since he had been looking down at an angle that foreshortened the outline of the silhouette very considerably.

"You know that Bates didn't do the job?" queried Durant harshly.

"Dave Bates never got drunk," said Reata, equally terse.

"Turn your friend over and we'll have a look at his face," said Durant.

Reata nodded and leaned to lift Anton's outthrown arm and, by that leverage, twisted the body over. As he raised that arm, he saw red letters scrawled on the floor beneath the shelter of it. Hastily he moved his foot in and obliterated the writing, making a red smudge of it, but what he had seen written on the floor by Anton as the Gypsy choked was the name of the murderer whose face at the window had been glimpsed while the knife, perhaps, was still in the air. And, as he lay gasping, Anton had written on the boards: **Durant.**

144

XI

"THE SHERIFF"

Durant had, after all, killed the man. Durant had dropped from the window. Durant, on soundless feet, had stolen back into the house and come to stand and look down at his victim. The rancher had on socks, and no boots. That would explain the silence with which he was able to move. Durant it must have been who, in the first place, had bought the help of the Gypsies. He had used them while he planned the murder of his brother, determined finally to have the whole property of the ranch in his own hands. No doubt Anton had returned to the place to extract another cash payment, or to levy a little additional blackmail.

The story began to straighten out in the mind of Reata, and he felt a powerful physical sense of loathing and repulsion. It was hard for him to remain in the same room with this perfect hypocrite. So great was his mental preoccupation with the rancher that he hardly was aware of the face of the Gypsy as he turned the body on its back. However, gradually, he saw it clearly. The handsomeness of Anton had departed in the agony of his death, and the mask that last looked on life contained all the vicious facts about the Gypsy's nature. A sleek and evil fellow he had been, and like a contorted snake he looked now.

Perhaps out of the murder of the Gypsy more events would follow than big Sam Durant bargained for. Queen Maggie would strike for her band. She would battle to avenge her fallen man.

Reata straightened the limbs of the dead man. He closed

the staring eyes. He tried to smooth and compose the features, but they kept pulling back faintly into the lines of the death agony.

"A lot of people might do some talking about you and this job," said the rancher. "Reata, there's a lot of gents that might think that maybe *you* jammed that knife into him and then dropped out the window and run around the house."

"A lot of people might think that," said Reata.

"You didn't make no holler. You just jumped through the window, according to what you say."

"That's what I did," said Reata. He kept looking down at the dead body. If he looked up, the rancher would plainly see the yellow devil in his eyes.

"Or, leavin' you out of it, suppose that your friend outside the house . . . what's his name?"

"Harry Quinn."

"Suppose that Quinn crossed you all up and done this murder, partner?"

Reata started a little. The thing was not totally impossible. If there was enough money to buy Gypsy help, there was enough money to bribe Harry Quinn, of course. The flaw in this argument was that Harry Quinn certainly had been too far away to take part in the first crime — the destruction of Cleve Durant. The second and greater flaw was that the name written on the floor by Anton was Durant.

The rancher was saying: "Go saddle a hoss and ride to Boyden Lake. Get the sheriff up. Bring him out here, so's he can see things. Maybe we shouldn't 'a' turned this feller on his back."

"I don't want him lying on his face . . . on the floor," said Reata.

"His face is dead."

"Aye, but I don't want it."

The rancher snarled something. Then he said aloud: "Go, get on your way. Call in your friend, Quinn, first. As long as he's here, we'll have to try to use him."

They went down the stairs. The snoring of Porky Durant followed them, and at one point Sam Durant actually paused and growled: "Fat, half-witted fool!"

He went on. The heart of Reata suddenly warmed toward the fat fellow and the round, soft, good-natured face. Far better a half-wit, than the iron cruelty of the rancher.

From the front door he whistled in Harry Quinn, who came out of the darkness quickly.

"Here you are, eh?" said Sam Durant. "Quinn, your partner thinks that the killer of the Gypsy is still somewhere in this house. We've got to pull out away from the place and keep a guard over it. Reata is going to ride into town and get Sheriff Greely. He'll be out here about sunrise or before, and, when it's daylight, we'll search the house. Meantime, you and I'll keep a close watch. Reata, get going!"

Reata nodded. He went by Quinn and muttered rapidly, softly: "Watch Durant."

Then he went to the corral, snagged a mustang, saddled the horse, and rode up the lane. The low, black silhouette of the house pointed after him like the barrel of a clumsy gun. He was glad to get on the main road and start the mustang away toward Boyden Lake. There was no weariness in him. He possessed one of those bodies that can defy fatigue as long as there remains a well of nervous strength to draw upon.

Now he walked, now he trotted, now he loped the tough little horse. And all the way, until he had sight of the dark smudge of the town, rising against the dim sparkling of the water of the lake, he kept thinking of Harry Quinn left alone on the ranch with the grim rancher. Poor Harry Quinn. In many ways he was as low a fellow as one could find, but, after

147

all, he was above murdering Sam Durant.

He remembered, also, the total silence in which the crime had been committed and the quiet that had followed it. Fat-faced Porky Durant had continued to snore. Cook had not been roused. And this soft-footed quiet made the death of Anton even more strange and horrible.

When he came into the town of Boyden Lake, it was dead, silent. He had to rouse a household to learn where he could find Sheriff Greely's house. Then down by the starlit lake he was presently tapping at a door. A window pulled up with a groan humanly deep.

"Who's there?" asked a man's gruff voice.

"News from the Durant Ranch. A Gypsy's been stabbed. He's lying dead out there. Want to have a look?"

There was an answering, wordless growl. He heard the man moving about inside the house. Lamplight glistened across a couple of windows. Then the door was opened, and he looked in on a half-dressed man of thirty-five, a range type, wind burned and sun blackened, fleshless, tough as rawhide. He had pale-blue eyes, very bright and steady, and always taking aim with a slight puckering of the lids.

Reata took a chair. He told, very briefly, the facts as they had happened. Then he slid out of the chair and stretched himself on the floor.

"When you're saddling up, saddle two broncs instead of one," he said. "I've got a spent horse out there. And I'm tuckered out. I'm going to rest here for a minute."

The sheriff said nothing. He rolled a cigarette, lighted it, and went silently out of the house. In the distance, Reata presently heard the racing of hoofs on the hard-beaten ground of a corral. He closed his eyes and drew in deep, regular breaths. The weariness began to flow out of his body into the coolness of the floor. Sleep, always at his command, stepped close to him. Wavering dimness of the senses soothed his mind. He was almost unconscious when he heard the bumping of hoofs and the squeaking of saddle leather coming around to the side of the house. Then he got up and went out to change the saddle from his tired mustang to a new mount. Instead, he discovered that the sheriff already had made the change and put the spent horse in the corral.

They were off together, the sheriff keeping to a continual, sharp trot. He was a man of iron in the saddle, and Reata accommodated himself quickly to this most trying of gaits. They rattled out of Boyden Lake onto the long road.

Only when the horses were pulled back to a walk, as they went up a very sharp, steep ditch, did Reata speak. "What sort of a fellow was Cleve Durant?"

"Best you ever seen," said the sheriff. "Always smilin'. The kind of a man it was good to hunt with, work with, drink with. You knew where he'd be all the while. Him and Sam was too different cuts. They was always wranglin'. Sam's a great worker, but Cleve was mighty fine."

After a moment he added: "Why d'you ask?"

"Because Sam killed the Gypsy . . . that means he killed his brother."

"That's a bit of news," said the sheriff.

"Maybe I'm wrong," said Reata. "But it's my guess. When I lifted that Gypsy's arm, I saw the name Durant scrawled out in his blood. He'd written that while he lay there, choking."

The sheriff whistled. "What did you do?"

"I rubbed the letters out with my foot."

"You fool," said the sheriff, "that spoils the case for us."

"Maybe not," said Reata, "and maybe so. But how could you hang a man just because his name's been written on the floor, even if it was written in blood? All that would have happened, if Sam Durant had seen that writing, would have been to put him on his guard. You can't catch a smart man when he's on his guard."

"That's right," admitted the sheriff. "But you sure thought fast when you were turning that body."

"I thought fast, all right," said Reata. "I thought just fast enough, I guess. He thinks that I believe somebody else did the job."

"We'll lay our heads together," answered the sheriff. "If Sam killed his brother, Cleve, he's the meanest skunk that ever rode a hoss. What's your name?"

"Reata."

"Reata, you're a bright feller. We're goin' to make something together out of this here case."

They jogged on into the gray of the morning before they saw the house looming. The dawn was brightening when they came up and found Sam Durant on one side of the building with a rifle across his knees as he sat on a rock and Harry Quinn, walking up and down, on the other side of the building. They had kept to their posts all the night.

"He's keeping up the bluff . . . that Durant," said Reata. "You've got to do your part now. Don't let him think you suspect him. Give him an extra hard handshake."

"I'd like to shake him into a hangman's rope!" snarled the sheriff.

He went straight up to the rancher, however, and grasped his hand.

"Reata's told me everything," said the sheriff. "You two fellows stay out here, will you? And Reata and me, we'll go inside and search the place."

That was the program. They went into the narrow, low cellar. There were only two small, empty rooms in it. Not even a rat could have hidden away from the first glance.

They climbed up to Doc's room. He sat up suddenly and

150

blinked at them, his old face wrinkling with surprise as he stared at the lantern light.

They went through every room in the house, and finally into Porky's.

Porky rolled over in bed. "All right," he groaned. "I'm goin' to get up . . . in a minute I'll be up." And he relaxed and began to snore again. He had slept all night with his window closed. The room smelled like a kennel.

"Bah!" said the sheriff as he stepped back into the hall with Reata. "There ought to be a way to get rid of the half-wits. They oughta be put off somewhere in an asylum where they can't do no harm."

"Get the murderers first and the half-wits will take care of themselves," said Reata.

They went up at last to Reata's own room. He had left Rags behind him. The little dog jumped down from his master's bed and bounded across the dead man. He began to whine and leap around Reata's knees until he was picked up and put on the shoulder of his master. From that vantage point he looked down on all that happened.

The sheriff said to Reata when he had completed his examination: "There's nothing to it. If you saw that name written on the floor, then it's a fact that Sam Durant killed the Gypsy, and that makes it ten to one that he murdered poor old Cleve. Ah, Reata, there was a man for you. One of the best in the world. And that sour-faced devil murdered his own brother! There's going to be some way of grabbing him and pinning it on him. If we can't prove it by the law, maybe a lynching mob is goin' to turn out to be a right thing for once in a lifetime."

Reata nodded.

"What'll we do with the body?" asked the sheriff.

"Leave it here," said Reata. "The Gypsies'll come for it likely."

151

"Shall we send word to 'em?"

"Why send word to 'em? They'll know. They know when one of their kind dies, almost the way a buzzard knows and comes a hundred miles to have a whack at a dead rabbit. The Gypsies are the same way. They always seem to know."

"You've been a lot with 'em?"

"I was with 'em a day, but it was a lot," answered Reata.

At that the sheriff smiled. He took out a bandanna, unfolded it, and laid it across the face of the dead man.

"If Anton was hired by Sam Durant, then what Anton knows is dead with him. Would any of the other Gypsies know anything?"

"Queen Maggie knows everything, of course."

"Can you make her talk?"

"Sure. String her up by the thumbs and light a fire under her feet. She may say something before her feet burn off . . . but it's not likely to be what you want to know."

The sheriff considered for some time. "What d'you think we ought to do?" he asked.

"Pretend that you think it was an outside job . . . go back to town . . . but be ready to come pelting out here the minute you get word. Something is going to break around here before long. I feel it in my bones. Aye, and in my throat, too, just where the knife sank into Anton."

XII

"VISITORS"

The sheriff left. He told Sam Durant that he had to get back to Boyden Lake, but that he would not let the case drop. There might be some connection, he remarked, between this murder and the unfortunate death of Cleve Durant. With a perfectly calm face, the sheriff shook hands with Sam Durant, begged him to keep looking for clues, and to send the first word of any importance to him at once. Then he rode away.

Reata saw him go, entered the bunkhouse, and promptly stretched himself on a bunk and fell asleep. Rags, curled up at his feet, would be his guard. There Reata remained until noon, when Porky Durant came in and shook him by the shoulder to wake him up.

"Hey, wake up, Reata!" Porky said. "Y'oughta see what's out here to see you. Hey, you just oughta see."

Reata wakened and saw Porky slapping his thigh and doubling over with mirth. The mouth of Porky was opened wide by laughter, but the cheeks of Porky were so fat that his mouth could not stretch very far. In that it was actually like the mouth of a pig. He seemed one who would have to take small bites.

"There's a man out there in a covered wagon," said Porky, "and he's askin' for you. He's got that dead Gypsy loaded into his wagon already. And you'd laugh to see the mules that are pullin' the wagon, and the way he rolled his cigar in his mouth. And the funny part is that he ain't no man at all. He's a woman! Come on and see, Reata."

Reata knew well enough that it must be Queen Maggie who

had come for the dead. He went out at once and found her sitting slued around in the driver's seat, resting one booted foot on the top of the right wheel. She had on her man's sombrero and coat, as usual, and the long, fat Havana stuck up at an angle in a corner of her great mouth. It always seemed to Reata as though coffee and tobacco, working together, had dyed her complexion to its present color. It looked like the sort of skin that would keep water out for a long time. The oil of the good tobacco seemed to have soaked through and through her body. She looked to Reata more like a big Indian than ever. And now she rolled the cigar across her huge mouth with a motion of her lips and said: "Hello, Reata. How's things?"

"Pretty good," he answered. "How's things with you?"

"Fair," she replied. "Pretty fair, I'd say. Except this fool goes and gets himself bumped off. He used to bring in a good pile of money to the tribe when we put on a show. You seen him ride. You know how good he was."

"Yeah, he was good on a horse," said Reata.

"You're right," said Queen Maggie. "He wasn't no good no place else. He was a lyin', sneakin', thievin', worthless hound, even for a Gypsy."

This frankness of hers did not surprise Reata. Nothing about her ever surprised him since their first meeting not so very long before.

"Well, I got him laid out in the wagon here and lashed down," she said. "And that makes me remember that things would be pretty good for you, if you wanted to join up with us now, Reata."

"You want me back?" he asked her curiously.

"Aye, we want you back bad," she stated.

"I'll bet you do," agreed Reata. "Every knife in the tribe would be good and sharp for me."

She shook her head, and the long ash at the end of her

154

cigar broke off and rolled down into the wrinkles of her coat.

"You don't understand," she answered. "We know when we lose a man . . . we know when we want a man to take his place. Your rope tricks, they'd make a lot of money for you and for us. It's an easy life, Reata. Besides, I need you. I ain't as young as I used to be, and I need a gent that I can kind of lean on. I could lean on you. Because you're a right man."

"Thanks," said Reata. "But I'm pretty busy."

"Where's Miriam in that hard head of yours?" asked Queen Maggie. "Ain't she got a place in it?"

"Sure she has," agreed Reata. "You don't forget a girl that's brought you as close to murder as she brought me."

"Now, now, now," murmured Maggie. "You wouldn't go and hold that ag'in' her, would you? And there she is, yearnin' and mournin' for you. There'll never be no man for her except you, Reata."

"No?" said Reata. He tried to smile, but a sigh was rising in his throat as he remembered.

"Chuck this ranch job, and hop up here with me," said Queen Maggie. "We sure need you, and we sure want you. There won't be any knives out for you. Now that Anton's dead, there ain't anybody that hates you enough to count."

"No, you wouldn't use knives. Guns would do just as well," said Reata. "And the tribe has plenty of guns."

"Is that the way you figger us?" asked Queen Maggie.

"That's the way," said Reata.

"So long, then, and the devil with you," answered Maggie, and whacked the mules with a long stick that she pulled out of the back of the wagon.

The mules lurched ahead. At a little dog trot that carried them hardly faster than a walk, they pulled the wagon bumping over the irregularities of the lane, and so drew off onto the main road.

155

Porky was standing beside Reata, shading his eyes with his plump hand as he stared after the wagon.

"She wanted you to come back, eh? You been with 'em, Reata? I guess you been pretty nigh every place in the world. That's the way you look. Like you been around a lot of places. Who's Miriam?"

"She's a gal the Gypsies stole . . . I don't know where. And they're taking her . . . I don't know where. To hell, I suppose."

He went back into the bunkhouse and stretched himself on the same bunk, for he was still very tired. Rags, as before, sat up at the feet of his master and guarded him. It was the whining of Rags that wakened Reata from a doze. Big Sam Durant stood beside him, his keen, hard eyes drilling into the younger man.

"Are you all petered out, or up to riding range with me?" asked Durant.

"Petered out," said Reata.

"Me and Quinn and Porky are goin' to do some work down the line. There's a stretch of fence that needs some work on it. Reata, I wanta know how long you'll keep on here at the ranch?"

"D'you want me to go?" asked Reata.

"You've brought me no luck," said the rancher bluntly.

"I'll go tomorrow, if you want me out of the way."

"I'll pay you for your full month," said Sam Durant. "But I'd rather have you gone. Tomorrow will be all right."

"Thanks," said Reata tersely. He closed his eyes again and heard the boots of the rancher thumping noisily out of the bunkhouse. *It was a little too patent, this speech of the rancher's,* thought Reata. He might have waited a few days before trying to elbow Reata off the place. If, in fact, he was to pretend that the Gypsy had been murdered by outside agencies, then he ought to pretend that he needed more protection than ever before. But even in the best criminal mind there are bound to be flaws. It was clear that the removal of the Gypsy had been a great gain for Sam Durant. Perhaps he had now removed the one man who could intimately have been witness to the process by which Cleve Durant had been destroyed.

So Reata closed his eyes tighter and summoned sleep from a distance. It came gradually closer. Finally unconsciousness came. His dreams were not good. He thought that he lay in a powerful furnace, scorched by the heat, and that Miriam sat by the open door of the furnace, laughing, throwing in bits of fuel to increase the blaze. The heat was not actually burning his flesh, but he was stifling for the lack of air to breathe. Finally he heard the whining of Rags, and he wakened.

The brilliance of a burning furnace was around him. The sun was far in the west, and the slant tide of its golden light washed through the room and painted and gilded the wall at the farther end. Rags stood on the chest of his master, and, with his rat-like tail straight and one little paw lifted, he was pointing like a hunting dog toward the doorway.

A shadow now fell obscurely on the end wall of the room, and Reata, turning and lifting on one elbow, saw that Miriam was there on the threshold.

She was not as he had seen her last. There was not a single slash of color in her outfit. She was all olive-drab in her loose riding clothes. There were fringed gloves on her hands, and a quirt hung from her wrist by its loop. She might have stood as the regular image of the typical range girl out on a long ride, but the roughest of clothes could not diminish the grace of her carriage. Under the deep shadow of her Stetson he probed for the blue of her eyes and found it.

She waved to him, saying: "Am I coming in or staying out?"

"Staying out," he said.

157

XIII

"THE TRAP"

He lay down again quickly. He wanted to wink her out of his memory and clear his eyes of her, because far down in his heart there was a region of pain and dizzy joy that she occupied. He had to forget her. He had to cut her out of his thoughts. Because even if her blood was white, her life and soul were Gypsy.

"All right," said her voice from the doorway. "I'm coming."

Rags began to wag his tail and whine an eager welcome. Her heels tapped on the floor.

"I told you to stay out," said Reata brutally.

She came up to the bunk and looked down at him. "You only said it twice," she said. "Three times would have made it true."

He could smell the dust on her clothes and see it in the wrinkles. He could smell the horse sweat, but also he found in the air a thin scent of lavender. It reminded Reata of riding over a white, summer road at the end of a day and having the first breeze of the evening carry down from the uplands a breath of coolness and of sweetness.

"Move over there a little," said Miriam.

He closed his eyes and waved his hand. "You ought not to be here," he said.

Although he kept his eyes closed, he could see her and more clearly. He decided that it would be better to look at the reality than at the thought. So he opened his eyes again.

She sat down on the mere edge of the bunk.

"It's no use our talking to each other," said Reata. "You'd better go away."

She pulled off her gloves, folded her arms, and held her chin between a thumb and forefinger.

"How does it feel," she said, "all at once having a girl that you like so close to you?"

He stroked the head of Rags and said nothing.

"I thought you were bigger," went on the girl. "But you're not such a big fellow, after all."

In spite of himself, he found that he was taking a big breath.

"When you're on your feet, then you're big enough," she said.

He kept patting Rags. He wanted to smile, so he made himself frown.

"It's pretty good to be like this, isn't it?" said Miriam. "The other things stop."

He did not see, but he could feel the shadow of her gesture.

"The Gypsies just turn into shadows," she told him. "All the years of my life flicker and go out. It's so nice to be here, Reata, that I even like this rotten old bunkhouse. What do you say? Isn't it pretty good to have me here?"

"Quit it."

"Aw, open up and be honest. Some of the chills that are wriggling inside me, they're working in you, too."

He groaned.

"Sit up and talk, will you?" she pleaded.

He sat up. After that, rising, he walked over to the long table and sat down on the end of it, swinging one leg and watching her. "It's no good, Miriam," he said.

"Why isn't it any good?"

"We know each other too well to be silly about the old game."

She stood up in her turn and smiled at him. In the slouchy clothes she was more exquisitely feminine than Gypsy finery could ever make her.

"All right," admitted Reata. "I feel trapped when I see you, but, believe me, I'm going to get out of the trap."

She kept her silence. He felt her eyes travel on him, half amused and half contented.

"You say that if a fellow struggles against the trap he just tears himself up," he went on.

She shook her head. "I'm not saying anything," she answered.

The fact is, he thought, *that she does not have to say very much, because to look at her is enough, and to keep waiting and listening for her to speak again.* "What sort of a sap do you think I am, Miriam?" he asked her. "I can see the facts, can't I? I can see you, can't I?"

"I hope so."

"What would it turn out? Suppose we marry . . . there's Miriam and Reata. Reata, the pickpocket, with his rope tricks . . . and Miriam, the bareback rider and Gypsy. Would it be a bust? Of course, it would be a bust. You want your own sweet way, and I simply wouldn't have it."

"Of course, you wouldn't."

"There'd have to be a master in my house," he declared.

"I've always wanted to find a master."

"The fact is that it wouldn't work. There's something fine about you . . . there's something in you that the right sort of a man could bring out. By Jove, Miriam, how clearly I can see you fixed up in a fine place with everything that a woman could want, from servants to blood horses. You could be happy like that, with nothing but velvet ever to come under your hands. But the way you'd have to live with me, starting at nothing in a shack, eating beans twice a day, roughening up your hands on a scrubbing board, wearing calico, getting down at the heels, would that be a life? No, you'd hate it. I'd hate it, too, when I saw you begin to change. You see how it is?"

She said nothing, but watched him, and he felt the gentle traveling of her eyes.

"Well, say what you think," he finally snapped.

"I'm not thinking."

"I mean, about what I was just telling you. Don't you admit that it's all true?"

"I don't know."

"Why don't you know? It was all English, wasn't it? Or do I have to talk Gypsy gibberish to you?"

"I wasn't hearing you."

"Now, you look here, Miriam!" exclaimed Reata. "I want to tell you one thing."

"I want you to tell me," she said gravely.

He snapped his fingers in the air, scowling.

She snapped her fingers in the air, smiling.

"Quit it, will you?"

"All right," she said.

He started to stride around the room, taking bigger and bigger steps. "I'm making a fool of myself," said Reata.

"Yes, but it's sort of nice," said the girl.

At that he walked straight up to her and stood so close that he could look down into her face, which, in fact, she made easy by tilting back her head.

"You make me so mad that I'd like to put my hands on you," he told her.

"I wish you would."

He did throw out his arms at that, until they almost closed on her, but by degrees he fought himself away from that tiptoe attitude of expectancy, got back on his heels, and forced his arms away and clasped his hands behind his back.

"You'd better go on home," said Reata.

"I'll go if you'll go part of the way."

"What's the idea of that?"

"I've got what you want. I've got the answer to all of this riddle."

"What riddle? This one here on the ranch, you mean? About Anton . . . and Sam Durant, you mean?"

"I don't care about Anton. I don't bother with dead rats. But I've got the answer to the rest of it."

"Go ahead and tell me, then."

"I'm going to do better than tell you. I'm going to show you."

"Show me, then. Where?"

"Up in the hills."

"What sort of bunk is this?" he demanded.

"It isn't bunk. When Maggie admitted that she couldn't get you any other way, I begged her to let you in on the inside about all of this. I don't know what it is, but *she* knows, all right. She told me that if I could get you up into the hills, then she'd let you in on the inside."

He was frozen with amazement, with excitement, too. "Wait a minute. What would Maggie get out of this?"

"She hopes that she can get you back into the tribe for good and all."

This chimed so perfectly with the way that Maggie had talked to him that noon that he could not help being impressed. For a long moment he kept in a balance, tempted, striving against temptation, wondering if he would not be acting the part of a fool unless he accepted this invitation to learn the heart of the mystery.

All that time he felt the blue of her eyes like something unseen, but under the hand. At last he said: "All right. That goes with me. I'll saddle Sue and go along."

She had been under such a strain, in spite of her smiling, that the breath of relief she exhaled had a faint moan in it.

Reata went out to the corral, saddled Sue, and tossed Rags

162

up before him. Then he rode out and joined the girl. She was on one of those half dozen little silken stallions, little gems of the range, that the Gypsies always had in their string. With glaring, red eyes and nostrils showing their crimson lining, he could do nothing but dance and prance while the long, low-geared mare traveled smoothly over the trail. Reata wondered at the ability of the girl to keep the steady pull that the little stallion needed. But her slender arm seemed tireless.

It was sunset before they came to the rim of the foothills; it was dark before they had been long among them, and then a moon came up and showed them the rolling hill forms around them and the dark solemnity of the pines as the woods began.

She took off her hat and tied it behind the saddle. He knew that was because she wanted him to see her, and he was glad. Their horses had learned to travel side by side, nose to nose, while Rags scurried up the trail ahead of them, hunting here and there, always busy, whipping his tail from side to side so fast that it disappeared from the eye. And he could see her leaving the watching of the trail to him, while she kept her head turned up to him, smiling. And he was smiling, too. They spoke hardly at all.

Once he said: "It ought to be always like this."

She answered: "It's *going* to be always like this."

The moon was well up when they came to a narrowing of the trail among big rocks, the trail passing in a straight line uphill.

"How much farther?" he asked.

"Do you care?"

"No, I don't care."

They laughed together. All at once he heard Rags's shrill yipping of fear and anger, and saw the little dog come streaking down the trail toward him. The clang of a rifle and the waspish hum of a bullet past his ear followed instantly. He saw figures leaping up among the rocks and heard the outlandish voices of the Gypsies crying out to one another. This was the way Queen Maggie intended to let him into the mystery. Aye, into the greatest of all mysteries.

He was done — he was finished. He had hardly the sense to pull the mare around. Automatically he caught up Rags as the little dog leaped for him. Had the girl known? Had it been all acting on the part of Miriam? No, he saw her ride straight forward up the trail above him, throwing out her arms to either side as though that empty embrace of hers would shield her lover better from the bullets. He heard her crying out in the Gypsy lingo, her voice like a shrill, mournful song.

Well, they would not risk putting bullets into the jewel of their tribe. They would spread out to either side to shoot past her into their chosen target.

He had loosed the good mare. She was running down the hillside like a bounding stone with terrible, unmatchable speed.

XIV

"OUT OF THE DARK"

When the three came in that evening and found that the cook had seen Reata ride away with a girl just before sunset time, the rancher said nothing, merely shrugging his shoulders. But when Harry Quinn swore that Reata was not the sort of a fellow to leave in the middle of a job, the cook said: "He ain't comin' back. I seen the girl."

"What did she look like?" asked Harry Quinn.

"I didn't see her face. I just seen the back of her, and that was enough. Reata, he ain't comin' back till that girl wants to let him go."

Harry Quinn argued, but rather vaguely. He wondered at the emphatic way in which the rancher exclaimed: "What would a girl have to do with this here?"

Then the loud mouth of Porky Durant was saying: "Hi! I heard the Gypsy woman this noon talkin' about Miriam, that wanted Reata back. I heard her talkin'. Maybe it was Miriam that got Reata."

"Miriam?" cried Harry Quinn. Then he was silent in his turn.

"Who is Miriam?" asked Durant.

"Miriam? She's poison, that's all," said Harry Quinn.

For he remembered her from the time he had been held prisoner by the tribe. He felt her name as one feels the scar of a vital wound. It was always somewhere deep in his life that he had to look to find her image.

Afterward, they had supper in a silence imposed on them

by the scowling face of Sam Durant. When Porky Durant started to carry on with rambling words about the Gypsy woman and her cigar, his uncle said to him briefly: "If you can't talk sense like a man, shut up and give us a few minutes of peace, will you?"

At that Porky hung his head, sulking, and it seemed to Quinn that there were tears in the eyes of the young fellow. He got out of the way quickly after supper and could be heard moving about in his room. There was the sound of the squeaking bed springs as he turned in. The uncle, hearing this, merely muttered: "A swine from the day he was born to the day he'll go into his grave. So much pork. *Bah!*"

Having expressed himself in this manner, Sam Durant rose. He said good night, and then, at the door of the room, added: "Reata's leaving tomorrow. I won't be needing you after that, Quinn." Then he went up the stairs that creaked steadily beneath him.

Quinn was so angered by this curt dismissal that he stamped across the room and threw open the door leading to the stairs. However, the sound of the squeaking, mounting steps checked his shout in some manner. He closed the door with a slam and listened to the echo go walking through the place. He turned about, growling in his throat that the place was a tomb, where everybody went to bed at the end of the day. No talk. No sitting around. Nothing to drink.

When he had said that to himself, he realized he could be wrong on that count and proceeded to look around the kitchen for a jug. He couldn't find a jug, but he discovered a pint bottle, half empty, then got himself a glass — a big one — and carried the bottle and the glass to the side of the kitchen, where he poured out his drink and set down the glass.

Here he settled down in some comfort. A good breeze came through the window and cooled his body. He rolled a cigarette, postponing the first taste of the whiskey until he should have finished half his smoke. That was the best way, in the opinion of Harry Quinn, to get the full relish out of whiskey. In the distance, thunder began to speak in a full, solemn voice. Quinn lighted his cigarette and drew two or three strong whiffs of the smoke into his lungs. Then, still breathing out smoke, he slowly lifted the glass.

At the good aroma of the whiskey, the dry gripping of a mighty thirst passed through him. He felt that the contents of that pint would never reach the roots of dusty dryness at the base of his throat. He lifted the glass, tasted one small swallow, and felt that the stuff was extraordinarily bitter. However, one meets all sorts of acrid stuff among the bar whiskies of the West. He merely shrugged his shoulders a little and then tossed off the dram. Bitter? Yes, it was so decidedly bitter that he hastily poured out another drink to wash from his mouth the memory of the first. Perhaps, thought Harry Quinn, something had gathered at the top of the pint of whiskey. Something alkaline, puckering the tongue and the inside of the mouth. He took another sip and, although the bitterness was still there, he settled back in his chair to enjoy a good evening.

In fact, he did not require a great deal of company, for on occasion he was able to let his memory wander through the dim forest of the past and find many a pleasant spot. He began to daydream over the times that had been in this manner, puffing leisurely at his second cigarette, when he found himself nodding, almost overcome by a great sleepiness. It was such a surprise that he jerked up his head, wondering. Only the moment before he had been feeling fresh, ready to put in a good time. Now he was dull, drowsy, full of yawning. He shook his head again, but that gesture did not serve to clear his wits. Instead, there was a strong and gripping numbness that settled across his eyes. It was like the pressure of a hot hand.

He regarded this sensation with bewilderment until something hot prickled between his fingers. He looked down and saw that his cigarette had burned up to the skin. He dropped it. Between his fingers there was a large white blister, and he had actually been almost insensitive to the pain. Sleep was charging over him. The soft beating of many feet was trampling over his brain, and in his ears, more and more audible, he heard the loud roaring of his pulse. Thunder rolled outside the house, but it was dim and befogged.

Harry Quinn had come to his feet, and there reeled back and forth like a hopeless drunkard. But terror that was springing ice-cold in his breast helped to give to his mind an instant of clearness. This was the way the thing had been done before.

The entire testimony that Dave Bates had given to the jury now swept back over the mind of Harry Quinn. Dave had said that he had sat down and had a drink — one drink. And then he had grown sleepy, very sleepy. It was strange that a single drink could overcome the steel nerves and the hard, grim mind of Dave Bates. But, then, perhaps there had been in that first drink — if only Dave had remembered to speak about that — a strange bitterness?

The terror ran wild in Harry Quinn. He knew that a criminal is likely to use the same method in successive crimes. If a man kills with a knife once, he'll use the same tool again. If he kills with a hammer, he'll murder with a hammer the next time. And now the murderer of the Durant Ranch was commencing his work again.

Quinn had to get out of the place. But as he turned toward the door, he realized that he would not be able to take more than a few steps. He would be found and dragged back and put into position by the murderer, and his gun would be found, the next day, with at least one chamber discharged — and a dead man would be sitting in the chair opposite

168

him. What man would that be?

He had to get rid of his gun, then. He pulled it out of the holster and tried to throw it through the window, but it merely struck the sill and fell heavily to the floor. It was strange. There was no force in his arm. It was limp. He leaned and picked up the weapon. He raised it as high as the window sill, when it fell from his nerveless fingers. He tried to pick it up again, but his body collapsed to the floor. He could not lift the revolver now. It was as impossible as though the little Colt weighed a ton.

He might cry out, though who could hear him except Porky Durant? The good-natured, foolish Porky seemed to Harry Quinn the one base and resting point of his salvation. He parted his lips. His own voice sounded like the roar of a sea lion on a rock, a noise submerged by the noise of the sea. Then all at once the body of Harry Quinn went limp along the floor.

XV

"THE WHISPERER"

The sleep of Sam Durant was generally very sound, but since the death of his brother there had been a tension on his nerves that rarely would relax. Because of that tension, the mere whistling of a draft though his room caused him to waken on this night. He listened for a moment and then heard the dull booming of thunder in the distance and the murmur of the wind around the edges of the house. A storm was coming up, and that would explain the whistling draft through his window.

Suddenly the draft ceased almost entirely. This was a trifle strange, he thought, for the wind was still murmuring around the corners of the building. It was as though the door of his room had been shut softly. Gradually he relaxed, thinking again about that which had occupied his mind before he fell asleep — the disappearance of Reata. The man was too dangerous to be entirely safe. The manner in which he had handled formidable Bill Chester was proof enough of that. Above all, it was strange that Chester had not tried to retaliate in some manner, but perhaps the explanation was not only in the things that Reata had done to Chester, but also in the faint yellow gleam that came into Reata's eyes when he was excited. A fellow who had seen that light once might not care to see it again.

Just as the body of the rancher grew slack again, and his thoughts were growing obscure, he distinctly heard the fall of some metal body in the lower part of the house, from the direction of the kitchen. This puzzled him, since the cook was already in bed. But perhaps Harry Quinn was rummaging around in the kitchen for food, though he had eaten plenty for supper. A moment later the sound came again. The same pan, perhaps, had slipped from the hand of the clumsy forager. The rancher frowned, but, while he was still frowning, he heard a cry so bestial, yet so human, so filled with despair and with horror, so unlike anything he had ever heard before in his life, that Durant sprang out of his bed. So doing, it seemed to him that he saw, very vaguely outlined near the door, the form of another man.

"Who's there?" he demanded.

But the form was not near the door. That was an illusion caused by the faintness of the light. Something rushed in the air. A crushing blow fell on the side of Sam Durant's head and knocked him to his knees. He was still stunned and helpless as the noose of a rope was tightened around his wrists. Then a gag was crammed between his teeth.

A whispering voice said at his ear: "Stand up, Durant."

He rose.

"It's your turn," said the whispering voice. "You remember Cleve? You're going to sit in the same kind of chair, dead as hell. You'll like that, Durant. You're going to be wiped out. There's going to be nobody left but the fat-faced half-wit, Porky. He'll have the Durant Ranch and the Durant money. Understand what I say?"

He nodded.

The thing was clear to him. Reata had been the outside agent who had killed Cleve Durant. Reata was also the fellow who came looking for a job in order that he might find his chance to destroy Cleve's brother. This shadowy form was about the height of Reata and must, in fact, be he.

What devilish malevolence was behind the thing? Perhaps the desire was simply to wipe out the two older Durants, knowing that Porky could easily be handled in whatever way shrewd, hard men desired. This explanation was enough. The only strange thing was that he, Sam Durant, with all his experience of men in this world had not realized that in his new hired hand he had a man too dangerous to be used on a ranch. Well, he would pay for that blindness now, and he would pay in full.

The whisper at his ear said: "Come on now, Durant. Walk straight through the door. Don't try to bolt. Don't even try to stomp or make a noise, or I'll bash your brains out here. Besides, noise won't help you. Poor Porky's snoring, I suppose, and Doc is half deaf. That's why I didn't have to get rid of Doc . . . because he's half deaf."

Durant obeyed orders. As beaten men will do, he moved steadily on according to command. The door was opened for him from behind. He went down the stairs toward the kitchen, and the rope was kept taut about his wrists from behind.

"Wait a minute," said the whisper at his ear.

He paused, and a bit of cloth was wrapped about his head. When he was so blinded, the door in front of him was pushed open, and he knew that he was entering into the presence of light. He was guided across the room, both his elbows being held in a powerful grasp. Then he was made to sit in a chair, and at once a long length of rope was wound around him. A man cannot be more helpless than he is when he's tied into a chair. There is nothing that he can do, no way in which he can move. But Sam Durant was tired of this life, anyway, he told himself. It was far, far better to relax and let the thing be ended for him by the hand of another man.

The whisper at his ear was saying: "Now you see the idea, Durant? Harry Quinn is lying on the floor by the window. He's been drugged with stuff in his whiskey. The fool! I drugged him. As the drug began to take hold, he realized what was happening. He tried to throw his gun away. That's what you

172

heard fall on the floor twice, but you lay there in your bed like a swine. You had no brain to work with.

"Then Quinn tried again to throw out the gun, so that you couldn't be shot with his Colt. But he failed again. The dope was working in him. He couldn't do it. Then he yelled, and that yell was what got you out of bed and in position to get a sock on the side of the head. You see!"

The whisperer chuckled. Durant sat rigid, waiting.

"Now," said the whisperer, "I've got you sitting pretty good, and all I have to do is to cross the floor and get hold of that gun. Understand? And after I have it, I come up close to you and shoot. And where would you rather have it, Durant? In the head? Or in the heart? Nod once for the head and twice for the heart. I'm a kind fellow, Durant, and I give dead men anything they ask for." He chuckled again.

Durant nodded his head once.

"You want it quick and sweet, eh?" said the whisperer. "All right. I'll aim the slug right at your mouth. I've wanted to smash a bullet through that mug of yours many a time before this. Because I know you, Durant, and you know me. You know me, but not as well as you think. Are you ready to die, Durant?"

Durant nodded. For it seemed to him, just then, that there was nothing in the world he wanted so much as the cessation of that frightful whispering. He heard the footfall cross the floor. The thunder was rolling loudly again, but he heard the rasping of metal against wood as the fallen gun was picked up. As they had found Cleve, so in the morning they would find his body sitting freely in the chair, the ropes removed, a bullet through his head.

XVI

"REATA RETURNS"

Reata, as the mare fled like a falling stone down the slope, was brought to safety by a sweep of the trail to the side, so that a crowd of vast boulders projected between him and his pursuers. He heard their frantic voices, screeching behind him, tearing through the air, and then the pelting hoofs of horses. Well, Sue had traveled a good distance this day, but she would travel still farther, and at a rate that would make the best horses among the Gypsies dizzy before long.

The way flattened out, running in a shallow valley with hills to either side, and behind him he heard the tumult of the horses and the shrill cries of the Gypsies to one another. He could see the dark of their faces and the brightness of their eyes without turning his head to look. They saw him, and a few bullets rattled among the rocks, but now he was around a farther bend, and every stride of the racing mare would put a safer distance between him and his hunters.

And the girl? They would curse her and rage against her, no doubt, but they would not touch her. She meant too much to them. It was savagely in his mind to suspect that she had known the trap into which she was leading him, but in his heart he knew that she had been innocent. And never would he see, in all his days, a braver thing than that picture of her riding before him toward the guns to cover his retreat, her arms thrown out wide.

In the white of the moon or the thick black shadow of the hills, he wove a way out of the highlands and into the flat of the valley of Boyden Lake below. For half a mile he kept waiting for the pursuit to appear. Then he realized that they had surrendered their chase. They knew Sue of old, and that they could not keep pace with her long, easy stride.

So he rated her back to an easy lope that she could continue forever, it seemed, without fatigue, flowing smoothly along over the ground. She was still at that gait, with hardly a break, when he came to the Durant Ranch. Half the sky was now adrift with thunderheads, and the noise of the storm was blowing up louder and louder out of the west. Still, he had moonlight to guide him, but that moon was almost hidden by the clouds as he approached the ranch house.

He pulled off the saddle and bridle and turned the mare into the shed, where he fed her. He was barely through giving her grain when he heard, or thought he heard, a strange cry from the direction of the house. No doubt it was an error of his mind. For the wind, when it is howling, can make strange sounds. And yet, as he finished giving the mare grain and then rubbed her down with some twists of hay, he was seriously troubled. He hardly knew by what, and he had to turn back the pages of his memory for a few moments before striking again on the voice that he thought he had heard. At once he gave up his work on Sue and strode from the barn without so much as closing the door behind him.

There was a light in the kitchen, that he had noticed as he came in and attributed to Doc, doing some late work — making bread, perhaps. But when he came closer, he saw, even from the near distance, a man bending down behind the window to the floor, lifting something, and against the opposite wall, lashed firmly into a chair, was a masked man. The rope went around and around his body and limbs, so that he could not stir.

Now the burden that was being raised behind the window

appeared as Reata drew near, and he saw that it was Quinn, looking like a dead man. His head was hanging. His arms flopped down. His mouth hung senselessly open.

He who lifted that burden could not be seen for a moment. And Reata exclaimed, not loudly, but in intense horror and surprise. Harry Quinn was dropped like a sack to the floor, and now, staring out the window, his red hair bristling it seemed, and his face working like the face of a beast, young Porky Durant glared from the yellow lamplight into the dull white of the moonshine in which Reata stood.

A gun flashed in Porky's hand. Reata was already racing, not away — distance would do him no good — but straight for the wall of the house. As he ran, the subtle coils of his lariat were in his hand, and he cast full for the window. The noose gripped at the flash of the gun. Reata jerked back. He heard a yell. The gun exploded. He saw the Colt fall outside the window, and the loosening noose come off the extended hand of Porky. Instead of running to the side, Reata dashed straight on at the window itself.

Porky had sprung aside, and, as Reata came up, he saw the chunky fellow standing with legs spread out, as though to receive a shock and withstand it — but he was facing now the open door, instead of the window. It had not occurred to him that any man would choose to enter the room by the window. There he stood, braced, and with another Colt balanced in his hand. The whole thing was perfectly clear.

As Cleve Durant had died, so was Sam to go. *Durant* was the name that Anton had written as he died. Durant . . . with Porky in mind. It was Porky who had planned, so simply, to wipe out his two uncles and possess himself of the entire property without loss of time. It was Porky, again, who had made the bargain with the Gypsies when he first needed help. It was Porky who, on this day, had twice tried to get Reata away from the ranch as a man too dangerous to have around when he was working out the last half of his schemes.

These things Reata saw clearly as he rushed for the window. He could not get through it before Porky had a chance to turn and fire into him. He could not enter the guarded door. And he carried no gun. It was not the first time in his life that he had had occasion to curse his fixed resolution never to wear a gun. But he had that agent which could enter the room for him.

It was not easy. He had to build a noose so small that it would pass through the narrow of the window, so broad that it would drop over the shoulders of Porky. One gesture made that noose. One gesture threw it through the window, making a soft, slithering whisper through the air.

And Porky, crouched a little, wavering a bit from side to side in the animal intensity of his hunger to kill, heard that whisper in the air. He seemed to know what it meant, and that it was too late for him to side-step. Instead, he twisted about as the rope descended above him, and with a bullet from his gun knocked the sombrero from Reata's head. It was good shooting. But the next moment a powerful tug on the lariat had jerked Porky forward.

Reata went through that window like a cat. The gun was still in Porky's hand. He tried to twist around and use it, till Reata stamped on his wrist. The bones crunched softly inside the fat of the flesh, and Porky lay still. A few twists of the little reata tied the fat fellow hand and foot. Then Reata stepped to the rancher and made him free.

Big Sam Durant leaned from his chair, staring, staring. Reata, working busily over the inert body of Harry Quinn, would never forget how Durant said slowly: "I only thought he was a pig. I forgot . . . that swine eat meat."

But Porky said nothing. He did not even nurse his crushed wrist. All the life of his body and of his soul was concentrated in the red stain of fire in his eyes.

It seemed to Reata afterward that there was no regret in Porky for what he had done. He had saved himself all his life, realizing his own vicious capacities, masking them under his affectation of simplicity that gave him idle days, saving himself for the great moment when he could strike to kill. There was only one real folly in his plan, and that was the exactitude with which he had copied the first crime in preparing for the second.

"When I seen you the first time," said Porky to Reata, later on, "I knew that you might make things go wrong. I knew it by the damn' cool look of you. I seen the yaller in your eyes the first shot out of the box. How I wish that I'd cut your throat while you were asleep!"

That was all he would say. They could not make him speak even at his trial. In silence he was to go to the end of his life, as far as legal answers went. But the proof that was gathered about him was too complete and too exact for him to wriggle out of the net.

Harry Quinn went to the penitentiary to get Dave Bates. He wanted Reata to do it because, as he said, Dave would think a lot of the first friend he saw when he was freed from prison. But Reata wanted to go back to Rusty Gulch alone, slowly. He wanted to pass under long leagues of the blue of the Western sky, and to let the honest sun burn out of him some of the memories of the Durant Ranch.

Sam Durant did not beg him to stay. He did not insist, even when Reata refused the thick sheaf of bank notes that he offered to his rescuer. Durant said: "I know what it means to you. It's been like a lot of bad weather. On top of timberline. No sun to see. You wanta forget. Well, you'll never forget, Reata. No more'n we'll ever forget you."

Then Reata rode south, leisurely. He had Rags for company. In that company, he felt more than secure, because for the second time, the little scrap of a dog had given him the warning that enabled him to save his life. And there was only one shadow on the soul of Reata all the way, and that was the thought of the girl. But it was better that he should not try to find her. There was too much Gypsy in her soul. She would be irreclaimable to the last moment of her life. One could not be in her company without finding the bright face of danger too often at hand. And yet the thought of her was always near him like a presence on the farther side of a door, like someone whispering on the other side of a corner.

When he came down into Rusty Gulch, he came by twilight, ten days after he had left the house of Durant. After he had put up Sue in the box stall that was her special place in the establishment of Pop Dickerman, Reata knew, as he patted her head, that she was two-thirds his own.

From the house, as he approached it, he heard only one voice sounding, loudly, and that was the voice of Harry Quinn. So Reata came up stealthily and peered through the window. What he saw was Pop Dickerman waiting on his two men at supper, filling their plates and their coffee cups, stepping here and there in soundless slippers, with a cat curled securely on his shoulder, a scrawny, yellow-eyed tomcat.

Harry Quinn was enlarging himself over a glass of whiskey that stood beside his plate of food. But his words had no meaning to the mind of Reata, who was staring fixedly at the little man who sat at the table. The face of Dave Bates was so thin that, in fact, it looked like only half of a normal face. It was twisted and crooked. The brow alone was noble and wide, and the eyes were as cold as stones. Never in his life had Reata seen a thing so evil. And it was for this that he had rubbed elbows with that whispering death on the Durant Ranch.

IN MEDIAS RES

THE LOST VALLEY

The short novel that follows Frederick Faust titled "The Lost Valley." It was first published as "The Emerald Trail" by John Frederick in Street & Smith's *Western Story Magazine* (2/25/22). This is the first time it has appeared in book form.

I

"BURNING MONEY"

When it happened, there were divided opinions. Some said that beginners have luck. Others declared that the devil takes care of his own. And last of all the cynics nodded their heads and admitted — old miner, old fool. But when all the talking was ended, the fact remained that the man who struck pay dirt and started the wild gold rush was young Billy Neilan, far better and more widely known as Chuck.

Of course, there was no reason in the world why Chuck should have struck it rich. He knew infinitely more about ropes and branding irons than he did about "color" and the ways of getting at it. He knew vastly more about poker than he knew about ropes and irons. And he knew far, far more about guns than he knew about poker. In fact, work was never a thing that troubled Chuck Neilan. What sent him out prospecting was simply the fact that he had never prospected before. And the third day he made the strike.

With typically careless exuberance, he took a well-to-do miner up to the claim and offered to sell out for five thousand dollars. But a miracle happened. The miner was too rich to be dishonest — at least, dishonest to *that* extent. He merely bought a half interest, and he paid for that half interest four times the price for which Chuck had stipulated to sell his entire share in the claim.

Twelve hours later a big gang of laborers was tearing into the mountainside and opening up the treasures of The Roanoke Queen. But Chuck Neilan was not on hand to watch the proceedings. He had swung his lithe body onto a vicious pinto and spurred the tough little beast toward town, for in Chuck's pocket was a stuffed wallet that rubbed against his ribs. And in the wallet the stuffing consisted of greenbacks of large denominations totaling twenty thousand dollars that clamored with eagerness to be spent.

All the way down the trail the thirst of Chuck, brought to a fine edge by the drought of Prohibition days, increased in sharpness. It became a consuming fire in time, and he struck the town of Sitting Bull like a whirlwind seeking action.

Sitting Bull was not a quiet, pastoral village. The epidermis of that community had been thickened by many a perilous year of existence in gold-rush times and out of them. The town had seen riots beyond number, and in the early term of its life it had regularly burned to the ground three times a year. Among the old-timers in that city were men whose names had rung and echoed up and down the length of the mountain desert, and yet the hardiest of these looked askance with the expression of men who feel that a storm is about to break when the rattle of hoofs and the whooping voice tore past the window.

"What young fool is that?" they would ask.

"It ain't no fool. It's Chuck Neilan," would be the answer of him who went to look. Soon as that answer was received, men looked to one another foolishly, pushed hats back on heads, and scratched speculatively, then looked to their guns.

Not that Chuck Neilan was a bully or a fight picker. By no means. If he had been, he must inevitably have left a red trail behind him during the first year or two of his vigorous manhood and come to a quick end himself. But, as a matter of fact, Chuck was the best-natured man who ever loved a fight from the bottom of his heart. He was very, very partial to fist fighting, but where his ability was known and some burly fellow wished to close and rough it, Chuck was perfectly willing to accommodate the hardiest of them in a whirl at rough-and-tumble. He would, much against his will, meet the desires of those who wished knife work. But the special domain, the *sanctum sanctorum* of Chuck, was gun play. He looked upon it not as a means of killing enemies and defending one's life. It was not that to Chuck. It was, above all, an art.

Chuck would talk with a hushed voice and subdued manner about the grace with which one fellow handled a gun, about the neatness of another, and about the speed of a third. Those were, as may be seen, the three chief articles in his creed: speed, neatness, and grace. He would hold forth at length upon the degree of polish that various gunfighters in the mountains possessed. As a matter of fact, he stood apart and above the rest of them, and he was recognized for his skill.

As has been said before, he was not a bully. Like all men who truly love battle, the only manner of battle in which he rejoiced was fair fight with no odds except on the side opposed to him. Nothing could induce him to attack a man smaller than himself, even though pushed to the wall in self-defense, and he had been known to back out of a room and literally take water rather than lay one of his formidable hands upon some obstreperous youth not yet familiar with the uses of a razor.

Indeed, as the reputation of Chuck Neilan spread and his formidable qualities became well known, he fell into a dearth of trouble, in spite of the maxim about those who hunt for it. Hardboiled battlers avoided him like poison, and law-abiding citizens would by no means risk their necks to subdue a noise maker who, as they were perfectly well aware, had not an ounce of malice in his entire make-up. Yet, although one may be perfectly sure that the lightning will not strike, it often serves to make the cheek change color and the eye grow smaller. Such was the effect of the advent of Chuck Neilan upon even the hardy citizens of Sitting Bull.

He galloped past with a whoop and a cloud of dust, and in the course of the day he plunged into and emerged from three separate parties built around various and sundry proportions of moonshine red-eye. Behold him, therefore, in the early evening striding down the streets of Sitting Bull with the carriage of a wavering reed in the wind and steps as irregular as the first halting paces of a child. His eye, however, remained clear, his voice steady, though somewhat shrill, and, when it was not necessary for him to move about, few would have guessed that he was inebriated, except for the reddened brilliance of his glance.

Of course, a crowd gathered around him. It spread behind like the tail behind a comet. If he sang, they echoed him in a chorus. If he halted, they halted likewise. Most of them were mean spirits who hungered to pick up a few wild tales to tell about the latest coming of this celebrity to Sitting Bull. Those who were actually his friends dared not argue with him about his course of action. For Chuck Neilan was very, very averse to meeting argument from a sturdy, full-grown man. He liked to have such arguments expressed in actions rather than words, and his preferences being well known, his friends gave him a wide swath when he started on a rampage. For that matter, none of the crowd was at all disposed to cross him in the least of his whims. And, though a halting, old woman came in his path and shook her cane at him and rated him soundly and passed quite unscathed in spite of her rashness, there was no stalwart man who would not rather have signed his own death warrant than have taken such action.

So, when he whirled suddenly and with an imperious gesture bade them scatter, they obeyed at once and fled to the four corners of the street like leaves before the wind. Chuck Neilan, staggering and laughing as he watched them flee, now turned again and pursued his uncertain way until a flare of light and a well-remembered window brought him to an abrupt halt in the middle of the block. It was the pawnbroker's window. There in the very center stood the most brilliant decoration of all, the silver-and-gold mounted saddle which, since his earliest recollections, had always shone in that window, apparently a fixture there for eternity, and far too beautiful for actual use. Many and many a dream had seen him seated in that saddle, rushing against onleaping hordes of Indians perhaps, or prancing through the center of this same street with familiar faces on either side.

He gazed on it now with his heart beating in his throat. Impossible to most perhaps, but nothing was impossible to a man who had twenty thousand dollars struggling to burn a way out of his wallet and again enjoy the air of a free circulation from hand to hand. Chuck lingered only in order to note that the gold spurs were also there beside the saddle, and then he turned and plunged through the door and into the cobwebbed silence of the shop.

That silence, the warmth, and the lack of fresh air caused the excited brain of Chuck Neilan to spin for a moment. His brain cleared as he saw through the cloud the familiar countenance of Mr. Isaac Sylvester. The first Sylvester had founded this pawnshop. The second Sylvester, who was the man who now confronted Chuck with his big hands spread palms down on the top of the glass-covered case, had carried on the same business. The first Sylvester was lean; the second Sylvester was broad. His face was a triangle. The base was the enormous breadth of his jowls. The apex was the stubborn tuft of hair that jutted out at the top of his narrowing forehead. His mouth was a shapeless slit. His nose was a pudgy mass made distinguishable only by the flaring, fishhook nostrils. His eyebrows darted out in the shape familiar to those who have seen a Mephistopheles made up for the stage. Under them were little, beady, black eyes that could glitter with complacence, shine with piercing distrust, or glow invitingly. They glowed in this manner at the newcomer, though a spot of white appeared in the exact center of each of Sylvester's cheeks. The cowpuncher-miner looked over the pawnbroker with intense distrust and dislike.

"Well, Sylvester," he said, "how come?"

"Fair . . . only fair," protestingly responded Sylvester, turning his hands palms up and shrugging shoulders that seemed capable of lifting a ton's weight. "Times ain't what they used to be when my father was running things."

"Huh," said Chuck, and made a wry face. Then he swallowed the ideas that came storming to his teeth.

"That saddle there in the window," he said. "How much?"

The glance of Sylvester flickered to the saddle and back at the face of Chuck Neilan. By the step with which Chuck approached, he now saw that the man was drunk, very drunk. But would it be wise to cheat him, nevertheless? Other men had cheated Mr. Neilan on occasion, and they had not lived long to boast of their cleverness. In reality, Sylvester hated Chuck more than he feared him. He had long promised himself that, if he could ever lay hands on the formidable cowpuncher, one crunching grip of his massive fingers would serve to end the battle before it was well begun. But the trouble was that, while he was reaching for his man, many, many things might happen. Sylvester looked again at the saddle and moistened his dry lips. And the heart of the cheat in him was dry also as a desert calling for rain.

"That saddle," he declared, "is all gold work and silver work and leather work made by hand, Mister Neilan."

"When you call me Mister Neilan," Chuck said, grinning, "I

know you're going to boost the price on me. How much, I say?"

The pawnbroker burst into perspiration. "It cost two thousand to make," he said and glanced at it aside. It was rotted with time. It was not worth, now, more than the value of the ornaments — say three or four hundred dollars.

"Two thousand?"

"But time has brought it down some," said Sylvester, seeing a tremendous profit in the grip of his fingers, and hardly daring to close them over the bargain. "Down to about eighteen hundred . . . or . . . seeing it's you . . . sixteen hundred dollars, Chuck."

In agony he had brought down the price that four hundred dollars, and now his brain reeled as he heard the tall man say: "Dirt cheap, Sylvester. Dirt cheap. That ol' saddle's mine. Trot it out. Trot it out!"

Weak with the conviction that the entire two thousand would have been paid without demure, the pawnbroker staggered to the window and returned, carrying the saddle. It was flashing enough and brilliant enough to make an eye-catching window display, but the leather was either warped or rotted out of all semblance to a saddle.

"I'll throw in the blankets," he declared generously, and he swathed the saddle at once in a great sheeting of wool. Then he breathed more easily. The hungry eyes of Chuck, the eyes of one intent on purchasing, were still wandering about unsatisfied.

"I seen a pair of gold spurs out in that window," he said. "Maybe . . . ?"

The spurs were instantly produced and turned back and forth in the fat hands of the broker, so that the light would catch on them and gleam. A price was named and instantly taken. The crisp bank notes once again rustled on the top of the glass case. The spurs were wrapped and became the property of the miner.

"Now," said Sylvester, "what d'you think of these?" And under the eyes of Chuck he slid a tray of diamonds.

There was no satisfactory light in the pawnshop, but from the two lamps sufficient radiance fell to make the tray come instantly awash with light, and Sylvester manipulated it slightly back and forth — just a bare fraction of an inch, so that the gems might have the better chance to scintillate. While his hand worked, his brain worked with tenfold speed, estimating how high he might boost the price on each diamond. To his dismay the other was shaking his head.

"Never took to diamonds much," he declared. "Just as soon have a bunch of old junk glass, pretty near. I like color, son, and lots of it."

Inspiration descended upon Sylvester. The tray of diamonds disappeared with the speed and many of the other properties of light, and in its place a second tray was produced, burning with the colors of a sunset — rubies, emeralds, topaz, pearls, none of them in any remarkable size, but all in such numbers that the color effect instantly charmed the eye. Hundreds of Mexicans had left this wealth here in exchange for gold. And many and many a gaudy scarf pin had been despoiled to increase the tray in Sylvester's shop. He looked upon it now with a sad sort of satisfaction. It was his particular hobby, this collection. He would almost as soon keep the tray as sell anything from it — unless he received his price.

The big, brown hand of Chuck shot across the tray with precision. Sylvester quaked. All his insides became suddenly the consistency of jelly. Then he remembered that the integrity of this wild battler was known, and his fear abated. There would be no cunning sleight-of-hand work from this customer. The hand drew back, and into the palm of it fell an earring from which was suspended a long, narrow, beautiful emerald.

"I sure like green," murmured Chuck Neilan, moving his hand so that the jewel showed a pool of light within it. "I sure like green, but I never seen green before that would match up with this. How much?"

It was worth, perhaps, two hundred; it had been purchased for fifty; Sylvester determined to take a snap chance. "Seven hundred," he said, "is what I'll sell that emerald to you for, Chuck Neilan. I like to see a gem like that come to a gent that will know how to appreciate it. Only seven hundred to you, Chuck." Again his head swam.

"Cheap . . . dirt cheap," the madman was chanting. "Gimme that earring, Sylvester. Got another like it?"

II

"THE NEED FOR ACTION"

Not even those men who had gone through times of stress with Chuck Neilan, who had proved his integrity, his fearlessness, his indomitable faith — not even these men could call him a handsome fellow. And the next morning it seemed to big Sylvester that the tall man who came and leaned in his doorway was the ugliest of mortals. The nose was as crooked and high as the beak of an eagle. The face was lean and of a bronze that verged on redness at the high cheekbones. The jaw was square, the mouth straight and broad, and the eye was like the eagle again, steady, unwinking, inscrutable, so that men never could tell whether Chuck was on the verge of laughter, oaths, or a gun play.

Certainly not a handsome man and yet a most interesting one. Few men could pass him over with a glance. Big Sylvester, thinking of the prices he had charged the evening before, moistened his white lips and rolled his eyes. And still the tall man leaned there in the doorway with his big, bony right hand draped carelessly on his hip just a little distance above the hand-worn butt of his revolver. Sylvester stared fascinated at that hand and at the drooping fingers that, he knew, could move with the speed of a whiplash as it snaps.

"Good morning," said Sylvester, and then, finding that his dry lips had moved without an audible sound, he managed to say huskily: " 'Morning, Chuck."

The terrible Chuck replied with not so much as a friendly nod. His silence was, to Sylvester, hardly less awful than the explosion of a gun and the tear of a bullet through flesh and bone.

"I done considerable buying in here last night, it seems," said Chuck at length, with his usual directness coming straight to the point.

"Yep," answered the miserable Sylvester, "you seemed to hanker after some of the things in the store."

"I sure did," agreed the other. "I hankered so bad that I didn't look at what I bought." He paused, running his cold eye carelessly over the burly frame of the pawnbroker.

Who could tell — thought Sylvester — *perhaps this devil of a man was even now selecting the spot where his bullets should strike home.* "You were considerable hurried," said the nervous Sylvester. "Didn't stop to do no bargaining. You just grabbed off everything at the first price and walked away with it. Well . . . that's good business for me, but not so good for you."

This candor surely would disarm the very devil himself. And even the cheated miner smiled, although for the life of him Sylvester could not detect an iota of real mirth in that smile.

Now Chuck Neilan lounged toward the proprietor, and there, resting his gaunt elbow on the top of the glass case, he brought his bright, steady eyes intolerably close to the face of Sylvester.

"I bought a pair of spurs," he said.

Sylvester nodded.

"They busted before I got 'em home," said Chuck Neilan.

Sylvester winced under this unexpected stroke. He had no reason to believe that there was anything wrong with those spurs. They had stood ten years in his window — but what was time to gold?

"I'll fix them for you . . . for nothing," he said.

Chuck grinned. "I bought a saddle, too."

Perspiration poured out on the forehead of the proprietor. "Yes," he breathed.

"The leather was all warped, and the lining was rotten. It rubbed away to dust almost when I touched it."

"I didn't know," stammered Sylvester. "Matter of fact, I ain't looked close at that saddle for a good many years. You wouldn't wait, Chuck. You just up and walked out with things. You didn't give me no chance to look things over and find out. . . ."

He was interrupted by the remorseless Chuck. "I bought this here, too," he said, and held forth on his fingertips the emerald earring. On the brown skin it was the rarest of rare greens. There was a slight tremor of the fingers. Slight though it was, it filled the jewel with quivering lights. The pawnbroker stared at the stone with wide eyes. Surely he had not committed a great wrong in the sale of this little emerald. He had hardly more than doubled the price, but plainly Chuck Neilan was merely producing all the evidence and adding up the deeds that had been wrought against him. When all was done, he would strike a swift balance with a touch of the trigger and call the account quits.

Slowly, slowly Sylvester made his laboring eyes rise, until they rested on the face of Neilan. To his unutterable astonishment, that face was strangely softened, and the cold eyes for the moment were staring into pleasant distance as one who hears music. Sylvester waited, too stunned to make surmises.

"Where's the other emerald? Where's the mate to this?" asked Neilan.

"I dunno," said Sylvester. "I dunno where it is. Only this one was brought in."

"That a fact?" murmured Neilan. "That a straight fact?"

The pawnbroker nodded anxiously.

"I was looking at it this morning," muttered Neilan. "Seemed to me, looking it over, that this here must have belonged to some young girl. Eh? Nobody but a young girl would want to wear it, I guess. A green like this would not be becoming to an older woman's skin."

"Maybe," said the other, still anxious.

"Maybe?" echoed Chuck. "Why ain't you sure? Don't you remember what she was like . . . and what her name was?"

Sylvester blinked. For the first time he began to catch his clue to what was going on in the mind of Chuck. The latter had dreamed over this paltry, low-grade gem until he had visualized the owner and original wearer. He had built her into a fascinating creature of the mind, no doubt.

"It was a man brung it in, Chuck," he answered.

"A man?" growled Chuck, fierce with disappointment. He brooded with sullen eyes. "How come a man brung it in?" he asked suddenly. "What business had a man with it?"

"I dunno. He just brung it in. That's all I know."

"A man," echoed Chuck, deeper and deeper in the slough of despondency. Then his brow contracted in a murderous frown. His strong, bony fingers closed over the fat arm of his interlocutor. "Did he say where he got it?"

"Why," said Sylvester, "d'you think he done murder for it? Might've been his sister's or his mother's? Or maybe he bought it, figuring on having it set for a stickpin."

"Huh," grunted Chuck Neilan, by no means satisfied with this matter-of-fact explanation. "When did he bring it in?"

"Yesterday afternoon."

"Late as that? Sylvester, I've smelled out some sort of a queer story behind this here emerald. I dunno why. I dunno how I got at the feeling."

"It's the way the morning after has hit you, son," said Sylvester kindly. "Strong drink does that, sometimes. Some

195

folks see their snakes when they're drunk, and some sees 'em when they're just finished being drunk. You were sure lit up last night, Chuck."

Chuck nodded. "What sort of a looking gent was him that brought it in?" he asked.

"Can't tell you that, son," answered Sylvester. "You see, he was kind of partial to not having his name knowed."

"Eh?"

"He asked me not to say nothing about him."

A flush ran up the thin cheeks of Chuck Neilan. "Sylvester," he cried, "don't that prove I'm right? Don't that prove they's something queer about this earring, him not wanting to have anybody know where it come from?"

Sylvester shook his head, smiling. "No use jumpin' to conclusions, Chuck. It don't mean nothing. Maybe it's something that was give to him, and he's ashamed to let it be known that he's sold it again. Maybe . . . well, they's a thousand ways of explaining about it, Chuck."

But Chuck slowly and obstinately shook his head. "I got a feeling about it," he persisted. "Nothing rides easy in me. I'm all upset. Me having just struck it rich don't make no difference. Gold don't mean nothing. All I want is some kind of action since I took a look at that earring this morning. And I figure, Sylvester, that I'm going to get it."

"Go out and try," the other advised, deeply relieved at the prospect of getting rid of this troublesome guest. "And good luck be with you."

But Neilan lingered. "You ain't told me what his name is," he insisted.

"Eh? I told you I couldn't."

"You ain't told me his name," said Chuck Neilan, his mouth drawing to a straight line. "Listen here, you low-down, flat-headed, money-hogging swine . . . listen to me, will you? I'd

196

ought to salt you away with lead so's you'd be an example to other gents of your kind not to cheat us simple folks in Sitting Bull. But I ain't touching a gun, Sylvester. I'm letting you give bail . . . and you're going to give bail by telling me the name of the gent that sold this to you."

Sylvester hesitated an instant — but in that instant his eyes, meeting the glance of the other, saw death, and they recoiled from what they saw. "He didn't give no name," said Sylvester, his olive skin turning a sickly, wan yellow. "He didn't give no name at all, but, if you're dead set on it, I'll tell you what sort of a looking gent he was. Big fellow with a blond beard . . . sort of faded yaller. Big chest sticking out under his chin. Wears two guns. Looks tough. And. . . ."

But the other rocked back on his heels, withdrawing from the counter for the first time. "You don't need to tell me no more," he said. "That's enough to locate him pretty handy, if he's stayed long enough in these parts for any of the boys to watch which way he started. Yesterday afternoon you say he was here?"

"Right."

There was no chance for a further exchange of words. Tall Chuck Neilan slid through the door, and the next moment the hoofs of his pinto thudded in the dust.

III

"CHALMERS IS SURPRISED"

A scant twenty minutes later the little mustang was scattering the gravel on the south trail out of Sitting Bull, for Chuck had located and named his man. The blond fellow of the deep chest and the yellow beard had spent the night in the hotel, given the name of Chalmers, and departed hardly an hour before Chuck arrived with his inquiries at the center of the town's social life. Chuck now rode the trail with a head held high, and with gleaming eyes. He was in his glory, riding a trail that no other man would have dreamed of taking, hunting a goal that no other man would have dreamed of desiring to reach, and throwing away the hours and the days of his youth with a wild abandon.

His man in this instance rode slowly enough. With an hour and a half of frantic galloping, he brought his sweating mustang over a hilltop and saw in the hollow beneath a square-shouldered man jogging steadily along on a tall horse — a heavy rider he was, and a glint of yellow hair showed under the back of the brim of his sombrero. So heavy of shoulders, indeed, was the man who turned in the saddle as Chuck thundered down the slope, hallooing, that the slowness with which his horse had traveled was readily explained. Neilan drew back the pinto to a rocking canter and presently drew rein on the tough little beast, directly confronting the stranger.

"Chalmers?" inquired Chuck heartily as he drew near.

"That's me, kid. What's your name?"

"I'm Billy Neilan."

"Well, Billy, what you want with me? You seem hurried by something."

"I'll tell you," said Chuck. "I seen this in the pawnbroker's place, and I bought it. I asked him where was the mate to it, and he said that he only had the single one. Here it is."

He showed the emerald, and from the corner of his eye he saw the big, blond stranger color to the brim of his hat.

"Sylvester wouldn't tell me who sold him the emerald," went on Chuck artlessly, "but I looked over the gents that was in town lately, and I couldn't figure nobody but you would be carrying around emeralds for sale. Most gents that float through on hossback ain't apt to be more'n a week's pay ahead of the game, let alone a emerald like this one. Is it yours?"

"No," answered Chalmers. "You got me figured wrong, son." He added: "Besides, what makes you so keen to find out about it?"

"I want to find the mate to it," said Chuck carelessly. "I'm starting in collecting emeralds."

"Ain't you starting kind of cheap?" said the other.

"Cheap?" said Chuck. "Not so's you could notice it. Would you call seven hundred for a dinky bit of stone like this cheap?"

"Seven hundred!" cried the other. "Good Lord! Did you pay that much after the skunk only forked over fifty to . . . ?" He stopped, his mouth agape on the next word, realizing that he had been trapped into a confession. Chuck Neilan was quietly grinning at him.

"All right, partner," said Chuck. "Now tell me some more about this here emerald, will you? Tell me where the mate to it is, and where's the girl that used to wear 'em?"

But Chalmers jerked his horse around and started on down the trail, growling: "To the devil with you and your questions, both."

Chuck spurred the pinto past his man and whirled the little

beast around on its hind legs.

"You and me ain't through talking," he declared, as the pinto came down with a crash on its forefeet. "I'm still right here asking questions, Chalmers."

"Ask and be hanged. Why, you skinny fool, I'll throw you off your hoss and break your neck if you keep spoiling my view like this. Are you plumb crazy?"

"Only half," answered the imperturbable Chuck. "Only half, friend. I say, are you ready to talk now?"

A light of understanding came into the eyes of Chalmers. He seemed to be gradually remembering. And as he remembered, his color paled rapidly.

"You're Chuck Neilan," he said suddenly. "You're Chuck Neilan that I've heard about, I guess?"

"I'm more or less him, I guess," admitted Chuck. "But don't let that make any difference if you got any designs on busting my neck, partner."

The other scowled but made no answer. Twice his hands contracted into fists, and twice his glance sought the revolver in the saddle holster on Chuck's horse, and his fingers uncurled.

"If that's the way of it," said Chuck, "swing out of the saddle, and we'll have it out on foot. I aim to hear you talk quite a pile about this here emerald, son."

The other blinked, then grinned in savage satisfaction as he gathered that Chuck really meant what he said, and instantly he was out of the saddle and on the ground, a huge man with a brutish face now lighted with anticipation of pleasure. Chuck threw his reins and readily joined him, but he was not yet firmly on the ground — hardly more than in the act of landing and quite off balance — when the big man came charging in. He came snarling and with his lips grinned back so hard that his eyes were well nigh covered with a mass of wrinkles. He struck with a pile-driver right. It landed high on the side of Chuck's head and shot him sprawling on his back.

Chalmers drove in to finish his man, his arms extended and his hands made into claws. Plainly he intended to go for the throat like the bulldog that he was. The horror of that distorted, bestial face and those reaching hands froze all the muscles of Chuck for an instant. But luckily the blow that threw him off balance had glanced and had not stunned him. He rose to his feet now, barely escaping that blind rush, and danced off. As Chalmers came in, he nailed the big man with a long right, bringing him up standing, and whipped a hard left fist instantly against his jaw.

The weight of the blows checked the rush of Chalmers, but they no more dazed him than if they had been delivered against a head of wood. In the very instant that he delivered the second punch, Chuck Neilan knew that he had no chance to batter down this heavy-handed, square-jawed fighter, and, changing his tactics at once, he dove like a football player for the knees of his enemy. His shoulder crashed home. The big man came down with a roar, too surprised to gain an effective hold on the slippery body of Chuck, and the next instant the latter was on top, holding his man securely with a half nelson and wrist lock, and jogging his face heavily into the stones on which he lay.

A dull groan, and then a yell of surrender immediately followed.

"Will you talk now?" asked Chuck.

"Aye . . . cuss you!" growled Chalmers. And Neilan slipped away and swung again into his saddle, with the revolver once again ready to his hand. Chalmers picked himself up slowly and wiped away the dust from his face. He still bore an expression of astonishment, as if he could not quite make out what had happened to him.

"First off," said Chuck calmly, "I want to know who owned this earring, and who has the mate to it now."

"Miss Harvey has it," answered Chalmers. "Old man Harvey's girl up in the Miller Hills. You know the place?"

"Think I've heard about it. How come she give you this earring?"

"She . . . she owed me some back pay," said the other. "This was to square things up. And it wasn't worth enough to square it up, at that."

Chuck Neilan caught at a passing thought. "You lie," he said fiercely. "She never gave it to you. Listen here, Chalmers," he went on, as he saw the big man wince in a manner that was a sufficient admission that he had lied, "I know something about this. I know enough to tell when you're keeping off the truth. And the truth is what I'm going to have, Chalmers, or else I'll blow that head of yours into a sieve. Now talk out."

Chalmers verified the threat by looking first at the fiercely set features of Chuck and then at his right hand perilously near to the butt of the gun. If he had been in his right senses, he would have known that murder was not in the province of Chuck Neilan. But Chalmers was not in his right senses. He was still bewildered by the manner in which victory in the late fight had slipped out from between his two hands in the very moment when he thought all was over. And his nerves were shaken by the mysterious way in which he had found himself prostrate on the ground held in an inescapable grip. To him the slender fellow on the horse seemed capable of anything.

"She give me the emerald," he said, "to take to Joe Purchass. You know him?"

"I've heard about him, too. He's up in the Miller Hills, I guess?"

"Yep."

"But instead of taking it to Purchass, you . . . well, why did she want to send it to Purchass?"

"I dunno. I got tired of trying to make head or tail out of the way that things was going on that ranch of hers. It sure made me plumb sick to see a fine ranch go to pieces and nothing done to stop it. They had as pretty a herd of cows as you ever seen, a couple of years back. And now look at 'em."

"Rustling?" asked Chuck.

"Maybe. I dunno. Rustling? Sure it was rustling. But who done the work, I don't know. And who's doing it now, I don't know. But it's worked as slick as though The Wolf himself had a hand in it. I guess you know The Wolf?"

"The Wolf?" echoed Chuck Neilan. "Good Lord. Is they anybody in the range that don't know The Wolf?" And his mind darted off into the haze of part legend and part indubitable fact with which the name of The Wolf was surrounded. "But The Wolf's gone," he continued. "He ain't been working in these parts for close on to six years, I guess."

"Then maybe it's his ghost," answered Chalmers, shrugging his shoulders. "But I was working for the Henry boys eight years ago, when The Wolf starved 'em out with his rustling gang. And the way the cows fade away on the Harvey place sure reminds me a lot of the goings-on at the old Henry outfit. Nobody knowed who did it. Everybody suspected everybody else. It was sure the devil."

"And she was sending you to Purchass, you say?" went on Chuck Neilan, drawing the other back to the facts and away from the imaginary parts of the narrative.

"She was."

"You got no idea why she wanted to send this to him?"

"None in the world. Unless. . . ."

"What?"

"Purchass used to hang around a pile. Maybe. . . ."

"Maybe she's sort of fond of him, eh?"

"Maybe."

"I guess that lets you out, Chalmers. So long."

There was no answer to this salutation, and Chuck cantered the pinto slowly back up the grade, looking over his shoulder to make sure that the disgruntled cowpuncher did not take a pot shot to even up matters. But although Chalmers gazed long and steadily after his late companion, he made no effort to draw his gun, and presently he climbed into the saddle on the tall horse and vented some of his rage and shame by spurring his mount cruelly and then driving at a sharp gallop down the hollow and up the grade on the far side.

Chuck made sure that he was no longer in range for a rear attack, then he drew back the hardy pinto to a walk.

IV

"THE LURE OF COMBAT"

The horse had need for some rest after the sharp gallop out of Sitting Bull, and Chuck himself had need for quiet for hard thinking. So far as he could make out, the matter was closed to him — as though a wall had been built between him and the silly dreams and fancies that had taken possession of him that morning when he first looked at the jewel. There was, to be sure, a girl behind the emerald, just as he had suspected. But that girl, it seemed, was sending a present to another man; and, when a girl sends presents of this description, there could be only one meaning. They were a token of amity, at least.

He recalled now, what he knew about Joe Purchass. His knowledge was spotty and full of breaks. But, at least, he was certain that he had heard of the Purchass family as one rich in land and timber and cattle. And of Joe Purchass he knew he had heard him to be a strong man, a daring and combative man, capable of creditably upholding the repute of the old Purchass family, for all of that reputation was now fallen upon his single pair of shoulders.

This data he gathered out of the mist of his memory that refused to yield any further points. But it was sufficient for the nonce. If a girl in difficulties on her ranch was sending jewels to such a man as Joe Purchass, there could be only one conclusion. And he, Chuck Neilan, had far better keep out of the trouble. He would be making a fool of himself if he interfered.

And yet one thing drew him in spite of his reason, drew him as the magnet draws iron. Everything in his soul of souls responded to the name of The Wolf. The terrible and strange man was known through the whole expanse of the mountain desert, and he was known as an invincible enemy, a stealthy and sliding ghost of a man. What he had done was hardly to be summed up by even the longest memory. In the narrow space of two or three years at most he had crowded his days full of one atrocious crime after another. From cattle rustling to murder, he had run the gamut and even, it was said, had descended to lower levels and had committed small crimes merely for the sake of the excitement. Everything about the man was terrible, less than human and more than human. He was one of those rare and devilish men who sin for the sake of sinning. Money, it was apparent from the first, was no object to him. But the excitement of getting money that was not his was a lure beyond resistance.

Thinking of the man, the picture of him returned to the mind of Chuck Neilan as he had heard the demon described a hundred times. He was, of course, always masked. Yet there were distinctive features about his face. It was rather round, and the cheeks were pink. It was a handsome face, despite the mask — eyes sufficient in themselves to disarm an enemy by making him creep. But more distinctive of all, his head was bald — prematurely bald. He was large of frame, swift of hand, deadly in fighting of all kinds. This much was certain. He was, in short, so easily distinguished that it seemed impossible that he could have returned to work mischief on the ranges again without at once being recognized and the report spreading hundreds of miles in a few hours. This in itself seemed enough to discredit entirely the report of Chalmers, and, yet, with a thrill running in his veins, Chuck found that he could not dismiss the lingering belief that The Wolf in person had an actual part in the mischief that was now going on at the Harvey ranch.

Why should his heart leap when he considered this possibility? Why should the heart of the prize fighter, one might as well ask, leap in his throat when he heard of the return to the ring of some famous and undefeated champion who retired some time before because of lack of worthy opponents? No man in the town of Sitting Bull, no man in the environs of that village, no man for a weary journey in any direction, would lift a hand against Chuck Neilan once his name was known. Like Alexander, he had conquered the known world. There was no longer left any hero who dared to do battle against him, unless he hounded respectable, quiet citizens into a fight. And that, of course, was entirely alien to his nature. And now, into the very heart of his domain, so to speak, a great and famous champion had suddenly arisen like a ghost from the grave — a man on whom he could make a three-fold reputation.

For these reasons, then, the heart of Chuck leaped in his bosom, and he chanted a song to the unheeding ears of the pinto as he rode along. It was a small clue on which to ride far, but Chuck had ridden farther on smaller clues than this. Now he determined to seek out Joe Purchass and give him the emerald that Chalmers should have presented, but which, like a petty thief, he had sold and then ridden away.

With his mind made up to the journey, the mind of Chuck became perfectly calm, for the simple reason that he would not think a jot about what lay before him until he confronted Joe Purchass himself. Blithely he rode down into Sitting Bull, made up his pack, unsaddled the pinto, and gave him a heavy feed, let him rest for six hours, and then struck out, in the dusk of the day, across the mountains. It was a hundred and fifty miles to the Miller Hills, and, once among them, he might have another fifty to do before he reached the ranch of Joe Purchass. So he let the pinto jog on at his own pace, which was slow but tireless, and that night, not very long before the cold break of day, he camped far out from Sitting Bull.

His sleep was short and troubled by dreams at that camp, for half a dozen times he envisioned himself engaged with The Wolf. He saw clearly, as if he had once before seen the outlaw, the smooth, bald head, as though tonsured. He saw the smile for which The Wolf was famous. In the midst of murder itself, that faint smile, men said, was never quite extinguished.

He wakened before the day was well advanced and struck out at once. In the first stage he had covered fifty miles. By afternoon of the next day he was among the Miller Hills. And that evening he learned at a ranch house the location of the Purchass place. The following morning he rode into sight of it.

It needed only a glance to determine that this was a rich estate. The buildings stood on a slightly swelling rise of ground, though the entire space which they occupied was itself in the center of a great hollow with the hills ranged about the edges of the cup in protective rows. The house was far larger than common. The whitewashed outbuildings, barns, and sheds were innumerable, shambling off in all directions from the dwelling house, except to the east. On this side the prospect was kept clear of business. The slope of ground was loosely planted with trees, and the eye of Chuck rested on stretches of watered lawn here and there among the trees and even colorful beds of flowers, with the colors blurred and smudged by the distance and the morning mist.

If this were the scale on which Joe Purchass lived and acted, well for Chuck, indeed, if he kept out of the affairs of the rich man. To be sure, he had wealth of his own coming out of the mine, great wealth it might be, but never comparable to such an established power as this. Humility entered the soul of the cowpuncher, but it did not stay there long. He cast humility over his shoulder like a worn-out coat, and with a shrill whistle he started the pinto down the last slope of his long trail.

From the distance, when he could look on the ranch headquarters spread out beneath him like a map, it had been impressive enough, but, when he dropped into the lower level and approached the knoll on which the buildings stood, his awe was vastly increased, and he only kept himself whistling carelessly by a great effort of the will.

The trees were far taller than they had seemed. The grass plots expanded into wide-sweeping lawns — the sure proof that the householder was from the East — and the colorful spots of flowers expanded in turn into little, formal gardens. When he came out in front of the building, Chuck approached it with a constant stiffening of the back. He moved by instinct toward the side entrance, dismounted, threw the reins of his horse, and then walked up to the door and knocked.

V

"INSTINCTIVE DISTRUST"

The first glance at the stately figure of the proprietor made Chuck wonder how persons could possibly call such a man Joe. That he was not known everywhere as Joseph and perhaps with an initial after the full first name was a great tribute to the democracy of the West. He was in every way a big man, a full six feet and two inches in height, with ample proportions of breadth and thickness to match. His head was covered with a close-curling crop of black-brown hair, that also grew in side-boards and whiskers, almost covering his face and descending to a short, pointed beard — a tonsorial arrangement that made his head seem extremely long. The manner of the rich man was as dignified as his appearance. His voice was big in volume but carefully held down to a pleasant speaking note; training had enabled him to make it perfectly smooth and equable. Only when he laughed or exclaimed, the voice burst out and roared in the astonished ears of the listeners. For the rest, his clothes were ordinary by comparison.

He was not garbed poorly, after the fashion of many Westerners who make it a point that they may surprise strangers by the contrast between their bank accounts and the sums borne about on their backs. Joe Purchass was dressed very plainly, nevertheless, and he had in addition a habit of continually attempting to bring his manner to a more plain and matter-of-fact basis. One felt that this effort was not entirely true to his inner nature, and it merely made those about him ill at ease. It was a forcible reminder that Joe Purchass had spent all of his more youthful years in the East and had come West only a scant year before, to assume the management of the entire family property that had at length come into his hands. He took on this matter-of-fact manner as he greeted the rather embarrassed Chuck Neilan.

"I've heard about you, Mister Neilan," he said. "And I'm glad to meet you now. I've heard about you as a very honest man and a very dangerous enemy. I hope that you haven't come up here bringing trouble with you?"

He chuckled a little as he spoke, and Chuck felt a bristling of dislike go up his backbone. There was no reason for such an impulse. It was purely blind dislike. But the instinctive things we do and feel are doubtless far more powerful than our reasoned actions. On the spot, he distrusted instantly and disliked Joe Purchass. For that reason he smiled in his most amiable fashion.

"I dunno," said Chuck. "I guess this ain't trouble. Least-wise, it don't look like no trouble that I ever seen. I think this is coming to you?" As he spoke, he slipped the emerald earring from his vest pocket and extended it in the open palm of his hand to Purchass.

The effect upon Joe Purchass was startling. First he started a pace back. Then he snatched the jewel from the hand of Chuck, and he peered at it as though in the changing green lights of the jewel he expected to read a message. Next, as though recalling himself, he straightened, and, while he placed the emerald in his wallet, slipping it, Chuck noticed, into a little pocket by itself, he examined Chuck with keen eyes.

"You're a new man at the Harvey place?" he asked. "How are things over there? And what's happening? Are they still talking about rustling and such nonsense?"

"I dunno," answered Chuck. "I'm not from the Harvey place. I'm from Sitting Bull."

And then, very quickly and simply, omitting as many of the unusual details of the story as possible, he told what had happened, and why it was that he had taken the long ride through the mountains to the Purchass Ranch. Joe Purchass listened with a growing astonishment, and, in conclusion, he stretched out his hand and caught that of Chuck in an overwhelming grip. Plainly the man did not realize the extent of his own prodigious strength. Chuck gritted his teeth and prayed that no bones were broken in his hand. He managed to maintain a half smile of carelessness.

"You've done a mighty fine thing," said Joe Purchass. "All the finer because you did it on the spur of the moment. You don't know the Harveys. You don't know Kate Harvey, at least, and she's the important one. Certainly, you've never seen me before. Altogether, Mister Neilan, you've done a thing that I won't forget in a hurry. As a matter of fact, I want to show you my gratitude in a more substantial way immediately. I know you hard-riding, hard-drinking fellows. Money rolls away from you about as fast as it rolls to you. Now, Neilan, just step into the library with me and let me give you a check that. . . ."

Chuck raised his hand with no little natural dignity of his own.

"Purchass," he said, "a few days ago I hit it rich in the mines. No credit to me. Just luck. But the point is that I hit it rich, and I'll probably get more cash out of that mine than I can ever spend on myself. Well, sir, it was right after that I decided to ride up here and give you the emerald. Money ain't what I'm after."

Joe Purchass frowned. Strange to say, this profession of indifference to money did not seem to please him at all. "At least," he said, with a touch of coldness in both manner and voice, "you'll let me repay you the price of the emerald."

212

Chuck considered, and then shook his head.

"You don't owe me money," he said. "If anybody owes it to me, it's the girl."

"She couldn't pay you," answered Purchass. "She couldn't pay you, my quixotic friend. Her ranch is almost ready to fall to pieces under the load of mortgages her idiot of a father piled on it. No matter how cheaply you bought the emerald, it would be a great hardship for her to attempt to redeem the earring."

"I'm not going to ask her to," said Chuck with equal firmness, and frowning a little in his turn.

Joe Purchass blinked, for plainly he could not understand. "Just what are you after?" he asked bluntly, and his smooth voice roughened and increased marvelously in volume. "Just what are you after, my friend?"

"Action," said Chuck curtly. "I'm looking for excitement, not money. And action is what I figure on getting."

"I don't quite follow you," replied Purchass.

"No? Well, Chalmers, the hound, told me he figured that The Wolf had something to do with this business at the Harvey ranch."

"Good Lord! The Wolf!" breathed Purchass.

"Yep. That's what Chalmers said, and he talked as though he meant it. Said there was the same smooth sort of work."

Purchass seemed to have recovered from the first shock. He broke suddenly into ringing laughter, so loud that Chuck was pressed back a step or two by the noise.

"The Wolf?" he repeated, chuckling when he could speak. "That's nonsense, Neilan. Chalmers was drunk or dreaming. Rustling, in my estimation, has little to do with the ruin of the Harvey ranch. The insane extravagances of old Harvey, and the fact that the girl is trying to do a man's work and run the big place by herself now . . . those are the things which, combined, have run down the place and loaded it with debts

213

where it used to be a paying proposition. Of course, there has been some rustling. Up in those wild hills there are twenty good hiding places in every square mile, and rustlers could work pretty safely up there. No wonder if a few of them have collected and run off some cows now and then. No wonder at all. But, sir, that is not what has ruined Harvey, because he has ruined himself."

"Hmm," growled Chuck, forced to admit the self-evident truth of all this. "Just the same. . . ."

"My dear fellow," the rich man broke in, laughing again, "Chalmers was drunk. Don't you know that the day of cattle rustling is past? Too many already have been hung for that work."

"It was only six years ago," broke in Chuck, "that The Wolf was working around these parts."

"The devil!" cried the rancher. "Are you going to hark back to that myth of a man all the time? By heaven, I don't believe the villain ever existed. Be reasonable, Mister Neilan. Consider, also, that no one would be capable of robbing a girl like Kate Harvey."

"No one but The Wolf," vociferated Chuck. "Every word you say makes me surer and surer that devil of a man is really at work up yonder in the hills around the Harvey ranch."

Joe Purchass grew very red with anger, but immediately he controlled himself and stepped back. "Very well, sir," he said, "if you think that, the best thing for you to do is to go out and find your man . . . and good luck go with you. But if what they say about The Wolf is half true, you'll have a considerable task on your hands."

The sneer with which this was said made Chuck Neilan even more red than the rancher had been the moment before.

"Matter of fact," he admitted, "I haven't set up to be a better man than The Wolf. I know he's a devil. I've heard

214

enough about his murderings and how straight he could shoot and how fast he was at getting a gun out of the leather. I know all that, and that's why I wanted to talk to you. I thought that maybe we could go hunting together and that way. . . ."

"Hunting a ghost? Hunting a man who if he ever existed . . . which I doubt . . . has certainly been dead these six years?"

"Well," muttered Chuck, a little abashed by the conviction of the other, "I see that you're going to keep out of it, but that doesn't mean that I'm through. I'm going to stick on this trail till it comes to some sort of an end. So long, Mister Purchass!"

The rancher grumbled an answer and turned away, but almost immediately his good nature returned, and he ran after and overtook Chuck before the latter could leave the house.

"Look here," he cried, laying that tremendously heavy hand on the shoulder of Chuck and spinning him around very much as though he were a top, "you can't leave like this. You've done me a fine turn, Neilan, and I mean that you shall profit by it. Stay here and teach me some way I can serve you. You won't take money. I apologize for offering it to you. At least, stay on and spend the night after your long ride. I'm starting off at once, but I'll see that you're taken care of . . . and there's some real old stuff here, my boy . . . not moonshine, but the real article."

The last bit of information struck Chuck at his weakest point. For an instant he wavered. Then he shook his head.

"I'll stick by this trail. It's bad luck to leave off a trail before you've seen both ends of it. Good bye, Mister Purchass."

His last impression of the big man was that he had started to speak in protest but almost immediately changed his mind and, with a shrug of his massive shoulders, turned his back on his departing guest and went into the next room.

Outside, Chuck swung into the saddle on the pinto and rode down to the nearest barn. He found a spindling youngster stuffing straw into sacks.

"What's the way to the Harvey Ranch, son?" asked Chuck.

The youth turned as though struck, and blinked at Chuck. "You're another, eh?" he grunted. "You're another for the Harvey Ranch?"

"Sure."

"Funny they didn't tell you how to get there, then. But hit north, straight north, and you'll sure come to it or folks that can tell you *pronto* where it is. What's your job going to be up yonder?"

"To keep a quiet tongue in my head and not talk like King Solomon before I'm old enough to wear long pants," said Chuck reprovingly.

And he swung the pinto to the left and struck north.

VI

"AT THE HARVEY RANCH"

Sometimes our brains work strangely, refusing to take heed of what our eyes see and our ears hear, until a considerable time has passed. So it was with Chuck Neilan on this day. He had put many a mile behind him by means of the industrious hoof of the pinto before his brain harked back to what the stable boy at the Purchass Ranch had said to him. When he thought about it the second time, it seemed to Chuck to be of more than passing interest. How was it that the boy knew so much, or guessed so much, and seemed to think with such mingled scorn and disgust about the Harvey Ranch? Once, indeed, he grew so excited at the prospect that he stopped the pinto in the middle of the trail and was on the verge of turning back, when he realized after an instant of reflection that if he returned and opened the same subject again, the boy's suspicions would be aroused, and he would become silent. So, growling at himself for a fool because he had not pumped the boy for information when the occasion was before him, he sent the pinto on again.

It was only fifteen miles as a bird flies, but as the trail wound it was nearer to thirty, uphill and down. The sun was setting when he came to the Harvey Ranch. No such imposing group of buildings as the Purchass place lay before him now. On a hillside, bald of trees, stood the unpainted buildings of headquarters for the Harvey Ranch. The woods which rolled green through the hollow on either side made the bareness of that slope stand out in striking contrast, and it seemed to Chuck that even from the distance he could feel the atmosphere of poverty which beset the place. The journey down the last slope occupied enough time to bridge the gap between the colorful heart of the sunset to the early portion of the dusk. All the world was gray when he rapped at the front door of the house.

The knock echoed through the interior, and then a tapping sound approached the door, a tapping sound of a cane accompanied by a shuffling noise of footfalls. Presently the door opened, and a cripple looked out at Chuck.

He was a man apparently not more than sixty at the most, but in certain features he appeared much older. His thin, long hair, for instance, was the purest white and so scant that it fell down beside his face, stirring in the air like a morning mist. His brows were gathered in a frown that was rather whimsical than wrathful or pettish. In his right hand was the knob-head of a thick cane that, by infinite usage and much brushing against things in the house, was polished throughout its length. He rested much of his weight upon this staff while he peered out rather anxiously at Chuck.

"Don't appear to recollect you, son," he said, "but step right in and make yourself to home. You're a mite late for supper, but we'll get something together for you. Step right in."

Chuck accepted the invitation and then followed the invalid down the hall into the interior of the dwelling. As he studied the painful laboring of that bent back, it occurred to him that he had come here for no purpose that could be easily explained to anyone. Men did not ride two hundred miles for the sake of getting into a fight, particularly when the fight was to be with a personage who probably was non-existent — The Wolf. His embarrassment reached a climax when his guide kicked open a door and ushered Chuck into the kitchen. It was littered with the dirty pans and dishes of the supper, and at the sink, making a great clattering at her work, was a young girl who turned to face them.

By something in her eyes as she greeted the old man, Chuck knew that this was Kate, the daughter of Harvey, who was attempting to run the ranch, and who was making such a failure of it. No wonder, if in addition to her managerial capacity, she had to act as cook and dishwasher, which seemed to be also in her sphere of service.

She showed not the slightest embarrassment, however, in meeting the stranger.

"Here's a gent come in to spend the night with us. Name is . . . he told me while we were coming down the hall. I didn't catch it."

"Bill Neilan is my name," said the cowpuncher.

"And this is my daughter, Kate. Can you fix him up a snack, honey?"

She nodded, indicated a chair where he might sit at the table, whisked from in front of him a litter of dishes, and turned to the stove — all while her father was getting through the door and out of the room. Chuck regarded her with side glances. He had had his affairs of the heart before, but never had he found a girl who fitted into his mind with the exactness of Kate Harvey. In the space of ten seconds he was in the midst of a pleasant dream that he spun out. He was wakened by the glance of the girl falling on him as decisively as the hand of a man might have fallen upon his shoulder.

"You can wash over there. You'll find the basin hanging on a nail . . . that granite basin upside down. There's some soap in the soap rack to your left. If you want hot water, there's some in this kettle. Help yourself!"

Chuck followed these explicit and curt directions. He was extremely downhearted by this time. Would to heaven, he thought, that he could pay for his meal in cash. But he could not offer to pay for food in this house. And he was heaping extra work on her at the end of a day during which who could tell what household and range-riding duties she had performed. He was frowning over this thought, as he dried his hands on the circular runner that served as towel, when the girl spoke.

"I've been thinking about your name. Are you ever called Chuck Neilan?"

He nodded, and then noted with indescribable mortification that her face hardened and her lip curled a little. No doubt she had heard some of the worst tales that circulated through the mountains, with him for the main hero. The exploits of a fighter are sadly altered in the telling, and, though the distance to Sitting Bull was not so very great, it was enough to twist things into a queer mess. Chuck wondered what she could have heard as he studied her disdainful face — a labor he continued through side glances as she turned some cold, fried potatoes in thick bacon gravy into the frying pan to be warmed.

She must have heard something very bad, indeed, to judge by her coldness. On the whole, there was a great deal that was disagreeable about her. She was by no means the clinging-vine type. Her voice was as level as the voice of a man. And so were her eyes. And though her profile was turned with haunting delicacy about nose and mouth, there was an accompanying pride as stern and cold as the pride of a man. The hand that, a few moments later, deftly slipped the plates and saucers and cups before him, and the steaming food and coffee with them — that hand was amazingly slight. But the voice with which she asked if he wanted anything else was utterly without emotion. Chuck made a desperate attempt to break the ice and start up conversation.

"When you heard my name," he said, "I guess it wasn't with anything in my favor."

"I've almost forgotten the story."

She answered with a half glance over her shoulder, not at

him but partly toward him, as though he were not worth a full turn of the head. The dishes rattled again, and the steam from the dishwater rose. Chuck Neilan fortified himself with a gulp of hot coffee.

"Well," he said at length, "I'm sorry."

"Sorry that I've forgotten the story?"

"Sorry that the story you heard was so darned bad."

"I haven't said it was," answered the girl, as cold as ever.

"You've looked more'n words could say," responded Chuck. "A pile more."

At this, she whirled squarely toward him, parted her lips to speak, and then, at sight of his anxious face, changed her mind and turned back again.

"You see," went on Chuck Neilan, "it takes about two tellings of the same story to get it all twisted. I'm wondering how many ways the facts that got to you was twisted."

She made no pretense of turning now. "You've never done anything really bad, I guess," she said, with an intonation that contradicted the words.

"Sure I have," answered Chuck. "Plumb bad, lady. But I've never done nothing mean . . . and by the way you look I figure that you must have heard some pretty mean talk about me."

"What," she asked, "is the exact difference between badness and meanness?"

Chuck poised his fork meditatively. "Badness," he said, "is beating up a man-sized man . . . meanness is beating up a hoss that can't fight back."

At this, she turned again and remained turned, heedless of the water, yellowed with the stain of soap, that trickled from the dishcloth in a steady stream to the floor. There was a twinkle of appreciation in her eyes. She seemed to be seeing him for the first time. And he, certainly, was seeing Kate Harvey for the first time.

"You feel a bit better about me?" he asked.

At this, she laughed frankly, tossed the dish rag into the wash pan with a great sloshing of the water, and came opposite him at the table. She dropped her hands, red and shining from the suds, on the top of the unpainted kitchen chair, facing him.

"What are you doing up here, Chuck?" she asked.

He was unprepared for this sudden lowering of the bars. He seemed to be admitted to a footing of semi-intimacy by the very intonation of that voice. It filtered down into his heart of hearts, a thrilling experience to Chuck. But he must not think that he had succeeded too far.

"I don't know exactly why I've come," he said.

To his surprise she nodded, not at all put out by this shuffling away of reasons and causes.

"Near as I can make out," she said, "that's why most of you boys start out. You get tired of working in one place . . . then you light out and ride till a river stops you."

"A river don't," said Chuck, grinning. "My hoss swims like a fish."

She nodded again. Plainly she liked him much better than ever before. But what should he say to her? It occurred to Chuck that she was far from a romantic type of girl. And this being the case, would it not be wise to refrain from telling her the true story of how he came to be at that moment in her kitchen?

"I'll tell you why I'm here," he ventured at length. "I've heard that they's some rustling going on up here."

She nodded. "You've heard right, Chuck Neilan."

"And I've heard that The Wolf was doing the work."

She started. "The Wolf! That devil?"

She slipped back from him until her shoulders rested against the wall of the room, and there she leaned, almost out of breath, and staring at Chuck as though he were literally the man whom he had named.

"The Wolf? What put that name into your head?"

Chuck had risen from his chair, but now she advanced again with an effort at laughter.

"Don't mind me," she explained. "Once . . . oh, it must have been six years ago . . . The Wolf came here . . . The Wolf himself. He sneaked into the house. He was after a safe Dad kept in the attic. But when he got into my room, he made a noise, and it wakened me. I saw him . . . bald head . . . round face . . . mask . . . and all, and I screamed and fainted. Why he didn't murder me for disturbing him and rousing the house, I never could tell. At any rate, he was gone when I woke up. My father was beside me. I told him what I had seen, and he went out and got the boys out of the bunkhouse. They searched all around the ranch house, but they found no sign, and at length they decided that I had simply had a bad dream. But it wasn't a dream. I still can see him . . . that giant . . . standing there with the moonlight pouring around him and shining on his bald head. Oh!"

She pressed both hands over her face, but, when she dropped her hands, her expression was almost as calm as ever. She was about to speak again when a knocking came at the side door, and she went to open it.

VII

"CHUCK RIDES ALONE"

A messenger was there with a sweating horse behind him. He jerked up the brim of his hat when he saw her and presented a note.

"From Joe Purchass," he said. "How are ye, Miss Harvey?"

"Fine. Come in, Charlie."

"Can't do it. Got strict orders. Minute I get this into your hands, I'm to turn around and come back to Purchass *pronto*. Can't even stop for a drink of water or" — here he craned his neck and sniffed enviously — "coffee. So long and good luck, Miss Harvey."

He was into the saddle in a flash, and the broncho wheeled in true cow-horse style and darted out of view. The girl ripped open the envelope anxiously. She read with a frown at first and then with an exclamation of wonder. She tossed the letter aside and faced Chuck with heightened color.

"I wonder that you're still sitting there," she cried, "after the way I've treated you . . . and after what you've done for me. I've a letter from Joe Purchass there. He tells me everything . . . in short . . . that you've done. Well . . . what you've done is fine . . . mighty fine."

She went straight to him and shook his hand with almost the strength of a man. And all the time her eyes were shining with such a light that Chuck found it hard to meet them squarely. All in a moment, then, she released his hand, made him sit down again, and took the opposite chair.

"I've been ready to think that everybody except Joe Purchass is a crook. But now I see I was wrong . . . and, oh, I'm glad of it. But he barely hinted at what you've done. I want you to tell me everything . . . everything."

Chuck shook his head. "Can't do it," he said. "I just sort of followed my nose, and here I am. You see?"

The girl laughed, delighted again.

"Sometimes I think that men and women are a good deal alike, after all. But just when I'm almost convinced of it, along comes someone like you, Chuck Neilan, and shows me that I'm a thousand times wrong. Well, don't tell me, then, if you don't want to . . . but let's go back to what you said about The . . . The Wolf." She hesitated before she could enunciate that nightmare name. "Did you mean what you said about him?"

"It's what I got out of Chalmers," confessed Chuck. "And he . . . well, when Chalmers was talking, he wasn't in no mood to tell no more truth than he could help. Maybe he just threw in that about The Wolf by guess work. He said that he simply thought it might be The Wolf, because The Wolf worked so plumb smooth, and this gent that's bothering you ain't any bungler himself."

"Was that the only reason?" said the girl, sighing with relief.

"It was enough to start me going," said Chuck Neilan gravely. "It was enough reason to seem sound to me. And here I am ready for work, Miss Harvey, if you'll put me to work."

"If I'll put you to work? Oh, if I'd only had one man like you before. But none of the cowards would stay. They ran away, as Chalmers did, when they found there was danger up here. Why, I've almost rounded up two or three of the rustlers myself, Chuck, and each time they've slipped away from me, simply because I haven't had helpers with me and . . . I do a good many rough things, you know, but I can't shoot to kill."

"And were they just as polite as you?"

"They were." She nodded, very grave and puzzled. "I've often wondered at it. While I rode after them, shooting into the air, not once did they turn and try a pot shot at me . . . and yet, once I was almost on top of a rascal on a gray horse. . . ." She stopped and shook her head. "But there's no cause for worry after this. No cause at all. Do you know what's going to happen?"

"You're going to let me have a try at 'em," suggested Chuck, his lips drawing back thin on his teeth, so that he looked for the moment the picture of a savage terrier that sees the promise of a fight just ahead.

"I know you'd give them trouble enough," the girl said, her eyes shining out at him again in that singular way they had, "but a great fighter and a strong man with a lot of good fighters and strong men behind him is coming down to the ranch. And they'll clean out the rustlers. Oh, they'll find them and run them down and jail them. I . . . I. . . . The cowards! The low-down cowards! They've ruined the ranch . . . they've broken father's heart . . . they've nearly killed me with worry . . . and now they'll be paid back."

Her voice broke with her emotion. Chuck, excited and sympathetic, leaned toward her.

"Who's coming to take over the job, then?"

"Guess, guess."

"I don't know the folks around these parts."

"It's Joe Purchass that's coming," cried the girl. "Think of how. . . ."

She paused. The face of Chuck Neilan was dark as a thundercloud.

"Purchass?" was all he said. "Him?"

"Why, who on earth could be better for the work than big Joe and all his men? And Joe alone is a host. He's like lightning with a gun, and he doesn't fear a hundred." Her face lighted as she described her warrior.

"Well," said Chuck Neilan dryly, "I guess I'd ought to wish you happiness, you having Purchass coming along. And it's sure easy to see that there ain't going to be no call for me to do any work rounding up rustlers on your ranch. That being the case, and me being through the supper, I guess I'll slope. S'long, Miss Harvey."

"Good bye," said the girl stiffly.

He stalked to the door. Before he quite reached it, there was a rush of footfalls behind him, and then the girl darted in before him and set her shoulders against the door. Her eyes glimmered up at him angrily.

"Aren't you ashamed, Chuck Neilan?" she cried. "Aren't you ashamed?"

He fell back. His dignity broke into small bits and tumbled from his shoulders. He looked about him. There was no refuge from those remorseless eyes.

"Aren't you ashamed?" she repeated. "D'you mean to say you'd run off and sulk, simply because another man is coming in to fight for me?"

"He has the right . . . ," began Chuck, but he was interrupted by her burst of merry laughter. "Well," he said, "I guess I've been a fool, right enough. I'll stay on, if you think I'll be any good here."

"Of course, you'll stay!" cried the girl, still laughing. "Go back to that table and sit down. And if you want to work, why, you can start in tonight or tomorrow morning. Matter of fact, those fiends probably will get word that Joe Purchass is coming, and they may try to make a big scoop just before he arrives. You understand?"

"Try to clean you out of house and home before the fighter comes, eh?"

"Ah, they're cruel enough to try anything. Do you know, I

think that they've purposely stolen the cattle by small degrees instead of driving off every living thing on my range . . . and simply because they wanted to torment my father first and then me." Tears sprang from her eyes as she thought of it.

"Don't seem like there could be skunks like that west of the Rockies," muttered Chuck. "But, suppose you sit right down yonder and tell me where they hang out mostly. I might do a bit of herd riding tonight myself."

She shook her head. "You couldn't do anything by yourself."

"Gimme a try at 'em."

"But they'd outnumber you. . . ."

"Nothing like luck," said Chuck, "in a pinch. And I'm sure lucky, Miss Harvey."

"I believe it. Well, have it your own way, because if I don't give you permission, you'll go, anyway."

"Right," said Chuck.

The council of war began at once. On the top of the kitchen table, scrubbed to whiteness and softness, she drew with pencil a rude sketch of the ranch and pointed out to him the places of strategic importance, so far as the rustlers were concerned. There were a thousand such places, it seemed to Chuck, as she enumerated hill and dale and wood and meadow and twisting creekbeds, where hunted men could scurry through the highlands by shortcuts. After a time his powers of listening were blurred. Already, in thought, he was out in the open under the stars and under the moon hunting for action. And though he knew that the girl was planning ways and means, he could not to save himself follow her schemes. At length she ended.

"You have my idea?" she said.

"Exactly," Chuck said with a smile, and fortunately she believed him.

228

There was one trouble. The poor pinto was much too tired to be used for this night shift. But the trouble was remedied readily enough. Chuck went with the girl out to the corrals, and there he selected, following her advice, a fine-appearing brown mare, on whose back he cinched his own saddle. Kate Harvey followed him to the gate of the corral, pleading to the last that he give up this breakneck scheme, but he merely shook his head, and in a moment he was waving back to her and cantering lightly across the fields.

In the gathering darkness, for it was not yet quite full night, she dwindled and finally went out behind him, and then Chuck wakened to the necessities of the work that lay before him. It was a sobering thought. While he was in the company of the girl, it had seemed a slight enough thing to attack and route a whole army of desperadoes. Now he realized that he was playing a dangerous game in a country strange to him and, no doubt, against great odds, so far as numbers went. He jogged the first mile across the lowland at an easy pace. As he mounted to the first ridge, the moon pushed a yellow edge above the top of an eastern hill and showed him the district in which he must do the hunting of that night.

VIII

"THE MAN ON THE GRAY"

It was an extent of hills as deeply chopped and hollowed out as the face of the ocean on a windy day. There were no commanding elevations, nothing approaching to a mountain, but, as far as his eye commanded, he saw ridge on ridge of hills, with sharp-sided dales in between. One could hardly see a distance of a hundred yards in any direction, and, to confuse one further, there was a dense sprinkling of trees here and there. Even if he sighted a stranger in this brightening moonshine, it might be difficult, or well nigh impossible, for him to run down the man. Here and there he saw cattle browsing, indistinct figures moving toward the trees in the hollow just before him. At least that proved the rustlers had made no move for that night.

Chuck Neilan glanced over the ground ahead. He wanted a proof of the speed of his mount, and here was going good enough for a test. The first touch of the spur sent the brown away like a whirlwind. Down the gully they darted and came in a single instant, it seemed to the delighted Chuck, up to the top of the opposite ridge. Yes, the brown had plenty of speed, and it would be a well-mounted rover, indeed, who should escape him, once sighted, so long as sight could be kept.

With this comforting thought, and with the moon steadily rising so that the angle of the shadows cast by hill and tree grew less and less, Chuck wandered on through his domain, keeping a sharp lookout for mounted men. Not, indeed, that he really expected to find a marauder at work or even in passing.

But the narrative of the girl had enraged him to the point where he was hungry for action, and now he was determined to shoot first and ask his questions afterward.

He never departed from a trot or a walk, saving the strength and speed of the brown. There was one fault in his mount that early made him shake his head and swear under his breath. His horse was by no means sure-footed, and several times the leggy mare stumbled on roots or stones. Her speed, however, would make up for any other deficiency.

In the meantime, the white moon shine cut with increasing clearness through the trees among which he was riding, and it was by virtue of that clear light that he saw his man at last — a glimmer in the distance among the trees. It might be the sway of a leafy bough. It might be the passing of a cow. But in order to investigate even a shadow of a possibility, Chuck turned his mare and drove her at a round gallop straight in the direction of the thing that had caught his attention. He had not covered a hundred yards when he heard a stifled exclamation of a man's voice, and in another instant a gray horse burst from the edge of a covert and darted away across a clearing, with the rider lying flat along its back.

Honest men did not ride in such a fashion at the first sight of a stranger. Chuck Neilan, as he gathered the mare under him with a touch of the spurs, whipped out his revolver and tried a snap shot at the disappearing figure. A shout of defiance answered him, and he knew that he had missed. He had no chance for further thinking. The tall brown was shooting beneath the trees, across the clearing, and then into more trees. Up a hillside beyond the brown whirled him and, then, as they shot out of the veiling trees, he caught a second fleeting glimpse of the stranger, this time framed vividly against the sky above him. It was only the glance of an instant, with the discovery pointed by the explosion of a

231

revolver in the hand of the stranger.

The bullet missed, but it hummed terrifyingly near to Chuck's head and proved that his antagonist must be quite or nearly as good a marksman as himself. If so, it spiced the pleasure of the night ride for Chuck Neilan. Then he plunged over the ridge of that hill and bolted down into a fairly wide and shallow dale. And with a shout of delight Chuck saw that the speed of his mount was bringing him up with his quarry, hand over hand. Twice the man on the gray whirled in the saddle and fired; twice he missed by a narrow margin, while the brown decreased the interval with its prodigious leaps. Then, as he neared his man, Chuck poised his gun for his own second shot. But he could not shoot down a man at pointblank range with his back turned. He called a warning, his man turned in the saddle with a yell of alarm — and at that moment the brown floundered, pitched to its knees, and sent Chuck hurtling through the air.

He landed with stunning force on his back, but, luckily enough, the force of a fall that might well have broken his neck landed chiefly on that padding of thick muscles just above the shoulder blades. As it was, he was badly shaken, and with his wits barely returned to him, he dragged himself slowly to his knees. His mind was quickly cleared now. There were two explosions of a revolver in rapid succession, and with the second a pain shot across his forehead as though a razor edge, white hot, had seared him there. Immediately there was a warm flow down his face. That sting of a bullet saved him. He looked up to see the marauder, cursing his bad luck, steadying his hand for a finishing shot after his two misses.

Before the gun exploded, Chuck Neilan whipped his own weapon out of the holster and fired from the hip. It was more luck, he knew, than virtue, that enabled him to strike his target with that chance shot. The man on the gray horse pitched forward, then rolled to one side, and fell on the ground with an audible thump. The gray horse danced away a few paces, but lingered, poor beast, to whinny a soft inquiry as to the fate of its master.

But Chuck had no time to pity the horse. He was filled with a wild anger at the rider whom he could have shot through the back a dozen times during the pursuit, and who, in return for this chivalrous treatment, had attempted to shoot him down like a dog when he was helpless from his fall. In an instant he was at the prostrate victim, jerked him over on his back, and shoved the muzzle of his Colt into the hollow of the rascal's throat.

All this he accomplished before his man stirred, groaned, and opened his eyes. Now Chuck saw what had happened. The bullet had been a chance hit, indeed. It had chipped a short groove in the very apex of the man's skull. From this wound a slight trickle was running, but it would be stopped in a moment or two by coagulation. In truth, it was the veriest scratch of a hit, but the force of the blow had stunned the rider. In fact, he hardly saw his victim open his eyes before the mind of the latter cleared from his swoon, and he strove to tug a knife at his belt out of its sheath.

A harsh command from Chuck, and the chill and convincing pressure of the muzzle against his throat brought him to his senses in time. As Chuck rose, his captive obediently rolled upon his face, cursing savagely and steadily while Chuck tied his hands. Leaving him secure, Chuck now caught the horses, mounted his victim on the gray, tied his feet under his mount, fastened the bridle of the gray to the horn of his own saddle, swung up on the brown, and was ready to return triumphant. But he paused first to make some examination of his man.

Never in his life had he seen so low a specimen of humanity. Low brows beetled over little black eyes that were now snapping with malignity. His head was thrust forward on a chunky neck at a sharp angle from the erect. His face was almost a perfect square, and in profile the heavy brows projected well nigh as much as the nose itself. Chuck Neilan regarded the brute details of this countenance with a shiver. Well for him that he had not fallen into the power of the man. He would have been murdered remorselessly. Just as this thought came to him, he remembered what the girl had said about her pursuit of a man on a gray horse, and how he had refrained from shooting back at her. This was strange. It was more than strange. It was nearly a miracle.

"Friend," said Chuck, "are you the gent that Miss Harvey took after one day out here in the hills?"

The other regarded him with a grunt and an imprecation that made the hot blood of the cowpuncher spin in his brain.

"I'm talking for your good, not mine, son," he said. "You can come in with me and be turned over to the law, or else you can talk out free and give us some dope that'll be useful. That's all. I hold it in your favor that you're the gent the girl chased, because you didn't turn around and shoot back. At least you. . . ."

"Orders stopped me," gruffly informed the captive. "I'd've fixed her right and proper . . . that snip! . . . but orders stopped me. I couldn't drive a slug into her. Hadn't been for that, she wouldn't have drove me through the hills like she did. Not her nor no other woman!"

Chuck Neilan regarded the bestial face with a shudder of disgust and shame — shame that such a creature should be called a man. In his revolt and disgust he cast about in his mind for some means of inflicting torment on his man. But Joe Purchass would tend to that, and, from what he had seen of the big rancher, it would go hard, indeed, with his present companion when Purchass took charge of the prisoner.

"Maybe," said Chuck fiercely, "you ain't going to enjoy this nice little ride to the ranch house with me and the moon and all that. I'll give you a bit of news that'll make you cheer up, son. Joe Purchass himself is coming down to the ranch. And he'll be the one to take charge of you."

There was a gasp from the rider of the gray horse.

"Purchass? You lie!"

"I'm telling you the truth. Purchass is coming. You'll sweat for your work, son."

But there was more courage in his prisoner than Chuck had expected. He tossed back his heavy head on his wide shoulders and chuckled. "Leave me and my troubles be," he growled when he was done with his contemptuous laughter. "You can't bluff me. I'm going to stay in the house tonight for a good sleep in a good bed. But I ain't going to stay long. I got business other places. You or Purchass . . . or a dozen like you . . . you don't worry me none. Get along to the house. I'm tired. I need rest."

IX

"PURCHASS TAKES A HAND"

The calm insolence of the ruffian irritated Chuck almost to the point of striking a helpless man. He restrained himself with gritted teeth, and they made on steadily toward the old ranch house. A tumult of noise about the Harvey place — the barking of dogs and the trampling of many horses in the barn — announced the coming of Joe Purchass and his picked men for the clean-up on the Harvey ranch.

"There you are," said Chuck, pointing. "There's the men that are going to see you in a couple of minutes, you skunk. If they's any fear inside of you, get ready to shake."

But the man on the gray horse merely shrugged.

"What's your name?" asked Chuck fiercely.

"Bud Tucker."

"Bud, by my way of thinking, you got about half an hour to live. I'm damned near sorry for you, friend. They'll tear you to pieces, those boys will, when they see the gent that's been hounding a helpless girl here in the Miller Hills. And when they start for you, take care of yourself, because I ain't going to step in between. Now, get on!"

This last threat seemed to have some effect upon the bulky rustler. He rode with his head turning rapidly from side to side, as though even at this moment he was still in hope of rescue. In a moment more they were in front of the first barn, and half a dozen men poured out of it from their work of unsaddling and feeding their horses to cluster around Chuck and the man who sat, bound hand and foot, on the gray,

236

blinking at them with his little brute eyes.

"I caught this hound," explained Chuck to the quiet-eyed little semicircle. "I caught him over yonder in the hills. When he seen me, he took off and didn't wait for no questions to be asked. Ain't no doubt that he's one of the gents that've been bothering Miss Harvey. Look him over, boys. Ain't he a man-sized skunk for you?"

They voted slowly, one by one, but unanimously, that he was that and worse. At first there was no flare of rage among them such as Chuck had expected. He wondered at it while he untied the rope and allowed the man to slip down from the horse. But as he landed on his feet and stood blinking rapidly about him, a hoarse-throated murmur rose from the group. They closed more thickly about him.

"Well," said one, "what you got to say for yourself?"

He who had called himself Bud Tucker shrank back until his shoulders struck against the side of the gray.

"You-all wait till I'm examined regular and proper," he growled. "How come you talk so big to me? What d'you know about me?"

"I know you're a hound," quoth the first interrogator. "You might make tolerable good fertilizer, son, and we ain't got much other use for your kind around these parts. Understand?"

The broad-shouldered captive merely shrugged his shoulders.

"You do the talking now," he averred. "I'll do it later."

"Why," muttered one of the cowpunchers, "he ain't a bit flustered. Get Joe Purchass out, and see if that don't throw a scare into him. Joe's a devil when he gets started on anything. Eh?"

They nodded and smiled fiercely.

"Go get your Joe Purchass," said the rustler, quite indifferent to their chosen threat. "That don't bother me none. He'll see justice done, maybe." And he sneered at them, one by one.

He had carried his carelessness a step too far, however, and now a lean, tall man, hard as steel and as flexible, stepped close to him.

"Do I know you?" he said. "Ain't you Bud Thomas of Winterville?"

"Me? No. Name's Tucker."

"Tucker nothing!" shouted the cowpuncher. "I recollect you plumb perfect now. It was you that worked the crooked dice in a crap game that cleaned me up a couple of years back. I been waiting to pay you for that, son, and here's the first installment!"

As he spoke, without warning his brown fist whipped up and back and then shot into the face of Tucker-Thomas of Winterville, and the shorter, bulkier man dropped flat on his back as though he had been shot. There was a growl of savage agreement from the other cowpunchers. They closed in. A man who will cheat in a crap game is bad enough; a man who hounds a helpless girl is, of course, still worse; and a man who could do both of these things was lower than contempt. The faces of the cowboys were hard and set as they jerked the victim to his feet again, and even Chuck Neilan, that inveterate lover of fair play, looked on with a nod. If they beat the breath out of this scoundrel, he would be getting no more than was his due. Yet he would take no part in the maltreatment.

Standing back, he saw them close in like hungry greyhounds around a coyote. He heard their voices raised. They were pouring forth an increasingly hot indictment upon the head of Tucker-Thomas. Hands raised — fell — and a snarl, animal-like in quality, answered the blows.

"I seen a barrel of tar," said one inspired voice. "I seen it in the wagon shed. Let's give him a roll in it."

"And then roll him again in a pile of feathers," said a second.

A yell of approbation followed, and then the voice of Thomas rose.

"Purchass!" he screamed. "Joe Purchass! Help!"

"Shut up, you dog," cautioned one of the cowpunchers. "Shut up. It'll be all the worse for you if Purchass sees you and hears what you been doing. He's sweet on the girl, you fool, and he'll break you in pieces, inch by inch, when he comes."

But the wretched man persisted in screaming for Joe Purchass, and presently the kitchen door of the house banged open, and a tall form appeared, running toward them through the night.

"What's going on out here?" roared the great voice of Purchass, rolling out in a volume that Chuck Neilan had guessed was possible when he first had talked with the big rancher that day.

"They're aiming to kill me!" screamed Thomas. "They're talking about tar and feathers and . . . !"

"What the devil's all this?" queried Purchass. Striding through the group, he caught Thomas by the nape of the neck and jerked him to his feet.

"Keep 'em off!" groaned Thomas, clinging to the big man. "D'you see 'em? They're planning on killing me!"

"Keep away, you swine," commanded the rancher, kicking the smaller man breathlessly away from him.

Thomas stood now at arm's length and repaid the kick of his protector with a writhing back of his upper lip that exposed a row of dog-like fangs. Purchass looked down at the fellow as though there were pollution in merely laying eyes on him.

"Who got . . . this?" he asked.

A chorus of voices declared Chuck Neilan to be the man, and Chuck felt that there was something more than ordinary surprise in the start with which the big fellow turned to him.

"Hello, Neilan. I been hearing a lot about you. You've dropped down in the Miller Hills like young Lochinvar, and now I see that you've made a hero of yourself. Glad to see you again!"

He turned back to the others.

"I'll take care of this gent, boys. I know you'd like to do for him, with trimmings, but murder doesn't help anybody along these days. We'd have to answer for it to someone, even if it was only Thomas that we cleaned up. I'll take charge of him."

They growled protest, but they could not interfere. Joe Purchass was turning away when he remembered Chuck and turned to him again.

"Come along. Kate has been talking about you. Come along to the house. I think there's room enough for you in there. We'll make out some way."

Nevertheless, though he made his voice hearty, Chuck could not avoid an impression that the words were exactly the reverse of the real meaning of Purchass. There had been, Chuck thought, a strange malevolence in the glance with which Purchass had first singled him out. However, he was too glad of the results of that night's work, and too eager to see Kate Harvey again, to spend much time and thought on small details such as this. If there was any doubt about the criminality of Thomas, it was removed the moment he was brought inside the house and Kate's eyes fell on him. She shrank a little and then blazed into wrath. It was, indeed, the man she had seen riding the gray horse.

She had difficulty in finishing this speech, because of the howling of a dog in the upper part of the house — a strange, unearthly, and weird sound.

"Have you brought the kennels into the house, Kate?" asked Purchass with some irritability.

"It's that greyhound I brought over from Graham City," said the girl apologetically, but flushing at the sharpness in the voice of Purchass, Chuck thought. "He's homesick. He nearly goes frantic outdoors. So I put him in a room in the old wing of the house. I take him out for a run twice a day, and I go up to see him once in a while besides. He's growing accustomed to things by degrees. He's nowhere near as noisy now as he used to be."

"A dog in a house," broke out Purchass, and then swallowed the rest of his words before they got past his teeth. He had already spoken too much, however, and Chuck saw a flash of anger pass between them. Doubtless Purchass wanted to marry this girl. The sending of the emerald had been a message and a symbol, beyond question. But if ever they were united, Chuck shrewdly foresaw many a clash of opposing wills.

The big rancher rapidly diverted the talk to another topic, the first that came to his mind, and this happened to be the courage of Chuck Neilan, who had just brought home this captive. As for Thomas, he would rope the man like a dog, he said, and throw him in an upstairs room until tomorrow, when a buckboard could take the scoundrel to Graham City to wait for his trial. So saying, he strode out of the room and left the girl facing Chuck.

"You caught him all by yourself?" she said. "Why, even Joe Purchass hasn't been able to do as much as that."

"Plain luck," said Chuck modestly. "And even if it weren't, you'd better not tell Mister Purchass."

She started to protest, changed her mind, flushed, and immediately changed the subject. During the rest of the time that they spoke together that evening, her manner was constrained. Continually Chuck found her looking up and searching him with side glances. Plainly she was afraid that he had looked a little too deeply into the mind of her husband to be, and there were things in that mind of which the girl was frankly ashamed.

X

"A GIRL'S FEAR"

All of this made matter for serious reflection, and not altogether unpleasant reflection, for Chuck Neilan. It employed him on the way to the room to which he was assigned. It grew large in his sleepy imagination as he slipped between the sheets of his bed, and it passed into his dreams as the fatigue of that heavy day of labor swept over him and blotted out the world.

He was wakened in the earliest gray of the dawn by a clamor in the house, and then by the shrill wailing of the captive greyhound. Chuck rushed downstairs half dressed and learned from a raging Joe Purchass, who stormed up and down the living room like a maniac, what had happened. By some mysterious resource of deviltry, Thomas had managed to get a knife and cut his bonds during the night. Then he had sneaked out to the barn, picked out and saddled the matchless bay gelding Purchass rode, and slipped away like a ghost on this horse. And so great was the speed of the bay that no attempt was made at pursuit. There was nothing to be done except to send to Graham City as soon as possible and make the wires hot, informing every sheriff within a wide radius of what had happened.

At the conclusion of this narrative, Purchass dropped into a chair and buried his face in his hands in despair, from which even the pretty coaxing of Kate Harvey could not rouse him. Chuck himself, much as he had come to dislike and to envy the rancher, could not help pitying him now. The vicious little pinto itself had found a place deep in the heart of Chuck, and he pitied with all of his soul a man who had lost such a charger as the bay. But there was nothing more to be accomplished. Chuck went back to his bed and fell at once into a sounder sleep than ever.

When he wakened, it was with a guilty start, for the sun of the late morning was pouring into his room. Not in half a dozen years had he slept so late as this. When he hurried down the stairs, Kate Harvey met him with laughter, and her old father cackled behind her. All the men had ridden off long before. They had gone out with Purchass to scour the Miller Hills and hunt for the lost cattle of the Harvey ranch. When Chuck asked indignantly why he had not been called to join the hunt, he was told that they knew he had ridden a desperately long distance the day before. But if he wanted hunting, he could have his share on the succeeding days, for Purchass had announced his determination to run through every nook of the Miller Hills with a fine-tooth comb until he found the missing stock, even if he required a thousand men for the task.

This last item was confided to Chuck with pride by Mr. Harvey, who took an immense satisfaction in the wealth of his son-in-law to be. He was a talkative old fellow on all topics, as a matter of fact. While Kate hurried a breakfast onto the table for Chuck, Mr. Harvey overrode all of her hints and her suggestions and insisted on telling the whole story.

"Because," said Harvey, "there's nothing to be ashamed of in it. What happened was sure to happen. And it served you right. Can't deny that, Kate. It served you right for being as stubborn as a mule."

He went on with his narrative. It seemed that, when Joe Purchass came West to take charge of the family estate something over a year before, he had at once met and fallen desperately in love with Kate Harvey. But Kate was too occupied with business affairs to pay much heed to wooers. She had

244

been running the ranch for a year, and, under her direction, while it could not be said that the place was prosperous, at least she had arrested the rapid decline into which it was falling under the management of her crippled father. In vain, Purchass besieged her. At length she confessed to him that business meant more to her than men just now, and that, when it was otherwise, she would send to him for help so soon as the business at the ranch became too much for her to handle, as he had repeatedly warned her it would become. Out of the impulse of a romantic moment she had agreed on a symbol, which was to be one of a pair of emerald earrings that an old Mexican woman had sold to Mr. Harvey.

For some time things had gone very well, but after a while the cattle began to disappear with astonishing frequency, and it was plain that rustlers were at work. She had made frantic efforts to locate the thieves but always without avail, until at length she had given up — the ranch being on the point of bankruptcy — and had sent the emerald by Chalmers to Joe Purchass, who received it after it had traveled along the dubious route already described.

As for Chuck Neilan, he heard the tale with a singular leap of the heart. Business chains were not the sort of chains that could bind Kate Harvey. Little as he knew of her, he knew this. In that Joe Purchass had not perceived so much as this gave him a great sense of superiority over the rich man. More-over, there were immediate consolations for having missed the roundup of the rustlers that was underway today. Kate was about to take a gallop to exercise the greyhound, Emperor, and out went Chuck Neilan at her side. They kept a hot pace over the hills for half an hour or more — slow going was simply no exercise at all for Emperor, the girl averred — and then they swung in a slower circuit back toward the house, with Emperor straining at the leash and cutting off toward Graham

City. He tugged until the arm of Chuck ached from the pull, and the girl told how twice the hound had broken away from her on similar occasions and raced over the mountains all the half dozen miles to Graham City.

By the time that ride was finished and the dog restored to his room in the old, unoccupied wing of the house, the lower floor of which was used for storing supplies, Kate and Chuck had grown fairly intimate. She had told into his sympathetic ear, for instance, the full story of her struggle to make the ranch a paying proposition. And he, in return, had regaled her with a few tales extracted at random out of his own adventures. Last of all he told of the gold mine which he had fairly blundered upon.

"And why on earth," cried the girl, "didn't you stay to work it and watch it and develop it?"

Chuck rubbed his ear in embarrassment. "I'll tell you how it is," he confessed at length. "I have a hunch working in me that you never can get a thing that you don't work for. Well, I didn't work for that gold. I just bull lucked it and found the stuff. I didn't take no chances nor no risks. I'll simply make a fool of myself someday when I go back and spend what they're digging out of them rocks for me. But the money ain't got me yet, and I ain't got the money . . . all of it."

She listened to this unique exposition with a smile, but they had no chance to continue the talk, for they had reached the house, and the horses and dog had to be put away.

There followed a lazy time around the house. No one returned from Joe Purchass at noontime. The afternoon wore away, and still there was no messenger from the leader of the hunters. Chuck Neilan, toward dusk, began to grow wild with excitement.

"He's struck something in the line of big game," he declared, "because, otherwise, he wouldn't be riding his hosses this long.

Wouldn't be surprised if they's some powder burning some-wheres up yonder in them Miller Hills, Miss Harvey."

As he spoke, he fell into an agony of suspense at the very thought. The evening wore on. The sun set, the color faded from the west, and the streak of yellow-orange that banded the horizon went out by dim degrees. Looking up to the sky, in which these changes had been taking place, one saw that it still seemed comparatively bright, but, looking down to the earth, one became aware that deep night was about to descend upon the hills.

It was through this dusk that they came, a myriad of voices, a myriad of tossing heads and horns, and Kate and Chuck ran out to see and to cheer. For it was Joe Purchass returning, and before him and his men rolled a dense herd of cattle. In five minutes the triumphant hunter was sitting at the table with the dust not yet shaken from his shoulders, eating ravenously. Down the table sat four of his henchmen, silent, dour fellows. The men who had first come over from the Purchass ranch had been sent in to Graham City to spend the night, thence to ride back to the home ranch on the following day. These new hands had come down and joined during the day. As for the explanation of the finding of the cattle, it was extremely simple.

Joe Purchass, his heavy voice rolling and rumbling, told the tale of how the cattle had drifted off the ranch and down into the lower ravines, where they found better grass and more water, and where they were not discovered simply because she, a woman, had not known how to hire efficient cowhands, and because the lazy fellows she did hire had only made a pretense of searching for the stock. No doubt this herd he had found did not represent half of her losses. Beyond a question the numbers of wandering cows had drawn thieves. But the rustling would cease from this point. She could rest assured of that.

The hound who had stolen the bay gelding would spread among his fellows the word that Joe Purchass had come down to run the ranch, and this, Purchass felt, would put an end to the lawlessness.

He announced this, Chuck felt, with unpardonable swagger, while the four dark-faced henchmen at the lower end of the table grunted in acquiescence. The manner of Purchass, indeed, was growing intolerably possessive. He lolled back in his chair when he had finished his dinner and looked about him with dull, careless eyes, basking in the admiration old Harvey poured out on him, the admiration of withered age for youth and strength and victory above all.

But in the meantime, Chuck saw that Kate, sitting beside him at the table, was growing paler and paler and more and more silent. Whenever he stole a glance at her, he saw that she was rewarding the talkative Purchass with smiles, but he saw also that those smiles were purely automatic. Several times he invited her with significant looks to share her discontent with him, but she seemed to misunderstand or not to see his glances. It was not until the meal was come to dessert that she dropped her napkin, and Chuck, leaning to retrieve it for her, found that she was leaning also. He instantly knocked the napkin far under his chair and had to lean farther down to fumble for it. That delay gave her a chance to murmur in his ear. And what she said froze his blood.

"Chuck Neilan, there's something wrong. There's something wrong with the face of Joe Purchass. There's something devilish about it that I can't quite remember. What is he? Who is he? And why . . . why am I so filled with fear?"

XI

"THE WOLF EXPOSED"

The significance of that soul-chilling whisper made its way slowly into the brain of Chuck Neilan. Gradually he began to understand that what he himself had guessed at had not been entirely wrong. It had seemed to him that the rancher was, indeed, changed, that he had discarded something like a mask from his face. His eyes, as Chuck straightened and handed the napkin to the girl with a smile, were flaming straight at Neilan with such a glance as Chuck would never forget. And after that, no matter how the talk ran, no matter how Purchass chattered away to please the greedy ear of Mr. Harvey, he reserved time and attention, now and again, to dart a heart-withering glance at Chuck.

Just what was the meaning of those glances, Chuck could not be sure, but at least he was confident that the rancher was intensely hostile. And more than hostile, he was venomously suspicious of every word and glance Chuck directed at Kate Harvey. So much the cowpuncher could tell. In the meantime, Purchass became momentarily more and more the new self that had alarmed Kate. Confident, it seemed, that the sending of the emerald, and then his work in reclaiming so many of the lost cattle, represented facts that indicated the complete surrender of Kate, Purchass was letting down the bars. And the real self that was now discovered was complacent, careless, confident to a degree that had startled Kate herself, and that had drawn her on to further observations. Chief of these, perhaps, were the same eyes that had startled Chuck — the bright, steady gray eyes that gleamed out beneath the straight, closely penciled brows of the big man.

What did the girl mean by saying that the rancher reminded her of someone? Why should she not have seen the resemblance before today? But even now, Chuck could see she was struggling patiently with her memory, and twice she bowed her head and rested her forehead in her hand, a mute symbol of the effort of her concentration. From the face of Purchass, then, she looked earnestly down the table toward the four dark faces of the followers of Purchass. In fact, there was something strange about these men. They were as ill-omened a quartet as Chuck had ever observed in all the days of his wild experience in the mountain desert.

A peculiar alarm grew in him, unquestionably the result of the strange whisper of the girl. He remembered now, with a qualm, that he had left his cartridge belt and gun hanging on a peg against the wall in the wash shed. For who would go into a perfectly friendly house and sit down with the encumbrance of a six-shooter burdening one's thigh? Only after he was seated did he notice that each of the gloomy and silent four retained their guns, and the big rancher likewise. It had not troubled him before, but now it returned as an insidious source of worry.

Kate Harvey had risen slowly from her chair and crossed around the table until she came to the left of the chair of Purchass.

"Joe," she said solemnly, "I have a question to ask you before all these people as witnesses. Will you answer me on your word of honor?"

"Word of honor?" grumbled Joe Purchass. "My dear, has your friend across the table been pumping fool ideas in your head?"

"This is an idea of my own. Will you answer me, Joe?"

"Of course . . . of course. What is it, Kate?"

"Where were you six years ago tonight?"

The result was perfectly startling. First Chuck Neilan saw the four cowpunchers at the end of the table straighten out with a jerk, and their uneasy eyes worked from side to side as if to hunt for a loophole of escape. After that, he saw nothing save the face of Purchass himself. He had read about men changing color and the sweat pouring out on their foreheads — all as the result of a phrase or two. But he had never seen it until this moment when it was exemplified in the countenance of Purchass.

Now that portion of his face that was not obscured with a forest of beard and whiskers and sideburns turned from deep tan to a grisly gray, and this in turn gave place to a tinge of purple. At the same time the forehead became white and glistened with a thick dew of sweat. All of this, moreover, took place on the instant that he heard the question. He turned, strangely enough, not toward the girl, but toward Chuck Neilan, and his eyes glowed like the eyes of a demon. There was no question about it now. He was, as the saying went, bad medicine, and he was particularly bad for Chuck.

The effect of this change in the face of Purchass was indescribably great in Chuck. It was still greater in the girl, for she sank against the table, staring in fear at the half-averted face of the rancher.

"Six years ago?" said Purchass, but the careless words were uttered in a husky, almost choked voice. "Let me see. I'm trying to remember."

Then, as though he saw that the emotion in his voice was betraying him, he started around in his chair and glared at her.

"Why do you ask, Kate? Has Neilan put you up to this nonsense, my dear?"

Her reply was very strange. It did not consist in words, but, making a quick gesture, she buried her fingers in the dark brown, richly curling hair of Purchass and tore it from his head. Such literally was what she did. The whole mass of hair covering the top of the man's head came away and exposed the pale skin beneath. The startled brain of Chuck Neilan, working in stumbling fashion, had hardly grasped the fact that the girl had torn a wig from the head of the big man, when her own scream went ringing into his ears and thrilling and quivering along his nerves: "The Wolf! Good Lord! The Wolf!"

And she cowered away against the wall, burying her face in her hands.

Chuck Neilan waited, agape. Had the big rancher decided to act in the first instant, he could have blown Chuck to a thousand pieces. But for one moment, perhaps, he hesitated, uncertain as to whether he might not laugh the accusation to scorn. In that moment of indecision, some assurance returned to Chuck. His blood began to flow more freely, and when Purchass, finally realizing that the game he had played so long was up, pushed back his chair with set teeth and scowling brows, Chuck drew back his own and prepared to bolt for the door.

"You first," said Purchass. "You put this into her head. You've been my bad luck ever since you came across my trail. Now, Neilan. . . ."

But Chuck had dived for the door — literally dived to upset the aim of the other, if the rancher should fire. He swung one shoulder sidewise and smashed into the door, knocking it wide and catapulting through at the same time that the gun roared from the hand of The Wolf — who had been — Joe Purchass.

Once outside that door, Chuck rolled to his feet and, with a roar of footfalls and voices behind him, plunged down the hall. He made for the side door, but, when he crashed into it, he found that it was locked, and, as he reached for the key, a gun boomed loud as a cannon in the narrow hall behind him. There was no chance to wait even the split part of a second. The heavy .45-caliber slug crashed into the door beside his head. Chuck turned to his left and bounded up the stairs, as a second shot nipped him stingingly in the shoulder. But it was only a scratch that served as a spur to make him bolt up the steps in longer leaps. At the head of those stairs he turned to his right and rushed for the end room. He might gain the outside in this manner and so reach the horses.

His first glance out the window showed him one of Purchass's men standing outside with Colt poised in his hand, with the lamplight streaming over him from a window in the dining room. Back again Chuck Neilan bolted and thundered into the hallway in time to be greeted by the roar of three revolvers directly behind him. Purchass and two of his followers were coming for the assault.

There was only one thing to do, unless he preferred to rush into the flaming muzzles of those guns that had missed him so far only because of the dimness of the lights. Chuck took the other alternative, and, wheeling to the left, he bolted for the unoccupied old wing of the house where only the greyhound now lived. Down the hallway he plunged as he had never raced before, with a shout of savage triumph from the throat of Purchass behind him.

The end of the hall was the door to the room where the big dog was quartered. He wrenched it open, slammed it behind him, and turned the lock. The next instant a heavy weight crashed against it, and it sagged in with a great creaking. It was a barrier to the pursuit, but it was a barrier that would endure for only an instant.

He leaped across the room, with the dog whining with excitement at his feet, and smashed the window there. He looked down. The night was dark, but he could see the ground distinctly. It was instant death to drop that distance. Groaning with impotence, he turned away, while the hound reared, planted its forepaws on the window sill, and then whined with eagerness and fear as even it recoiled from the drop to the solid earth below.

With his brain whirling in the search for expedients, Chuck looked around him. It was plain enough, this catastrophe that had happened. The Wolf, a man of good family gone bad, had disappeared some six years ago, and then, trusting to a wig and a growth of hair to disguise a face never plainly seen by even his closest followers, he had come back to claim his heritage and incidentally to attempt to marry Kate Harvey. So much for this devil who merited, Chuck could see, all that had been said about him.

As for the plan of The Wolf now, it was equally simple. By killing Chuck, he removed the one strong witness against him. He could then take Harvey and the girl, through the agency of his four followers, up into the hills until she consented to marry him. This accomplished, he could return and take his place in the world, giving any number of good reasons for having killed Chuck Neilan.

There were things unexplained in this brief summary, but Chuck saw all of this in one flash. The next instant he groaned as the door sagged under the weight of a new assailant. If he were to find escape now, he must act with the speed of the wind. The dog, standing on his hind legs at the window, looked around over its shoulder and seemed to beg for speed with its whine.

That whine gave Chuck his idea. He tore off the coat and vest and ripped a section from the front of his shirt. That would do for something to write on. But ink?

He used the readiest alternative for ink. He jerked out a penknife, pricked the end of his right forefinger, jabbing it until the flow was free and then, spreading the cloth against the wall with his left hand, guessing at his letters in the dark, he wrote:

Murder. Harvey's ranch. The Wolf.

That message should convey his meaning, short though the words might be. He ran to the greyhound, tore one end of the cloth in two, and tied it in the collar. Then he lifted the heavy, sprawling brute to the window. There was a snarl, a frightened whine, and teeth clashed an inch from his face as the terrified dog discovered his purpose. But the next instant Emperor had been pushed out head foremost into empty air.

The door crashed down behind him, and a roar of voices filled the room. But Chuck Neilan crammed his shoulders into the narrow window and peered downward, regardless of what had happened elsewhere. He saw Emperor land with a thud, lie a moment inert, then rise, stagger, trot, and suddenly skim away into the night with great bounds.

The next moment he was torn away from the window and went crashing to the floor with the weight of two men bearing down upon him.

XII

"KATE'S ANSWER"

They brought him downstairs, Joe Purchass, alias The Wolf, carrying him with as much ease as though he had been a child. In the dining room they found old Harvey close to collapse, cowering in his chair in the corner. Kate Harvey stood beside the window, pale, but otherwise calm enough. The calm was broken for an instant as she saw Chuck Neilan brought, living, before her. What had passed made them close to each other. There was an impulsive gesture of both hands thrown out.

"Chuck!" she cried, and there was a world of meaning in the single word — so much that Purchass turned sharply on her.

He made no response, however, and beckoned to the guard, who had remained to watch these two, to lower his revolver and stand back. He was obeyed in silence. The fourth of the men now appeared and closed the outer door to the kitchen. He also took his place in silence, with an unperturbed expression. But the eyes of each of the four, like the eyes of so many dogs, followed every movement of the leader.

Purchass took up an easy position in the center of the room where he could keep everything in view.

"We're about to start on a little trip, Kate," he said. "We're going to leave a note or two to inform neighbors, perhaps. Then we're going for a jaunt up into the hills. No fear." His face blackened as he saw that her eyes were riveted upon Chuck Neilan. "No fear, Chuck is going with us. We can't leave dead men behind."

A faint cry came from the girl. But The Wolf raised his hand to silence her. "Stop that! Do you think we'll kill him and then take him? Nor your father, either, my dear. You good people are going on a little excursion with me, and with these four faithful fellows of mine to take care of us. Up there, I hope, you'll make up your mind to marry me, and I'll see that a book and a man are brought for the purpose, together with a license and all things necessary. That marriage, I think, will shut your mouth and the mouth of your father. As for Neilan, he's a very honest man, eh? Well, I'll extract a very solemn promise from Neilan. That will have to be our program."

As he spoke, he sent a dour glance at Chuck. No question about the nature of the promise he would extract. It would be a request pointed with the muzzle of a gun and signed in burning powder.

"I'm telling you this, Kate," said the leader, as the girl made no reply, "because I want you to understand immediately exactly where we are, and what we are doing. If you won't consent, I shall not carry you a step."

The girl exclaimed faintly, incredulously, and at the unbelieving hope in her face Purchass grew pale.

"Not a step would I carry you," he repeated. "And neither would I carry these two. I'd leave them behind in such shape that they'd never talk . . . never."

Chuck Neilan looked at the big man, wholly incredulous. It did not seem possible that there was a man living capable of such unscrupulous villainy. Again he glanced at the girl. She was utterly colorless, her glance roving swiftly in agony from his own face to the face of her father. That poor old man, broken by age and by his weakness of body, crumpled farther into the corner and watched what was happening with great, dumb eyes of fear.

"First," said Purchass, sitting on the table and swinging one

257

leg with a carelessness of manner that Chuck knew did not represent his true mind, "Kate, I want you to know some of the things which should be put on the right side of the page and added up in my favor. Along with it, I'll tell you the bad things. Go back to a night six years ago, a night when you woke up and saw The Wolf standing in the shaft of moon shine that streamed in through your window. That night, Kate, I saw your face for the first time. You were only a girl, but there was so much beauty and purity in you, my dear, that, when I got clear of the house, I began to think things over.

"You see, I had taken to deviltry . . . the life of The Wolf, who, by the way, was never as bad as the fools say . . . not because I was driven out of polite society, but simply because I wanted a few thrills. Well, I got 'em! I went from bad to worse. I was going downhill fast, until I saw you, Kate. That changed me. I saw that I'd have to put on the brakes. And I did. I left the country. I spent nearly five years getting used to a wig and growing a beard. When I came back, my own family in the East did not recognize me. And certainly nobody in the West knew me to be The Wolf. I've lived here a full year, and nobody would ever have learned it if it hadn't been for the working of your instinct tonight . . . and the working of a woman's instinct is a thing against which men have no defense. It can't be guarded against. Even now no one knows except a few members of the old gang.

"I had to use them to break down your defense, Kate. They were the cattle rustlers who stole your cattle. They were the fellows who broke you down to such a point that you had to send that blessed emerald to me. And these men won't speak to inform against me. As to the others, your father will do a good deal for the sake of a comfortable berth the rest of his life . . . he won't talk. And that leaves you and Neilan. As my wife, you'll be quiet, I suppose, and as for Neilan . . . well, I shall extract a promise, eh? Then I am free, Kate, to go back to the Purchase Ranch and continue my life exactly where I left off when I saddled and came over here yesterday, except that I'll have my wife with me. Kate, do you understand? Do you consent?"

She quivered as though she had been struck with a whip. But as she raised her head to answer, he checked her.

"Not yet," he said. "Take half an hour or so to think things over from every angle. At first, of course, you would detest me. But after a time I am sure that you would feel far otherwise about matters. I am going outside for a stroll. When I come back, you can say what you have to say."

With this he left the room, the outside door banged after him, and his footfalls departed.

There began what was for Chuck Neilan and the girl the longest period of waiting in their lives. Every moment was a year of life. While she struggled through that grim problem, Chuck found her eyes reaching to him across the room time and again, as though asking him mutely for advice that she knew he could not give.

At last he burst out: "For heaven's sake, do the thing that will keep you straight with yourself. Your father's an old man. And I'm a pretty hard one. If either of us keeps on living because you've gone into a living death, d'you think . . . ?"

A snarl from one of the guards cut his generous speech short, but his meaning had been made clear enough, and he was rewarded with a glint of moist eyes and a sad shake of the head from the girl. Then she dropped her face in her hands and waited, with strong shudders shaking her now and again. From without a whistled note drew two of the guards away. After five minutes more there was a sound of approaching horses and the faint squeaking of stirrups jouncing in the stirrup leathers. The Wolf was making ready to start his journey, and in a moment or so he would be among them ready to ask for the answer. How long it had been since he left the room, no one in it could have undertaken to guess, though surely it had been at least the half hour he had promised to give them.

A little later the door opened softly, and the big rancher stood before them with the wig once more in place on his head. That act of self-deception made Chuck Neilan nearly smile.

There was no doubt in Chuck's mind about what answer the girl would give. She answered the final question steadily enough: "I'll go with you, and I'll marry you . . . and heaven forgive you if men ever find out what you are. But these two are safe?"

She pointed to Chuck and her father.

"Absolutely," said The Wolf, nodding. "And. . . ."

A hiss from one of his followers made him start. Instantly the man who had been left outside called: "Chief! Quick!"

In a bound The Wolf was through the door, and then the cause of their alarm was audible to those within the room — the mutter of rapidly approaching hoofbeats — many and many of them — drumming up a blur of sound.

"Harry . . . Lou!" thundered a voice outside — the voice of The Wolf. "Come for your lives! The mountains have been turned into horsemen. But kill Neilan first . . . kill him before you come!"

But Chuck Neilan, at the first order, caught the chair beside him and hurled it across the room. It crashed against the lamp and flooded the place with darkness. Twice a revolver exploded, fired with malevolent abandon, and then the two stumbled through the doorway out to the wildly cursing Wolf.

They started off with a sudden outburst of hoofbeats that faded as the roar of the approaching party increased, swept nearer, and broke around the ranch house. Those frantic riders who had nearly killed their horses in the rush across the six miles of hills in response to the message written in blood — those ready fighters, guns in hand, saw no signs of the fugitives as the latter dipped down the hillside. The next moment they were in the darkened room with only the stifled, hysterical sobbing of a girl to guide them.

Someone flashed an electric torch. The round flare of light wavered a moment and then picked out the age-dulled eyes of the father, and then Kate Harvey, weeping in the arms of a tall, brown-faced stranger whose right forefinger was gashed at the tip.

MAX BRAND

MEN BEYOND THE LAW

These three short novels showcase Max Brand doing what he does best: exploring the wild, often dangerous life beyond the constraints of cities, beyond the reach of civilization . . . beyond the law. Whether he's a desperate man fleeing the tragic results of a gunfight, an innocent young man who stumbles onto the loot from a bank robbery, or the gentle giant named Bull Hunter—one of Brand's most famous characters—each protagonist is out on his own, facing two unknown frontiers: the Wild West . . . and his own future.

___4873-6 $4.50 US/$5.50 CAN

Dorchester Publishing Co., Inc.
P.O. Box 6640
Wayne, PA 19087-8640

Please add $2.50 for shipping and handling for the first book and $.75 for each book thereafter. NY, NYC, and PA residents, please add appropriate sales tax. No cash, stamps, or C.O.D.s. All orders shipped within 6 weeks via postal service book rate. Canadian orders require $2.50 extra postage and must be paid in U.S. dollars through a U.S. banking facility.

Name_____
Address_____
City_____ State_____ Zip_____
I have enclosed $ _____ in payment for the checked book(s).
Payment <u>must</u> accompany all orders. ❑ Please send a free catalog.
CHECK OUT OUR WEBSITE! www.dorchesterpub.com

MAX BRAND

RONICKY DOONE

First Time In Paperback!

"Brand is a topnotcher!"
—*New York Times*

Doone's name is famous throughout the Old West. From Tombstone to Sonora he's won the respect of every law-abiding citizen—and the hatred of every bushwhacking bandit. But Bill Gregg isn't one to let a living legend get in his way, and he'll shoot Doone dead as soon as look at him. What nobody tells Gregg is that Doone doesn't enjoy living his hard-riding, rip-roaring life unless he takes a chance on losing it once in a while.

_3738-6 $3.99 US/$4.99 CAN

THE MOUNTAIN FUGITIVE

First Time In Paperback!

"Brand is a topnotcher!"
—*New York Times*

A wild youth, Lee Porfilo is always in trouble. If he isn't knocking someone down, he is ready to battle any cowpoke who comes along. But a penniless brawler can't stand up to the power of rich ranchers, and the Chase brothers will do whatever it takes to defeat Lee—even frame him for murder.

Porfilo has to choose between the hangman's noose and a desperate bid to prove his innocence. His every move dogged by lawmen and bounty hunters, he flees into the wilderness. But a man can't run forever, and Lee Profilo would rather die facing his enemies head on than live as an outlaw and coward.

_3574-X $3.99 US/$4.99 CAN

MAX BRAND

THE WHISPERING OUTLAW

FIRST TIME IN PAPERBACK!

"Brand is a topnotcher!"
—*New York Times*

He is a mystery among frontier bandits—a masked gunman who never shows his true face or speaks in his honest voice. A loner by design, The Whisperer holds that it is above all foolishness for a man to have a partner in crime if he hopes to ride free. But a gent who plays a lone hand will never make a big killing.

So The Whisperer decides to do something either wildly desperate or extremely clever. He plans a spree of daring robberies that will make him a legend, and for a gang, he recruits a passel of ornery outlaws. All The Whisperer wants is one chance to strike it rich—all it will take to bring him down is one man who gets too greedy.

_3678-9 $3.99 US/$4.99 CAN

Dorchester Publishing Co., Inc.
65 Commerce Road
Stamford, CT 06902

Please add $1.75 for shipping and handling for the first book and $.50 for each book thereafter. NY, NYC, PA and CT residents, please add appropriate sales tax. No cash, stamps, or C.O.D.s. All orders shipped within 6 weeks via postal service book rate. Canadian orders require $2.00 extra postage and must be paid in U.S. dollars through a U.S. banking facility.

Name_____
Address_____
City _____ State_____Zip_____
I have enclosed $_____in payment for the checked book(s).
Payment <u>must</u> accompany all orders.☐ Please send a free catalog.

TIMBAL GULCH TRAIL

"Brand is a topnotcher!"
—*New York Times*

Les Burchard owns the local gambling palace, half the town, and most of the surrounding territory, and Walt Devon's thousand-acre ranch will make him king of the land. The trouble is, Devon doesn't want to sell. In a ruthless bid to claim the spread, Burchard tries everything from poker to murder. But Walt Devon is a betting man by nature, even when the stakes are his life. The way Devon figures, the odds are stacked against him, so he can either die alone or take his enemy to the grave with him.

__3828-5 $4.50 US/$5.50 CAN

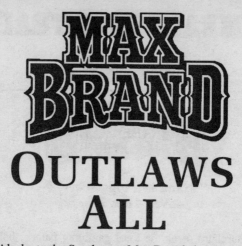

OUTLAWS ALL

From Alaska to the Southwest, Max Brand, the master of the Western tale, brings the excitement of the frontier to life like no one else. His characters live, breathe, struggle and triumph in a world so real you can hear the creaking of the saddle leather. Gathered in this collection are three classic short novels by Brand, all filled with the adventure and heroism, the guts and the gunsmoke, that made the West what it was.

___4398-X $4.50 US/$5.50 CAN

Dorchester Publishing Co., Inc.
P.O. Box 6640
Wayne, PA 19087-8640

Please add $1.75 for shipping and handling for the first book and $.50 for each book thereafter. NY, NYC, and PA residents, please add appropriate sales tax. No cash, stamps, or C.O.D.s. All orders shipped within 6 weeks via postal service book rate. Canadian orders require $2.00 extra postage and must be paid in U.S. dollars through a U.S. banking facility.

Name_____
Address_____
City_____ State_____ Zip_____
I have enclosed $_____ in payment for the checked book(s).
Payment <u>must</u> accompany all orders. ☐ Please send a free catalog.
        CHECK OUT OUR WEBSITE! www.dorchesterpub.com

The Lightning Warrior

The Indians call the great white wolf the Lightning Warrior because of the swiftness of his attack. But even the giant Colbolt isn't interested in the massive wolf until Sylvia Baird makes the beast's pelt the one condition for her hand in marriage. She thinks she is safe, but when he returns with not only the pelt, but the wolf itself, and demands his prize, Sylvia's only hope is a desperate flight for freedom. Colbolt sets out in determined pursuit, but he's forgotten Sylvia's newest ally. . .the Lightning Warrior.

___4420-X $4.50 US/$5.50 CAN

Dorchester Publishing Co., Inc.
P.O. Box 6640
Wayne, PA 19087-8640

Please add $1.75 for shipping and handling for the first book and $.50 for each book thereafter. NY, NYC, and PA residents, please add appropriate sales tax. No cash, stamps, or C.O.D.s. All orders shipped within 6 weeks via postal service book rate. Canadian orders require $2.00 extra postage and must be paid in U.S. dollars through a U.S. banking facility.

Name_____
Address_____
City_____ State_____ Zip_____
I have enclosed $_____ in payment for the checked book(s).
Payment <u>must</u> accompany all orders. ❑ Please send a free catalog.
      CHECK OUT OUR WEBSITE! www.dorchesterpub.com

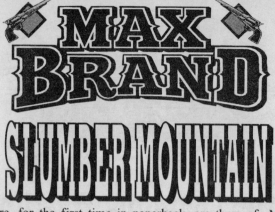

MAX BRAND
SLUMBER MOUNTAIN

Here, for the first time in paperback, are three of Max Brand's best short novels, all restored to their original glory from Brand's own typescripts and presented just as he intended. "Outland Crew" is an exciting tale of gold fever and survival in a frontier mining town. In "The Coward," a man humiliated in a gunfight finds a fiendishly clever way of exacting revenge. And in "Slumber Mountain," Brand presents a harrowing story of man versus the wilderness as a trapper fights for his life against the mighty wolf known as Silver King.

____4442-0 $4.99 US/$5.99 CAN

Dorchester Publishing Co., Inc.
P.O. Box 6640
Wayne, PA 19087-8640

Please add $1.75 for shipping and handling for the first book and $.50 for each book thereafter. NY, NYC, and PA residents, please add appropriate sales tax. No cash, stamps, or C.O.D.s. All orders shipped within 6 weeks via postal service book rate. Canadian orders require $2.00 extra postage and must be paid in U.S. dollars through a U.S. banking facility.

Name_____
Address_____
City_____State_____Zip_____
I have enclosed $_____ in payment for the checked book(s).
Payment <u>must</u> accompany all orders. ☐ Please send a free catalog.
          CHECK OUT OUR WEBSITE! www.dorchesterpub.com

SOFT METAL
MAX BRAND

Collected here for the first time in paperback are three of Max Brand's greatest short novels, all restored to their original splendor, just as the author intended. In "The Red Bandanna," Clancy Morgan returns to town to warn his best friend, Danny Travis, that Bill Orping is heading there, looking for a confrontation. But when he gets there he finds that Orping has arrived before him and was shot in the back—and it looks like Danny was the killer. "His Name His Fortune" is the story of a young gambler who falls in love with the daughter of a wealthy rancher who despises him. And in the final short novel, "Soft Metal," Larry Givain, fleeing from a posse, meets a beautiful woman at a deserted cabin belonging to one of the men in the posse. Her brother is also holed up in the cabin, pursed by a notorious gunfighter. With death drawing ever nearer, Givain realizes his life will never be the same again.

___4698-9 $4.50 US/$5.50 CAN

Dorchester Publishing Co., Inc.
P.O. Box 6640
Wayne, PA 19087-8640